Anthony Gilbert and The

Anthony Gilbert (1899–1973)

Anthony Gilbert was the pen name of Lucy Beatrice Malleson. Born in London, she spent all her life there, and her affection for the city is clear from the strong sense of character and place in evidence in her work. She published 69 crime novels, 51 of which featured her best known character, Arthur Crook, a vulgar London lawyer totally (and deliberately) unlike the aristocratic detectives, such as Lord Peter Wimsey, who dominated the mystery field at the time. She also wrote more than 25 radio plays, which were broadcast in Great Britain and overseas. Her thriller *The Woman in Red* (1941) was broadcast in the United States by CBS and made into a film in 1945 under the title *My Name is Julia Ross*. She was an early member of the British Detection Club, which, along with Dorothy L. Sayers, she prevented from disintegrating during World War II. Malleson published her autobiography, *Three-a-Penny*, in 1940, and wrote numerous short stories, which were published in several anthologies and in such periodicals as *Ellery Queen's Mystery Magazine* and *The Saint*. The short story 'You Can't Hang Twice' received a Queens award in 1946. She never married, and evidence of her feminism is elegantly expressed in much of her work.

By Anthony Gilbert

Scott Egerton series

Tragedy at Freyne (1927)

The Murder of Mrs
  Davenport (1928)

Death at Four Corners (1929)

The Mystery of the Open
  Window (1929)

The Night of the Fog (1930)

The Body on the Beam (1932)

The Long Shadow (1932)

The Musical Comedy
  Crime (1933)

An Old Lady Dies (1934)

The Man Who Was Too
  Clever (1935)

**Mr Crook Murder
  Mystery series**

Murder by Experts (1936)

The Man Who Wasn't
  There (1937)

Murder Has No Tongue (1937)

Treason in My Breast (1938)

The Bell of Death (1939)

Dear Dead Woman (1940)
  aka *Death Takes a Redhead*

The Vanishing Corpse (1941)
  aka *She Vanished in the Dawn*

The Woman in Red (1941)
  aka *The Mystery of the
  Woman in Red*

Death in the Blackout (1942)
  aka *The Case of the Tea-
  Cosy's Aunt*

Something Nasty in the
  Woodshed (1942)
  aka *Mystery in the Woodshed*

The Mouse Who Wouldn't
  Play Ball (1943)
  aka *30 Days to Live*

He Came by Night (1944)
  aka *Death at the Door*

The Scarlet Button (1944)
  aka *Murder Is Cheap*

A Spy for Mr Crook (1944)

The Black Stage (1945)
  aka *Murder Cheats the Bride*

Don't Open the Door (1945)
  aka *Death Lifts the Latch*

Lift Up the Lid (1945)
  aka *The Innocent Bottle*

The Spinster's Secret (1946)
  aka *By Hook or by Crook*

Death in the Wrong Room
  (1947)

Die in the Dark (1947)
  aka *The Missing Widow*

Death Knocks Three Times
  (1949)

Murder Comes Home (1950)

A Nice Cup of Tea (1950)
  aka *The Wrong Body*

Lady-Killer (1951)

Miss Pinnegar Disappears (1952)
 aka *A Case for Mr Crook*

Footsteps Behind Me (1953)
 aka *Black Death*

Snake in the Grass (1954)
 aka *Death Won't Wait*

Is She Dead Too? (1955)
 aka *A Question of Murder*

And Death Came Too (1956)

Riddle of a Lady (1956)

Give Death a Name (1957)

Death Against the Clock (1958)

Death Takes a Wife (1959)
 aka *Death Casts a Long Shadow*

Third Crime Lucky (1959)
 aka *Prelude to Murder*

Out for the Kill (1960)

She Shall Die (1961)
 aka *After the Verdict*

Uncertain Death (1961)

No Dust in the Attic (1962)

Ring for a Noose (1963)

The Fingerprint (1964)

The Voice (1964)
 aka *Knock, Knock! Who's There?*

Passenger to Nowhere (1965)

The Looking Glass Murder (1966)

The Visitor (1967)

Night Encounter (1968)
 aka *Murder Anonymous*

Missing from Her Home (1969)

Death Wears a Mask (1970)
 aka *Mr Crook Lifts the Mask*

Murder is a Waiting Game (1972)

Tenant for the Tomb (1971)

A Nice Little Killing (1974)

Standalone Novels

The Case Against Andrew Fane (1931)

Death in Fancy Dress (1933)

The Man in Button Boots (1934)

Courtier to Death (1936)
 aka *The Dover Train Mystery*

The Clock in the Hatbox (1939)

Courtier to Death

Anthony Gilbert

An Orion book

Copyright © Lucy Beatrice Malleson 1936

The right of Lucy Beatrice Malleson to be identified as the author of this work has been asserted in accordance with the Copyright, Designs and Patents Act 1988.

This edition published by
The Orion Publishing Group Ltd
Orion House
5 Upper St Martin's Lane
London WC2H 9EA

An Hachette UK company
A CIP catalogue record for this book is available from the British Library

ISBN 978 1 4719 1064 7

www.orionbooks.co.uk

Printed and bound by CPI Group (UK) Ltd, Croydon, CR0 4YY

CHAPTER I

THE GIRL was standing by herself against the cream panelling of the ballroom. As soon as he saw her Glyn knew she was unforgettable. Standing slightly aloof from one of the most brilliant gatherings even London could boast, she was neither intimidated nor angered by her isolation. Her attitude of indifference was expressed by her pose, the slight movements of her hand as she lifted the cigarette to her lips, the faint tilt of her head as she sent the smoke back into the room, in her tranquil appraisal of the vivid, restless faces surrounding her. Yet, he thought shrewdly, indifference isn't natural to her. It was like wearing an unfamiliar dress; she donned it and wore it with exquisite aplomb, but the moment of release would come when she might draw it off and resume the habiliments of everyday. And immediately, perceiving that, Glyn had eyes for no one else.

He was convinced that he had never seen her before, and since he attended most of London's more notable parties that argued that she was a new-comer to the town. She seemed very young and was dressed in a fashion that emphasised her slender immaturity. A white gown, with a slim high-waisted effect, rippled into flounce above sedate flounce down to her heels; she wore no ornaments and, so far as Glyn could decide, no make-up; her hands were ringless, her fingernails unstained; her small short face was pale and expressive, her fair hair bunched in curls on the nape of her neck. Above her brown eyes her eyebrows were like pale golden feathers, almost invisible against the white skin. She wore a little brown velvet coat of so austere a cut that it drew attention to the discreet femininity of the gown beneath it.

" I wonder who she is," thought Glyn. " Does she know no one here that she's completely alone? And why does no one trouble to entertain her?"

It seemed to him outrageous that anyone so young and so new to London society should be thus neglected. And yet you might have expected to find her surrounded. She was a provocative and, he thought, an endearing type. Her lack of effort to maintain a robust individuality, her refusal to underline her attractions by the use of lipstick and rouge, gave her a distinctiveness of which it was impossible to remain unaware.

He looked round for his hostess, a vivid, ugly woman with Spanish black hair and a brown skin. She was, as usual, surrounded by men, artists, politicians, notable among them Fleming, of the Foreign Office, who had surprised his supporters a few years ago by evincing a passionate interest in the film industry to which, said his detractors, he devoted more than a fair share of his time, and Julian Lane, the brilliant young producer who, it was rumoured, had been instrumental in persuading Fleming to invest in film companies—Glyn's roving eye stopped there. This was the first time he had met the fellow in the flesh. All sorts of stories were current about him, his daring, his enterprise, his originality. Starting his career as a painter of the macabre he had suddenly turned the full flood of his inspiration— torrential and sometimes misdirected, but you had to expect that of experimentalists—into the channel of the films. He had had one or two short films produced that had attracted no particular attention, and then about a year ago he had offered the world " In the Shadow of Paris," the film that had made his name and fortune. Glyn observed him with increasing interest. He was said to be the youngest English producer; he couldn't be above thirty, an ugly compelling fellow, with a startlingly white face that, in a woman, you'd have sworn had been treated with cosmetics, a great deal of black hair brushed, with no particular elegance, off the high forehead, the big nose that proclaimed Jewish blood, cleft chin, and strangely eloquent hands. Glyn watched him fascinated. Magnificent hands those were, what the barrister used to call speaking hands. They could tell a story by sheer force of gesture. Oh, an odd fellow altogether, but intelligent, and painstaking to the point of genius. Crazy about his work, too. It wasn't often that you saw him out at parties like this. Glyn began to wonder why he should be here to-night.

"Does he want more support?" he reflected, and the wild notion sprang for a moment into his mind that he himself might take an interest in such a proposition, were it put to him. He knew that there was talk of a new film that Lane would be producing in the near future, and it might be that the young man wanted money. Glyn, momentarily forgetting the girl, drew nearer to the group.

Lady Hunter, his hostess, discovering him, whirled suddenly and caught him by the arm.

"Come and tell us the latest legal scandal, Glyn," she invited him. "Oh, you won't, of course. You're so heart-breakingly discreet I believe, even if you had a wife, you wouldn't tell her anything. It isn't human."

Glyn, always rendered ill at ease by this derisive form of baiting, said in pedantic tones, "Ah, but Galt and Fleming here have only men's reputations in their hands. I have their lives."

"That's why your confidences would be so

fascinating. Come, lift the veil just an inch for us. This young Riddell you're going to defend. We're all longing to know what his chances are. In fact, we've made a book at the golf club. Can't you give us a tip?"

He drew a step distant, and she came after him, putting a big well-shaped hand on his arm.

"Glyn, how exasperating you are. I suppose that's why you have the reputation of being the most intriguing man in London. You go everywhere, you know everyone . . ."

"Not everyone," he interrupted. "I'm puzzled by that girl over there. The one in white, standing alone. Who is she?"

"Somebody's secretary brought instead of a wife, I daresay. I don't remember. I give my guests carte-blanche, you know, and I can't say they abuse it."

"You don't remember whom she came with?"

"I'm afraid I don't, darling. Does it matter?"

"She doesn't appear to know anyone," Glyn pointed out.

"Don't be tiresome," the woman besought him. "You know what my parties are. I expect people to know one another. You really can't expect me to go solemnly round introducing people, like a Vicar's wife."

Glyn said nothing and the woman continued, curiously, "Why do you want to meet her? Do you think you've seen her somewhere before? Or suspect her of something? You live such a sinister life, Glyn, always discovering drug-dealers in the most respectable-looking members of society. I've always longed to have a sensation of that sort in my house. I wish you could remember who she is."

"I've never seen her face before. That I'm certain."

"How disappointing! But perhaps your sub-conscious will re-assert itself and put a name to her."

Her flippancy angered him, but his desire to meet this girl, a desire strengthening momentarily to a resolution at all costs to learn more about her, kept his expression pleasant and his voice smooth. Once enrage a woman like Diana Hunter and you could whistle down the wind for any favour she was able to do you for months, perhaps even years, to come.

So he only said, "I couldn't forget that face," and he smiled so engagingly that she laughed back at him, exclaiming "You're dying to be introduced. Why not own it? Come along then."

Her fingers tightened on his sleeve, but he needed no urging to follow her across the room to where that strange unsmiling girl waited.

"This is Rodney Glyn. He wants to know you better." That was typical of Diana's introductions. It wouldn't embarrass her that she didn't know the girl's name; nor would she expect the girl to mind.

Glyn asked considerately whether his companion wouldn't prefer to sit down. "There are plenty of chairs, and you must be tired," he suggested.

But without moving, "I'm not easily tired," she assured him.

"Still, you've been standing a long time."

She turned her head, still without hurry, and her lips began to shape themselves into a smile, charming but faintly derisive.

"Have you been watching me so long, then?"

He was impatient with his own lack of poise. A girl so young should not be able to discompose him with the first words she uttered.

He returned, with none of his usual flair for light conversation, "I wondered why you preferred to stand alone, when there are so many people close by you."

"I don't know any of them," she told him carelessly, "and Lady Hunter didn't introduce me."

"Diana never does introduce people. Most of them know one another pretty well; and anyway these are informal affairs."

He saw the delicate almost invisible brows lift. "So in London this is an informal affair?" she said, and her eyes narrowed in amusement. "It seems very—intricate to me." Her eyes took in that brilliant assembly, the women gleaming with jewels, the men in severely formal evening dress, an array of white ties and tail coats, diamond studs and beautifully polished shoes, made by hand, she reflected shrewdly, with a Parisian's instinctive eye for detail.

He began to be irritated by the ease with which she discomfited him. "Perhaps we don't mean quite the same thing by informal," he suggested. "You don't know London very well?"

"This is my first—informal party."

"Perhaps Lady Hunter doesn't realise you are not a Londoner." He looked at her questioningly, hoping she would tell him something about herself.

But she afforded him scant satisfaction. "My father used to tell me that a clever man is a citizen of the country in which he finds himself. So therefore I am now a Londoner."

"And before that?"

She shrugged her shoulders. "A Parisian, an American, a Viennese . . ."

"You've made good use of your time, mademoiselle." He ought to have realised at a glance that she was French.

"It is kind of you to put it like that." Now she was openly laughing at him; a gay ironical spirit looked out of her brown eyes, twisted her mouth into elfish lines. He thought furiously, "I can't let myself be put out of countenance by a chit like this. Who the devil is she? And what's she doing here?"

He said with great formality, " Mademoiselle, I do not yet know your name. Lady Hunter . . ."

" Does not know it either. She did not hear it. I am Mademoiselle Dulac, and I am secretary to Mr. Fleming."

" Oh!" A light broke over him. " I see. The films," for you couldn't associate her with politics. " How stupid I am not to have thought of that at once. I should have guessed you were connected with that world. But Lady Hunter saying secretary put me off the track. I've never actually seen you on the screen have I? I'm what they call a fan, and I'm sure I should remember you."

" I don't see how you could, monsieur. I have never appeared on the screen."

" But I'm right in thinking that's your ambition?"

" Not even that, monsieur. Unlike almost all the girls I have met, there are two things I have never desired to do—to act in the films or on the stage, or to enter a convent."

" Perhaps you may change your mind. Perhaps Mr. Fleming could persuade you. He's more or less absorbed in film interests these days, isn't he?"

The girl stubbed out her cigarette in a mother-of-pearl tray. " I'm sure he'd tell you anything you wanted to know, monsieur."

Again a rebuff strengthening his own sense of resolution to overcome her defences. " I'm not asking you for advance information," he said, almost too bluntly. " It isn't Mr. Fleming's activities that interest me. I think you might have a great career on the films. Surely you don't want to stay a secretary all your life."

Her fairy brows lifted. She tilted back her head, assumed an angelic pose, clasping her hands, lowering her long pale golden lashes so that her eyes were almost invisible. "Oh but monsieur, there is only one answer to that. I should like a little cottage in the country and to keep a dog and a cat. I may not be on the films," she added, assuming a natural expression and taking a tiny gold cigarette-case from a pocket in the brown coat, "but that is what all film-stars wish to do—in the end." She had lighted the cigarette before he had recovered from his astonishment at her lightning changes of pose and speech.

Someone passing brushed his arm. Di Hunter's malicious voice whispered silkily in his ear, "Aren't you going to offer your companion any supper, my dear Glyn? Everyone else has gone down already."

Startled, he looked up to see that what she said was true. The great brilliant ballroom was practically empty. He turned, laying down his cigarette-case, and offered his arm to his companion.

"Will you?" he asked, but Mademoiselle Dulac said coolly that she was waiting for a message for her employer. "That is why I am here tonight; he cannot be interrupted, but the message is important. I must remain here, monseiur. But do not, I beseech you, rob yourself of supper on my account. As you saw, I can be quite happy alone."

For the first time he detected a note of genuine alarm in her voice, urgency in her manner. "She wants me to go," he thought. "And not because of any personal objection to my company. She wants to be left alone. Why, I wonder? A rendezvous with a lover? Something definite to be done while the room's empty?" His brow furrowed; he didn't like it. The girl was a stranger, known to none of them. Her story of the message seemed to him the flimsiest of excuses. She could have arranged to have it brought her in the supper-room.

"She's not my guest," Glyn told himself, "I'm not

responsible for her." But he looked with resentful eyes at the exposed back of his hostess as it disappeared round the curve of the staircase.

He asked abruptly, " Does Mr. Fleming expect you to go without any supper?"

"He doesn't think of that, of course. I'm his secretary, monsieur. That is not the same as being a wife or a dancing partner. Besides, I can have supper at home when the message has come."

"I shall hold myself responsible for you, see that you don't starve," he promised her. " For the moment, then, au revoir."

The supper-room was full of clamour. Jewels flashed, voices rang out, laughter was less subdued than it had been an hour ago. Glyn found himself detained by Lady Hunter.

"So you've left her," she jibed. " Couldn't you persuade her to come, too?"

"Apparently she's on duty for Fleming, waiting for a message. Ridiculous, of course, but the race of Casabiancas persists amazingly, in spite of the cynics. Fleming," he added abruptly, " doesn't seem to think of his employees as human beings. He's more like a machine than a man. His work's everything to him."

Diana Hunter's eyes sparkled. " That's why he is so irresistible to women perhaps."

"She can starve for all he cares," Glyn said disgustedly.

"It's largely due to him that she hasn't starved," Lady Hunter taunted him. " You were so much interested I thought I'd do you a good turn and find out something about her for you. You should be grateful."

He nodded, refusing to commit himself. He knew Di's way of getting information. Already she would have spread the rumour that he had fallen headlong for the little nonentity in white flounces; if he wasn't mistaken, he'd be the laughing-stock of the evening before the party was over; and, being Di's party, it would probably go on to all hours of the morning.

"All very well for these women," he thought, hotly. "They can lie down all the afternoon and stay in bed till midday. I suppose that child has been at it since nine—Fleming's a byword for work— and will have to be at the desk at nine to-morrow morning."

"Have you lost interest already?" Lady Hunter teased him, but she was a little anxious, too. She had hoped for some amusement in baiting the serious-minded K.C., whose lack of interest in women was notorious.

"I'm dying to know what you've learned," he returned, truthfully.

"It seems that Fleming found her in a rather third-rate cabaret show in Paris a few months ago; he was taken by her and offered her a job as his secretary. Why, no one quite knows."

"Or why she took it. I gather she doesn't hanker for a film career, and being part of the machinery by which Fleming orders his life can't be much of a prospect for any young woman."

"Perhaps she's long-sighted," suggested Lady Hunter. "There's no getting away from the fact that the French are a shrewd nation and Fleming is a very rich man, richer than ever since he started investing in films. Though he had a fair amount of money before that."

"He hasn't the name of paying his employees too well."

"As I said, she may be long-sighted, taking small dividends in the hope of an ultimate scoop. Like the rest of us, my dear Glyn, she probably knows which side her bread's buttered. And you're not forgetting that, with the possible exception of yourself, Fleming's the most eligible bachelor in London."

"I'm not," agreed Glyn politely, "but perhaps, like Alice, Mlle. Dulac likes only the best butter."

His companion chuckled maliciously. "You're like Lucifer in the swiftness of your fall. What is it, I wonder, about these innocent-looking young women that undermines your strong man? It's always happening, though you'll have to admit that a girl who has sung in a cheap Parisian cabaret must know something about life."

"And you're looking to Fleming to teach her the rest?"

"I think you wouldn't mind helping. Give me one of your marvellous cigarettes."

He slipped his hand into his pocket. "That's odd," he exclaimed. "I had the case a minute ago. Ah, I must have left it in the ballroom. One moment." He had reached the door before she opened her mouth to tell him it didn't matter. He went lightly up the stairs, sick at the cheap turn the talk had taken, cursing himself for being too weak-minded to refuse to discuss the girl further. He understood well enough the construction Diana Hunter put on the younger woman's motives, and scowled. A commonplace mind, for all its flashes of fineness, its genuine culture, and a certain fastidiousness in personal relationships.

Not that he personally had any fears as to Fleming's motive in making the girl his secretary. A man in his position wasn't going to risk scandal; if he'd wanted some passing adventure with the girl he'd have kept her in France. But it angered the lawyer to think that her position should lay her open to such misconception, and even more to realise that if she knew what people said about her, as very probably she did, she wouldn't care.

The door of the ballroom stood ajar; the polished floor glittered with reflections of the myriad lights that blazed from ceiling and wall; at the further end French windows opened on to the sparkling night. Beyond the window the Park lay in patches of darkness lighted by a string of lamps; and in the window itself, outlined against the distant view, stood the girl who occupied his thoughts, and a tall dark figure whom an instant later he identified as Julian Lane. Involuntarily he drew back a step, and as he did so he heard the girl's voice, low and penetrating, urgent with a fear that thrilled and shocked him.

"There will just be time, Julian," she said. "We must take no unnecessary risk."

"For him or for ourselves?"

Her hand came out and touched his arm. "Ah Julian," she said. "You feel as I do about this. But remember—he may be armed. Be very careful. You have just time. 11.54 at Victoria."

She turned from the window, letting the elaborate tapestry fall into place. Glyn walked into the room.

"My cigarette-case?" he began. "Ah, mademoiselle. Is there still no hope of persuading you to come down to supper?"

The girl hesitated, but Lane said in masterful tones, "Mademoiselle has a headache, and I am seeing her into a taxi, thank you, sir. Come, Eve." He laid his hand on her arm.

Glyn said, "Shall I tell Fleming, if he asks for you?" and now her glance was innocent and surprised as she said, "Oh, but he won't ask. He won't expect me to stay. It was only for this message that I came."

There was nothing Glyn could do but stand back and wish the pair good-night. Then he picked up his cigarette-case and went slowly down the stairs in their wake. Complete disinclination for the party and all its remaining members overwhelmed him, but he did not belong to a generation that consults no tastes but its own and he returned reluctantly to the supper-room where his hostess awaited him. For himself, now that Eve Dulac had gone, it was as if all the lights had been lowered and the band gone home.

The heat and noise of the crowded room struck him with a fresh stab of distaste as he made his way towards the spot where Lady Hunter stood.

"I thought you had succumbed to the wiles of your charmer," she greeted him. "Come and sit at Fleming's table. I want to ask him about his new film and you want to ask him about his new secretary."

Regardless of his protests that he wanted to do nothing of the kind, she dragged him across the room to a rather noisy group collected round a small table. Fleming looked like a stage politician, tall, hawk-nosed, lean, with an incisive manner and a smile of great charm and subtlety. "You'd think a fellow that looked as fictional as that must be a fool," was Glyn's characteristic reaction; but his experience had taught him that Fleming was nothing of the kind. He was, on the contrary, a man who set tremendous store on detail, and his success in every walk of life that he had so far attempted was generally held to be due to the fact that he distrusted most of his underlings and attended to the work in hand himself. He was a man who seemed to need practically no sleep; his brilliant eyes dominated to-night's gathering, that hung on his words.

"You must give us a little stable information," a woman in a red silk frock was exclaiming. "This new film of yours—all sorts of rumours are going about, and I expect they're all untrue."

"And all dissimilar," smiled Fleming. "Well, that's natural enough. Precious few people know anything about it, beyond Lane and myself, and neither of us is exactly a chatterbox."

"So he's producing for you again, is he? He's an expensive young man, they say."

"He can have the bottom of my purse," was Fleming's unvarnished retort, "if he produces me another masterpiece. I've never had much sympathy with half-measures. If you really want a thing you want it so badly that you'll take any chances to get it. I wanted The Shadow of Paris, and I wanted it perfect. On the whole, I think I got it. I want The Judge, and I want that perfect, too, and I'm taking steps for which most people would condemn me to a lunatic asylum to get that, too."

"Well, we've learnt the name of the new master-piece, anyway. What's it about?"

"Ask my producer," suggested Fleming. But Lane was nowhere to be seen.

"He said he'd have to go early," explained Lady Hunter. "You're living up to your reputation of slave-driver, Fleming," and everyone laughed.

"Who's the star?" they clamoured.

"That's my shock for you. I daresay you'll call it either rank insanity or else a bid for publicity, though I think I might claim without vanity that at the moment I don't stand in need of that. But if this new picture we're putting out does anything to rival its predecessor it won't be my money, or even Lane's genius, that will account for it—but the man who acts the leading part."

"I suppose you know you're tantalising us all abominably," said his hostess in brusque tones. "You're as bad as a film actress trying to make a wretched reporter guess which of the new stars she's taking over as her next husband. Don't be so cheap, Fleming, and tell us the man's name at once."

"All right." A theatrical fellow for all his departmental discipline, Glyn decided, seeing the handsome head tip back, noting the momentary pause during which everyone waited on tiptoe as it were, for his announcement. "It's not often I'm accused of being womanish. Incidentally, mine isn't the dashing type of film, magnificent lover, shrinking but indomitable heroine, thrills galore. The chief character's an old Jew, a withered embittered old creature, and what you see is the last year of his life. I'm making a definite break from the romantic tradition, and Lane is with me. He's got ideas, that young man."

"And who's consented to play this senile old wreck?"

Fleming held them all with his magnetic eyes. "Rene Tessier," he said, and waited for the storm to break.

He didn't have to wait long. There was an incredulous gasp from the assembly, and then a jabber of voices.

"Tessier! My dear chap, have you seen him lately? He was pointed out to me when I was in Paris a few months ago. To all intents and purposes he's a dead man."

"They say he drinks like a fish—drugs, too. He's beyond redemption."

"The death of that son of his broke him up. Some mystery there. A woman, I believe."

"Mad as a hatter," confirmed someone else.

With some difficulty Fleming made his voice heard above the melee. "You're wrong, and I'm going to prove it to you. Tessier isn't dead. He's simply under the weather."

"You'll never be able to pull him out far enough

to star him in the kind of play you contemplate. You'll only land yourself in the Bankruptcy Court."

"I don't think so. I told you I didn't mind taking chances. It will be a risk; I've faced that. But it may also be the opportunity of a lifetime. The man's a genius, and that's a word I hesitate to use of anyone. He's an artist right in his bones. Once he can be persuaded to start work there'll be no more trouble. He doesn't just enact a personality, he becomes it. He won't be ruined, shattered Rene Tessier any more; he'll be the Judge. You've all seen him, I expect."

"I have, in every play he's ever acted in," responded Glyn, warmly, "and I appreciate what you say. It's uncanny, the way in which he penetrates under the other fellow's skin; he can change not only his appearance and his character but even his nationality. You can watch it happening. I can think of no other living man who so impresses me. You've got a contract with him?"

"It's waiting to be signed."

"Where are you making the picture?" asked Lady Hunter.

"In the new studios at Eden End."

"You haven't had any difficulty about getting permission for him to act over here."

Fleming smiled discreetly. "These things can be arranged."

"Of course, you're hand in glove with authority."

"It's the famous and much-lauded policy of not letting your right hand know what you left hand does. In any case, I'm utterly opposed to the notion that you can nationalise art. Its universal, not an affair for patriotism. No one but Tessier can make this picture as Lane and I are resolved it shall be made. I'd stretch a lot more points than I've had to in this instance in such a cause. Why, there's no man living can equal him for technique and gesture. You know that strange face of his, more like a vulture than ever since he had his bad luck, but vivid—you can't put it out of your mind. I remember the first film in which I saw him, some unknown man's story of the French Terror. Tessier played the part of an old man whose daughter was ridden down by an aristocrat's coach while she was trying to save her child from the wheels. It was superb. I couldn't by any words of mine chill your blood as mine was chilled that July afternoon. The face, the dumb eloquence—that man can talk with every limb he's got; the hate and the scorn and the bitterness that never forgets. . . He didn't get his effects by shouting or shaking his fist—I've seldom seen a man move so little—but he awed a packed house—and he was a minor character. The film was nothing, except for his work. It went out of circulation long ago. When compliments were being showered on Lane for The Shadow of Paris a year ago I remember his saying to me that the one that made him feel on top of the world was when Appleton referred to him as the second Rene Tessier. He produced his own things in those days, and if he did produce you'd know you could expect perfection, not a detail out of place, not a gesture wasted. Oh, he was a king among men and he will be again."

His glowing voice silenced them all; his words had conjured up a vision of that magnificent little man, shoulders bent, deep-set eyes terrorising his audience, his golden voice holding them spell-bound.

"If you do bring him back to the screen," Glyn heard himself say, " you'll have done your art a service for which it will never sufficiently thank you. I also remember that film. Sometimes I feel I'd give the world to forget it. It's strange that such a man

17

should let even a tragedy like the death of his son break him so completely."

"What did happen, darlings?" enquired Lady Hunter. "Why haven't I seen the film? You're making me feel horribly in the cold."

"Oh, jumped off the Arc de Triomphe. Some unhappy love affair that the youngster took too hard. Tessier idolised him, and when he was gone he seemed to lose all interest in life. But he's too good to be lost. The man who discovered him believed he'd discovered a miracle."

"He had discovered a miracle," said Glyn dryly, "and if you're successful, you'll have worked one. And all luck to you. When does Tessier land?"

"To-night. I've just had a wire." He took it out of his pocket and spread it on the table before him.

It said:

Arriving Victoria 11.54.

CHAPTER II

THE rain, that had begun shortly before eleven, had swelled into a rushing torrent before the boat train from Dover reached London. Water streamed down the smooth sides of the engine, hissing on the metals; it thundered on the roofs of the carriages, came sweeping against the windows, so that even the meagre lights of the countryside were blotted out. The train was crowded; the third class carriage in which a little foreigner, with a large head, was huddled into a corner-seat, was full of women, talking with the peculiar stridency of voice that distinguishes a certain type of Englishwoman.

"Now, mind what I say, Gwen, the minute we get in, you put your head out and get a porter. You know what this station's like, about six porters for the whole train, and the men always get them if they can."

"Funny, how porters seem to like men. Get bigger tips, p'haps."

"Men have more money to throw away than us girls. Don't have to do so much with it."

A plump lady, with feathers round an elaborate satin hat, joined in genteelly, " They do these things so much better in France. I'm sure at every turn there were those men in blue blouses simply clamouring to help you. And it's no use telling me the French are an acquisitive nation; you don't have to tip them a penny more than you would our own men and they look ever so much more grateful."

A fourth voice broke in from a further corner, " What I miss most when I'm abroad is my afternoon tea. These foreigners don't seem to have any cosy notions at all. And if you go into a teashop all you can get is a bit of pastry costing twice as much as it does at home and half the size."

The unhappy little Frenchman listened to these criticisms of his country without resentment. His thoughts at this moment were concerned entirely with himself. It had been an abominable journey; he had been fearfully sick on the boat, and had felt more like a rat than a man as he stepped off, keeping an anxious eye on the solitary suit-case that now contained all his possessions. He was unaccustomed to this kind of travelling; last time he had come to London, eight years ago, the reception he had received would not have disgraced royalty. There had been eager crowds waiting on the platform, and they'd cheered him as he came benignly out of his first-class carriage, with servants to look after his ample luggage, and run ahead and arrange about his car. He had stayed at the Ritz and people had hung about in corridors, ostensibly to catch their friends, or pausing to light a cigarette, but actually, as he knew, to see him at close quarters. His table had been mobbed on the rare occasions when he hadn't had his meals sent up to his suite; and once— this made him proudest of all—he had been on the pavement, waiting to get into his car, and a London omnibus had drawn up close by. The conductor had struck his head inside, and instead of calling Ritz Hotel as he always did, he'd said, " Anyone for Rene Tessier? Rene Tessier? Right, mum," and he'd helped a plump lady to alight. Tessier himself had been so much enchanted by this tribute that he had remained on the pavement, to the delight of onlookers, who nudged one another and exclaimed, " Isn't that sweet of him? Standing there to let everyone have a good look. I think he's marvellous, don't you?"

" Oh, I do, my dear. Definitely marvellous."

He had got into his car then and been driven off, through the Park, with all the chestnuts in flower, and the may-trees coming out and tulips in bright beds at Hyde Park Corner and the Stanhope Gate. It was a different sort of welcome he would get now. Rene Tessier, so far as the public was concerned, was a dead man. He knew what they said about him. That the death of his son had broken him utterly, that he'd become a hanger-on at cheap cafés, touting for a, drink from any fourth-rate fool who'd stand him the price of it and afterwards boast of his conquest, that he mixed with all the rabble of Paris —very likely that he was a thief and blackmailer into the bargain: that he was in debt, and constantly on the run from his creditors and the wretched women who trusted him for the rent of his single room. Oh, a back number, my dear, hadn't saved a cent, of course, these actors never do and if he had, it would have gone into the publican's pocket long ago. And there was a divine American called George Weyman, definitely the most amazing man the screen had ever portrayed. A mincing, jabbering ape, thought Tessier, but without indignation. He had so little passion left now, and what there was he must safeguard for the work he had to do; he had no energy to waste on the third-rate men who had stepped into his shoes. Besides, he'd got another chance, and he had come to England to take it. After two years the opportunity had sprung up; it would take all his wits, but at least he shouldn't go down to posterity as one of the men who'd gone under. All the essential fire of the man's nature burned up in him, stiffening the bowed back, lightening the haggard face.

A woman who had left the carriage a few moments previously suddenly stuck her head through the door and said, " They're saying the train's on fire. Think it's true?"

The women to whom she spoke didn't lose their heads. They said, " Oh, I shouldn't think so," in comfortable tones, and continued their reminiscences. Tessier rose slowly and stiffly, inch by inch; his hand gripped the frame of the carriage. Fire, whispered his terrified heart. All his life he had been haunted by this dread. But he mustn't show his fear. He stood there panting and sweating, keeping himself rigid by a pure effort of the will, and those God-damned women went on commenting in their ignorant ill-bred fashion on the country of his birth and their extremely limited travels, quite oblivious of his obvious Parisian derivation.

" I am Rene Tessier," he muttered to himself. " I am Rene Tessier. I am not afraid," and the wheels took up the maddening refrain, " You are Rene Tessier. Rene Tessier. And you are terribly afraid." A groan escaped him, and a thin lady, smelling of peppermint, across the gangway, leaned forward and said gravely, "Tooth-ache, mossoo? I have some aspros . . ." But he smiled with difficulty and waved them away. It was nothing, he said. A little migraine, and then the woman came back and said it was a false alarm and everybody laughed and began to chat eagerly about other false alarms, and Tessier slid back into his seat. And at once his mind reverted, as it always did, to that chill morning almost before it was light, when he'd been called from his bed by a gendarme and taken down to the morgue to see a body laid out on a stone slab—the body of his son, who had destroyed himself by leaping, in a frenzy of despair, from the Arc de Triomphe. Rene had identified the corpse and attended the inquest; and when he came out into blinding sunlight he had to face a tornado of reporters and questions and the stares of the curious heartless multitude. For days after that he never opened a paper without seeing headlines that practically everyone else had already forgotten.

Dramatic Leap to Death
Film Star's Son falls from Arc de Triomphe
Midnight Tragedy

Wherever he turned, on young shoulders and old, in the faces of sages and cretins, he saw only that dead white face, vacant and still streaked with mud, that bore no resemblance, in essence, to the face of his only beloved son. It was after that that he had dropped out, till now he was scarcely a name to the majority. Till now. He might never do another piece of work, but by this he would be remembered.

"By God!" he whispered, and the words were less an oath than a vow.

The train raced along the gleaming rails and entered the station. This was dimly-lighted and drab in the rain that thundered still on the dingy roof. Tessier drew in his small elegant feet to let the rapacious women scramble out and make their frenzied struggle for porters before he rescued his suit-case from the rack and climbed out. The platform was almost empty; only far ahead he saw the serviceable shapeless backs of some of his fellow travellers or their counterparts—these women were as alike as peas in a pod—and heard a dim clamour of voices as they argued with ticket-collectors and one another. At this hour, he reflected, Paris would be preparing for carnival; London seemed like a city of the dead. Yet he knew that under hundreds of roofs lights were blazing, lovely women in exquisite gowns were dancing, dicing, making love; suave finely-tailored men, who hadn't been dragged from their beds on a dark May morning to identify a body, would be ordering drinks, chatting, all enjoying the luxury that only money can provide. While he, Rene Tessier, stood forlornly on the platform, wondering how he would drag his exhausted limbs as far as the hotel where he had booked a room, on the advice of a man he'd met in one of the little cafés on the outskirts of Paris where he was so often to be found.

"It is not very comfortable," he had acknowledged. "But no one will trace you there. And it is quiet. As for the food," he shrugged his shoulders. "Well, one knows what food is like in these poor English hostelries." Only Tessier didn't know. Still, after his squalid Parisian experiences he didn't suppose whatever this place was like it would daunt him. "I will take a cab," he thought. "The driver will know the place," and he stooped to pick up his case, for, true enough, there wasn't a porter in sight. At that moment a dark lithe figure came running past the ticket-collector and approached him. He wore a wide-brimmed black hat and a black overcoat; between the two was a scarf no whiter than his face.

"I beg your pardon, monsieur," he said courteously. "I should have been here earlier, but for the weather. It was impossible for some time to get a cab." He took off the black hat that was dripping, and Tessier saw that it was no blacker than his hair and eyes. A striking fellow, thought the perplexed Frenchman, but one whom for the moment he didn't recognise.

"I don't quite understand," he began, and the new-comer said at once, "I beg your pardon. My name's Lane—Julian Lane. I'm producing Fleming's new film. If you'll permit me," he took the bag from the other's frozen fingers. "The honour's mine, believe me. It didn't occur to me till quite late that you might perhaps be travelling alone. You have reserved a room? If not, I've a spare room in my flat . . ."

"You are very good, monsieur. I have a room." He gave the address, watching his companion's face. But Lane's expression did not flicker.

"Yes, I know the neighbourhood. We can get a cab now, I think. The rain's clearing a bit." They came through the barrier and Lane called imperiously to a porter, "Taxi, please." One materialised out of the dark night and the young man handed his companion in and stepped in beside him.

"You'll let me travel with you and see you settled?" he suggested. "Some of these small hotels haven't much notion of comfort." And he added gracefully, "May I say, monsieur, how proud I am of this opportunity that you and Mr. Fleming are giving me? I hadn't dared hope for so much luck."

"Did Fleming tell you what train I was coming by?" asked Tessier.

"No. His secretary, Mademoiselle Dulac. It was she," he added honestly, "who was anxious that you should have some sort of reception."

"Ah!" The stranger's deep-sunken brilliant eyes inquisitively examined his companion. "You know Mlle. Dulac?"

"Yes," responded the young man steadily. "And I hope to know her better. I feel," he added, in a less restrained tone, "that she must have at least some faith in me, even some liking for me, that she entrusted me with to-night's errand. It's obviously a matter that concerns her a good deal."

"You know, of course, that she was to have married my son?" said Tessier so abruptly that Lane flushed in embarrassment.

"I heard it from her own lips," he agreed. "But naturally it's not a subject on which you could expect her to elaborate. You don't, I hope," he added, observing his companion's drawn resolute face, "hold her responsible for what happened?"

Tessier lay back; he spoke so quietly that the other had to lean towards him to hear what he said. "My son died because Eve Dulac refused to marry him," he said. "You can't ask me to forget that."

"Yet you're prepared to make use of her," broke out the young man impulsively.

Tessier smiled, an odd harsh movement of bloodless lips. "Oh, I'd use the devil to further my plans," he said, and then the cab turned the corner into a villainous little side-street and stopped before a door with a garish illumination—HOTEL—over the gateway.

"We seem to have arrived," said Lane, superfluously, leaning forward to open the door.

"Have you," he asked—the thought had

apparently not occurred to him earlier, "had any dinner?"

"I could eat nothing," said Tessier hurriedly, adding to himself as he stepped out of the vehicle, "this cold freezes one's bones."

Yet as he stood in the hall of the shabby little hotel to which his compatriot had sent him, there was a nobility, even a magnificence about him that no exhaustion or poverty could wholly disguise. Lane thought, "He could do that part of the Judge even now" and when he took the old man's arm he was surprised at the hardness of the muscles, his power of resistance.

"Thank you. I am perfectly well now," he said, and turned to speak to the proprietor, a large olive-complexioned man who came forward to examine the new arrivals in a doubtful way. He couldn't quite make the couple out; the old man was shabby and his luggage meagre, whereas his companion was well-dressed and had the air of a man to whom such hotels as his were a novelty, and not a pleasant one at that.

"M. Tessier?" he said, looking enquiringly from one to the other. There was not a shadow of recognition in his voice as he mentioned that once-famous name; he even seemed doubtful whether the older man might not be a servant, and the other a man perhaps attempting to conceal himself from pursuers.

Rene Tessier raised his head. "I booked a room here," he said proudly, and at the unexpected authority in that voice Pecheron changed his manner. It became not more pleasant—and it had not been pleasant at the outset—but more suspicious, as though here was a mystery and he was not a man who cared for mysteries. Indeed, he could not afford them. "Is there a fire in my room?" his client continued.

"It has not been lighted. No orders were given . . ."

"Have it lighted at once, then. It is a coal fire?"

"It's a gas fire. Monsieur's room is at the top of the house."

"Why's that?" broke in Lane, warmly.

"Because Monsieur asked for a room with access to the fire escape. I took it," he added insolently, "that monsieur was afraid of fire."

Lane looked up as though he would break into a furious protest, but Tessier said with an unassailable dignity, "You were right. I am very much afraid of fire. And with reason. But of that I do not speak. I will go up now, and you will please send someone to carry my bag."

Pecheron twitched a greasy-looking book from the counter of the manager's recess.

"If monsieur will sign," he suggested, leisurely pulling forward an ink-pot and a villainous pen.

"Surely that can wait till the morning," protested Lane. "M. Tessier has had a bad journey and has not dined."

Tessier, however, taking no notice of either man, moved forward and unscrewing a pen that he drew from his coat-pocket, scrawled his almost indecipherable signature. Then he returned the pen, that was cased in gold. "One of my few remaining tributes," he told Lane, who had put down the suit-case, and now asked, "Would you like me to leave you now, or could I be of service to you perhaps?"

"I'm feeling extremely ill," Tessier confessed, in tones too low for the proprietor to hear him. And indeed his appearance was alarming, and he could scarcely keep on his feet. Lane gave him an arm, murmuring as they ascended the stairs together, "I had a message for you from Mademoiselle. She would be glad to see you in in the morning, here, if you wish. Or at her rooms. Fleming won't be wanting her before midday. And then he, too, hopes to see you . . ."

"I shall be glad to see Mademoiselle as soon as she cares to call," Tessier agreed. "Say, eleven o'clock. But I have a second engagement later in the morning. Perhaps after dejeuner it would be convenient for me to see Fleming." He asked one or two questions about the work in prospect, that Lane answered with alacrity. The stairs were steep and numerous and he was beginning to be afraid his companion would find them overwhelming, "and that," he reflected, "will mean this old fox ahead of us will claim the price of the room and send Tessier to a hospital. If I can keep him going . . ."

It was almost a losing fight. At the door of the huge, gaunt room that had been allotted to him, Tessier reeled and only Lane's supporting arm got him as far as the black iron bedstead on to which he collapsed, letting his forehead, damp with sweat, lie against the chill coarse surface of the sheets.

"I don't believe even they are clean," thought Lane in disgust. "They've been slept in since they were last laundered," and he looked anxiously at Tessier to see whether he also would notice.

Tessier, however, was either too sick to notice anything or had slept in too many strange places to be fastidious, for he made no comment. Pecheron stood away from the bed observing the pair, with sullen anger in his expression.

"Monsieur is ill," he burst out at last. "He should not come to an hotel. You're staying with him?" he added resentfully to Lane. "I had orders only for one room."

"I shall stay with him till monsieur's better. Fetch some brandy," he added, "the best you have. And you needn't be afraid that he's going to die on your hands," he wound up contemptuously, "this is the effect of a shocking crossing and no food."

With no very good grace Pecheron departed on his errand, and Lane gently urged his companion into the creaking basket-work armchair that stood by the bubbling little gas fire. The room was bitterly cold, with a single electric light that left a great patch at the further end in darkness. There was a huge square window over which thin blue curtains were inadequately drawn. The rest of the furnishings consisted of a cheap dressing-table, a chair or two, a writing-table and a commode cupboard on which stood a chipped basin and ewer.

"A bad place for a rat to die in," said Tessier suddenly, opening his eyes and looking round him. "That's what you were thinking, isn't it? But don't be afraid, Mr. Lane. I'm not going to die here. I haven't made this detestable journey in order to fail at the end of it. And I should be glad if you would not tell Mr. Fleming quite everything that has occurred to-night. To-morrow I shall be a new man."

"I shall say nothing," promised Lane. "You may rely upon me." At that moment Pecheron returned with a freshly-opened bottle of brandy and a plate of sandwiches that he placed on the table at the old man's elbow. Lane expected him to retire, but instead he hesitated near the door and repeated in dissatisfied tones, "The gentleman is not well. He should not be travelling alone."

Lane hustled him out of the room. "That's a pestilent fellow," he observed, as the door closed behind the heavy reluctant figure. "Indeed, if you'll permit me to say so, I don't find this the sort of hotel where you should be staying. If you take my advice you'll clear out in the morning. If I can be of service . . ." That was as near as he dared come with the old man in so overwrought a state to offering money. But Tessier didn't take offence.

" You are right," he said. " I had no idea . . . But I shall be well enough. A little brandy . . ." He took the bottle off the table and with a steady hand poured what appeared to his companion to be a good quantity into the thick glass. He drank it practically neat.

"Habit perhaps, if all the stories they tell of him are true. I suppose the brandy's pretty rank," he added aloud, but to his surprise Tessier said, " It is wonderful. You must taste it. One would never have supposed such an oaf to have such golden magic in his cellar."

Lane had not moved from his position by the door that he had taken up after the departure of the landlord. Now, as his gaze moved in turn from that strange huddled figure in the battered armchair, with its indomitable face and resolute voice, to the bareness of the ugly room, to the darkness beyond the sphere of the electric bulb, to the window through which he could see a cluster of dimly-shining roofs, and while he listened to the faint sounds going on in the hotel, an extraordinary sensation seized him, such a sensation as men experience who have drunk, not enough to render them intoxicated but more than enough to stimulate them and engage their imaginations. He felt as though some force outside himself were compelling him, as if it would sweep him off his feet, and he actually made a physical effort to remain where he was. But the sensation— part excitement, part exaltation, part fear—possessed him. He had to go with that inexorable tide. For a minute he put his hands over his eyes as if to free himself from this peculiar domination. He had a moment of actual terror when he believed the old man to have supernatural powers; then the feeling became less acute. A sense of mystery remained, but once again he belonged to himself. Turning towards Tessier he saw that he was now pouring himself out a second glass of brandy. Catching his companion's eye, the former said, " You must take a glass with me. This sort of spirit is a treat to me after the kind of drink to which I've become accustomed."

" He's getting drunk," thought Lane, noticing the untouched sandwiches. " All that brandy on an empty stomach," and he was careful only to pour himself a very weak mixture. But even so the extraordinary quality of the spirit delighted him. At once he felt cool and enterprising. He knew it would be useless to try and shake Tessier back to sobriety, " and indeed," he reflected, " it's probably best that he should be in this semi-comatose state. Eve herself would agree as to that."

Tessier suddenly began to speak. " Mr. Lane," he said, " I have told you already how grateful I am to you for your kindness to-night. I believe I can trust you. There is one more thing I should like to ask, and I beg of you to tell me the truth." But even when Lane had said, " You can rely on me, sir," he seemed to find some difficulty in putting his thought into words. " It is this," he said at last. " I know I shall seem strange. You may think I'm delirious, but what I want to know is this. Were we followed to-night when we came here? Did anyone follow us from the station? Or perhaps," he added on a disappointed note, " you would not have noticed."

" I think I should," said Lane, " and I think I can say no one followed us. But—forgive me—have you been troubled in that way lately?"

It was now obvious that Tessier had drunk too much brandy. His head came forward, the eyes enormous and staring; his voice had the careful distinctness of an intoxicated man.

"I know too much," he said slowly, "and soon—in twenty-four hours perhaps—I shall know more. I'm—dangerous to a man like that."

"A man like whom?" Lane asked the question eagerly, but Tessier would give him no reply.

"You wouldn't think I was dangerous, would you?" he asked, cunningly. "But I am." He dropped back and not all Lane's cajolery could get another word from him on the subject. Suddenly he straightened himself and began to talk, not of the present but of the glittering unforgettable past, of triumphs and audacities, of encounters and risks, a hotch-potch of personalities such as no newspaper would dare publish, of trade secrets hitherto unknown. And as he spoke his failing voice grew stronger, he sketched scenes with a single gesture, an inflection, a turn of hand or head; he mimicked and caricatured till Lane stood transfixed at such an exhibition as he had never before beheld and in all probability would never see enacted again. Even for the moment he forgot why he was there.

"And now," wound up Tessier, "I play a new part, the Judge. The Judge! Tell me, does Fleming regret his offer?"

"I think he's prepared to abandon the film if you don't play the title-rôle," returned Lane, simply.

Some devil of vanity was attacking Tessier to-night; he seemed drunk, not merely with brandy, but with his own glory. He said, "I'm thirsty. Talking always makes me thirsty. Give me some brandy," and Lane took the bottle and poured him out a drink just out of his sight so that he shouldn't see how it was diluted.

When Tessier had drunk it he fell back exhaustedly, and Lane stooped and changed his shoes for him, putting on Moorish slippers that he found in the unlocked suit-case. The fellow was wrapped in a patterned silk dressing-gown, a relic of more fortunate days. Lane bent over the old man, wondering whether he could lift him into the bed, but he abandoned that notion, contenting himself by spreading the thick counterpane over the recumbent figure. As he moved towards the door he saw that Tessier's wallet had fallen to the floor, having presumably dropped out of his pocket during his moments of collapse on the bed. He picked it up to find it was stuffed with notes, some of them of remarkably high value.

"I wonder how honest Pecheron is, and if there's any guarantee he won't come prying as soon as I'm out of the way." He wondered for a moment if it might be wiser to keep the wallet till the next morning, but Tessier might wake up and look for it. For the same reason it would not be safe to hide it, so Lane made a note of the numbers, and laid the wallet on the table at its owner's elbow. Moving across to the window he stood for a moment staring out at a flight of roofs, rising like miniature ranges, as far as eye could reach. Tessier's room looked over the back of the building. Immediately beneath was a narrow alley in which a single lamp burned. The night was uncannily still; once a policeman stepped into that limited white radiance, but for the most part the place was as quiet as the grave. A spatter of stars had broken through the ragged clouds, and here and there a window still burned gold, but for the most part these were like blind eye-sockets.

"It's a queer neighbourhood," he said in a low voice. "I don't suppose anyone knows half the strange things that happen here." And the artist in him thought of that illimitable drama spread under his gaze, the tragedies, the beauty, the rapture those sordid little cells housed. It was some such vision that had inspired his latest and most famous picture. He drew a long breath at the thought of the future. Now he was pure fanatic; personalities ceased to be of account. He saw only his own work and the years ahead. A lean grey cat slid like a shadow along the gutter of an adjacent house; it seemed suddenly to see him, for it paused in its slinking progress, one paw lifted, its black shadow flat against the rain-wet roof of the house. Then like a spirit it had vanished, and he could not see it go. In the room behind him the man stirred noisily, and Lane turned back. There was nothing more he could do now. He had already offered to spend the night in the room, saying, " I assure you, monsieur, I could make myself quite comfortable on that chair," to which Tessier had replied, with a glimmer of malice, " No man, monsieur, could make himself comfortable on such a chair."

As he paused, with his hand on the knob of the door, he thought he detected stealthy footsteps outside, and flinging the door wide he saw Pecheron moving like a great dark cat towards the head of the stairs.

At the sound of the door opening the fellow turned. " I tell you I don't like this at all," he began in belligerent tones. " That friend of yours should be in a hospital. I don't want to have a man dying on my hands, a foreigner, too, which always makes more trouble. He should go to a hospital."

" If I know anything of hospitals," returned Lane easily, " we should spend half the night finding a vacant bed and filling up forms. And at that we should probably finish him by taking him out on such a night. I don't want to stand in the dock on a manslaughter charge on his behalf or any other man's." And then he began to ask about the brandy, saying he'd like a bottle for himself. "You may congratulate yourself that that brandy did M. Tessier more good this evening than a dozen doctors. Where do you find such stuff?"

Pecheron looked a little mollified, though he refused a straight answer. "Smuggled, I shouldn't be surprised," decided Lane. "Well, I could hardly expect him to tell me that. I'll be round in the morning," he added, "to see how M. Tessier is. I fancy he's staying with friends after to-night. Are you open every hour in the twenty-four?" he added, seeing that the front-door still stood ajar.

"For strangers chiefly," admitted Pecheron. "We are open all night."

"You're rather far from a station for that, surely," countered Lane, but Pecheron was more than his match on this ground. "This is a noisy part of London after midnight," he said. "And there are plenty who find it—inconvenient—to go home so late." He smiled blandly, and Lane grinned. That word—inconvenient—showed humour of a type, if not the best. With a final commendation of Tessier to his landlord's care, the young producer passed out into the dark street.

The rain had ceased some time ago, and stars were multiplying overhead; but down here on the pavements there was still little light; the moon was invisible and the lamps few and dim. Lane looked up and down the street. "Must be a paradise for criminals," he murmured. "One policeman couldn't do much here, and if he's a wise fellow he'd probably emulate Nelson and go conveniently blind, if the odds were too outrageous."

A hundred yards distant he saw what he wanted, a tall box like an up-ended coffin painted scarlet. It was close to a coffee-stall where a few people, including a short aggressive young man with a prominent nose, were drinking bovril and execrable coffee. Lane dived into the box and pulled the door to, but there was something wrong with the catch, and it wouldn't remain shut. He called a number, knowing that Diana Hunter's parties were generally dusk to dawn affairs, and guessing that Fleming would still be there. No need, he reflected, waiting for his connection, to telephone to Eve Dulac and say he'd executed her commission. She anticipated from her friends the efficient loyalty she was prepared to give. Anyway, the only telephone at her block of flats stood in the hall, and he had no intention of calling her from her bed to tell her what had happened. Lady Hunter's butler answered the phone and said that Fleming was still on the premises. Lane held his arm sideways to catch a streak of light from the coffee-stall on the face of his watch.

"Just after one! I suppose they'll keep it up till four or after, but I'm not going back."

Then Fleming's voice said, "Hullo! What's up?"

"This is Julian Lane. I thought you might like to know I've seen Tessier. Mlle. Dulac asked me to meet him. I've just put him to bed, figuratively speaking, at the foul hotel someone told him to go to. The Robespierre—wouldn't you think the name would warn you? The landlord's a rogue if ever I saw one. I only hope he doesn't rob the poor devil. Still, he didn't know the name of Tessier, which shows you how the fellow's dropped out."

The door of the telephone cabinet swung a little wider in the wind; the young man with the prominent nose put down the thick china mug from which he had been drinking bovril, and moved a step nearer; he had a nose for scandal like a mouse for cheese and ears like a Red Indian's.

"He's all right?"

"Perfectly.   The journey pulled him to pieces rather, but there's nothing to get anxious about.   He spoke of two appointments in the morning—one, I fancy, with Mlle. Dulac and the other—he didn't say.   I left word that I'd go round to the hotel in the morning, make sure everything's all right.   I don't much care for the look of that landlord."

He heard the sound of a slight scuffle at the other end of the telephone, and then Diana Hunter's voice said cheerfully, "I ought to warn you that everything you say is being overheard.   You've got a lovely clear voice.   Why did you go away so soon? And aren't you coming back?"

But Lane excused himself; he had work to do, he said, hanging up the receiver and moving to the coffee-stall for a hot drink.   So much engrossed was he with his own thoughts that he didn't notice the hawk-nosed young man slip away like a shadow in the direction of the Robespierre Hotel.

In spite of his plea to Lady Hunter, he did not at once return home.   He thought he would leave a pencilled card at Eve Dulac's house, letting her know that he had met the old man, that he wasn't armed, and that he was expecting to see her in the morning at 11 a.m.   His nerves were wide-awake; he had no thought of going to bed, and presently he found himself walking slowly along the Embankment, watching the gradual lightening of the sky, as the dark blue was shot by a growing white radiance heralding dawn.   Scarcely any life moved on the water; he saw a launch, that probably belonged to the river police, move like a dark shadow, with a single gold eye, through a world of shadows; the cranes and wharves were deserted, and indeed in that ghostly light it was like moving in a world where life had once moved and would not move again.   He paused by the great golden bird that does perpetual

honour to the men of the Air Force who perished in
the War, and let his mind fill for an instant, as
water fills a sinking jar, with thoughts that it
aroused. Unlimited freedom, the whole sky for its
kingdom—his perverse, ambitious and dominating
temperament was intrigued by the conception. But
soon enough he was back at the present time, thinking of the future, of what he was going to do, of Eve
and of Fleming, and of that sunken, shrunken little
creature in a sordid top-floor room in a Soho byway.

Big Ben struck three and Lane thrust his hands
into his coat pockets, realising for the first time that
he was shivering.

"I'm a fool to loiter about," he told himself, and
turning, hailed a stray taxi that had almost
abandoned hope of a fare.

At approximately the same hour a man stood in
Tessier's room in Soho Square, and waited for the
policeman to pass through the pool of light flung by
the solitary lamp into the anonymous shadows,
before making his get-away.

CHAPTER III

CONTRARY to the belief of platitudinarians, there is
not more privacy in London than in the country.
In the country you may travel for miles and hours
never seeing a human creature or a homestead, as
anyone who has had the misfortune to lose his way
or his purse can testify. But in London there is no
privacy at all, except by accident. All day long the
casual town-dweller is under the eye of an illimitable
and curious public, a public, moreover, of which
many members are trained observers. The man
offering matches at the kerb, the drab trying to get

shop prices for her wired carnations, the woman with a baby on one arm and a tray of wilting white heather on the other—all these are keen psychologists, knowing almost at a glance who is likely to be amenable and whom to pass by with a gesture that magnificently or shabbily thrusts aside, even disintegrates, importunate distress. Then there is that mighty army, the embryo novelists, always on the hunt for copy and disdaining the advice of Sidney's muse, there are bus conductors and even policemen. You might think it would be better at night, but even then there remain the police, reinforced by rescue-walkers and that half-world that sleeps by day; and all the unemployed on the benches, the beggars and the homeless. The fact remains there is no real secrecy anywhere. Hide your needle in a haystack, drop gold into the river, put your corpse under the flags of your kitchen floor —sooner or later someone will unearth what you have been at such pains to conceal. Even if you're a broken-down film star, tucked away under the roof of an obscure hotel in Soho, you can't keep your privacy. Someone's going to drag you into the public eye. And not only the people who leave exhilarating parties to meet you on a wet platform and escort you to your wretched lodging, valet you, look after your money and promise, like the Good Samaritan, to return later, but mere curiosity-mongers, men with a nose for news, always on the look-out for a scoop in dull times, to whom your personal tragedy is nothing but so many words paid for at so much a line.

Glyn subscribed to three daily papers, one to keep him abreast of home and foreign developments, one to point him the blind alley down which an obstinate opposition continued to stray, and one to satisfy a curiosity as lively as any journalist's. He confessed unashamedly that his favourite page was the Police Court News, and a headline on a poster reading BODY FOUND IN CELLAR, for example, always sent his hand diving into his pocket for a copper.

On the morning after Diana Hunter's party he opened the third paper to find a column headed by Rene Tessier's name.

Former Film Star's Secret Visit to London
he read.

> Eight years ago, when Rene Tessier came to London, the city turned out to do him homage. This king of the screen received a welcome many a monarch might have envied. At that time his income was reputed to reach a total of six figures—in pounds sterling. Last night he paid his second visit but London knew nothing of it. A solitary admirer met him at the station and accompanied him to an obscure hotel. Here, high under the roof, forgotten even by those who used to applaud him, sleeps Rene Tessier, the genius of the screen, the man of mystery, whose reason for this unheralded visit is still undivulged. Does he plan, as is whispered in some quarters, to rise like the phoenix from the ashes of his own death-bed, more magnificent than before? . .

Glyn put down the paper, the remaining paragraphs unread.

"How do they churn it out?" he speculated in real admiration. "Phoenix indeed! But I'm with him on one point. Why the secrecy? I suppose Fleming's afraid he may take fright and skedaddle back to his native squalor." He remained quiet for a while, brooding over the tragedy, its uselessness, the pity of it. "And is there one hope in a hundred that he'll make good?" he thought, throwing down the newspaper and starting to walk up and down the room. "And where," he asked himself with a fervour that astonished even his own heart, "does that girl come in? And what's she afraid of?"

Glyn's curiosity, that always slept with one eye open, was keenly aroused. It was clear that Eve Dulac knew a good deal more than the journalists or Fleming; not, perhaps, more than Lane, in whom she seemed to have confided. More anyway, he decided, than he himself was ever likely to know.

His stock of knowledge was increased that afternoon when, returning from an appointment, by tube, he opened the evening edition of the Planet. Once again that fatal name occupied a prominent place.

FILM STAR'S DEATH

Rene Tessier, a former film star and producer, at one time reputed to be the richest man in his profession, was found dead in an hotel in Soho Square East this morning. A letter in his hand-writing was found on the table beside him. It is understood that M. Tessier was returning to the screen after an absence of two years to play a leading part in Mr. Julian Lane's new production.

"Suicide!" exclaimed Glyn softly. "So that's what mademoiselle was afraid of. And not all her precautions have been any use. I wonder—oh, I wonder how much this means to her."

Glyn was one of those men whose tortuous minds delight in problems, the more obscure the better. A practically insoluble cross-word, a jig-saw puzzle of some hundreds of pieces, practically all of which may be sea or sky or the blue of the lady's frock in the foreground, a mathematical dilemma that has perplexed the experts—all these delighted him. In addition, he was a lawyer, with the suspicious type of mind such a profession breeds. He was greedy, too. When a case was brought to him he didn't probe delicately, he tore the flesh off the bones and then set about discovering what had happened to the meat that wasn't there.

"It's the clues you haven't got that solve a case," he used to say.

And thinking about this tragedy of Rene Tessier he stumbled at once on a startling discrepancy. A man who's a bad sailor and short of cash doesn't travel to England in order to destroy himself in a fifth-rate hotel, when the Seine's so handy, he decided. What happened after he arrived? The answer, according to the paper, was that a nameless admirer met him. That, presumably, would be Julian Lane.

"What then?" he asked, his lively curiosity resolved to be satisfied. "He must have learnt something after his arrival. I suppose the inquest will reveal that," and immediately he set about a re-arrangement of his own plans to enable him to attend this. It would not be difficult for a man who had done as much police work as himself to find out the time and hour. He might even get it from the landlord of the hotel where the body was found. And he was sufficiently candid with himself to acknowledge that it was less the death of the poor little devil than his hope of meeting Eve Dulac again that made him eager to miss no detail of the proceedings.

Stepping out of the Tube he heard his name spoken and found Fleming at his side.

"I was just thinking of you," he exclaimed.

All Fleming's suavity and buoyancy seemed to have deserted him. This news that to him was so momentous filled his entire horizon, so that, although the paper was full of various paragraphs, it did not occur to him that any except this one should have attracted Glyn's attention.

"You've seen the news, of course," he said. "Was ever anything so ghastly? That poor fellow putting an end to himself in that dingy room, with everything he most wanted within reach, and he couldn't quite stand the course."

"Is it certain it's suicide?" asked Glyn, but without much surprise in view of the note about the letter found by the body.

"Lane has seen the proprietor, who appeared very talkative. There doesn't seem much doubt. Of course I shall be at the inquest to-morrow, since I was instrumental in getting him over here. It's a bad business in every way. Lane's nearly as hard hit as I am myself."

"There are other actors," the lawyer reminded him, feeling that this abysmal despair was rather blacker than even so tragic a situation warranted.

"Not for me," returned Fleming in quiet tones. "Not, that is, unless you can find me another man with the same gifts as Tessier had. But you won't. I've combed Europe for a man to play the Judge; I didn't choose Tessier very willingly. I knew the risk I ran. But he was my one chance. You can think me as crazy as you please—I can see you do— but I'm not exaggerating when I say that this affair is the biggest tragedy for me since the outbreak of war."

Glyn shot him a startled glance, but it was obvious that the man's violence was genuine. Temperament, thought Glyn, shrugging his shoulders. It's destroyed Tessier, having put him at the top of the ladder, and if he doesn't take things a bit more easily it'll end by destroying Fleming too. But aloud he only asked for details of the inquest. Fleming looked at him in some surprise.

"You being called?"

"I'd know the details if I were," returned Glyn, softly. "No, it's nothing but sheer vulgar curiosity that takes me to the court. I'm one of the people who keep up the circulation of the more sensational Sunday papers."

Fleming laughed. "Cause and effect?" he suggested delicately.

"Meaning that my bread and butter is involved? Perhaps you're right. I must admit I hadn't thought of it like that before."

2

Alone in his bachelor chambers—he lived very comfortably in Saracen Street, Mayfair—he had the courage to admit that his chief interest in the case was not the soi-disant celebrity, but the mysterious girl, whose interest in the dead man he had not yet fathomed, but whose fear had been apparent enough; who had routed without effort a man accustomed to hold his own in any society, and had given him nothing but a polite rap on the knuckles for his pains. Glyn subscribed to no philosophic doctrine that finds reason in the most casual contact, believing that patience achieves all things. He had no reason to imagine that Eve Dulac had the slightest desire to see him again, whereas his desire was intense. Therefore, he decided, I must make the opportunity. But how he should accomplish this he had no notion.

For the second time, however, Mademoiselle showed herself the leader of the two. That evening, as he lay smoking in his library, Glyn's servant came in with two cards on a salver.

"A lady and gentleman to see you, sir."

Glyn took up the cards.

Mademoiselle Eve Dulac.

Mr. Julian Lane.

"Bring them in," he said, standing up, aware of a strange nervousness at the thought of seeing this girl in his own home surroundings. Lane, he noticed, looked ill-at-ease as though he had only come because he had no choice; Eve Dulac was pale and composed, dressed this evening in a short black fur jacket open at the neck to disclose a white satin stock, and a narrow black cloth skirt above fashionably high-heeled shoes. A tiny hat was perched above her curls; her gloves were long and black with exaggerated cuffs.

It was clear that she was accustomed to dealing with busy men. Refusing the drink and cigarette her host offered, she came at once to the point, while Lane hesitated in the background.

"Mr. Glyn, you were kind enough to speak to me last night, because you thought you might be able to help me. Perhaps I was not so grateful as I should have been, for to-night I do need your advice. I am in a difficulty, and I am anxious not to involve strangers in this affair. It is very painful for me," she added, with a strange young dignity that he found amazingly touching, "even to speak of these affairs, and to take advice from a stranger—ah, that I cannot bear to think of."

"I'm more flattered than I can say that you should come to me," said Glyn with perfect sincerity. "You can count on me to do anything possible."

Lane here broke in, "It's a legal point, and neither of us quite knows our ground. Commercial law's one thing; I'm sound enough there. You have to be in my work, if you're not going to be ruined. But this is criminal law."

Glyn looked up, his brows lifting and the girl continued," "It is to do with M. Tessier. You saw his death perhaps in to-night's papers? Yes? Well, to-morrow they will make the enquiry, settle how he died. In fact, that is as good as arranged. Julian has been to see the proprietor of the hotel, the man who found him, and he has learnt that M. Tessier killed himself. To-morrow, it seems, everyone will know that."

"Well?" said Glyn in perplexity. "What can I do to help you?"

"That verdict must be prevented. It is not true."

"You mean to suggest foul play?"

"I say nothing, only that Rene Tessier did not take his own life. He despised all such cowards. I think if Louis had died in any other way he might have recovered. That he could never forgive."

Glyn was startled. "You want to bring in a verdict of murder?" he insisted, anxious that the young woman should realise the seriousness of her intentions.

She repeated with an obstinacy that he found exasperating, "He did not kill himself. Why, consider. If he had intended to die would he wait two years and then come here, to a country he does not know, not well, that is, and take his life like a rat under such a roof?"

"Surely the obvious answer is that he had no intention of taking his life when he crossed, but in a moment of exhaustion and despair he lost heart."

"If he had meant to lose heart he would have lost it two years ago. For two years he has waited. . . ."

"For what?"

"For his opportunity. Ask Mr. Lane. He will tell you that Tessier knew himself to be followed, to be a peril to men who were perhaps in his power. I tell you, he had enemies and he knew it."

"You know who they were?"

"No. But he wrote to me sometimes—oh, he gave no names, of course. But he was only waiting."

"You have his letters, perhaps?"

" No, no, I did not keep those. They were foolish. But I knew."

" You keep speaking of an opportunity, but for what?"

The girl's face grew so pale that Glyn thought she would fall; Julian Lane, however, made no move to support her and since he did not, Glyn felt he could not. Her eyes were black against that pallor as she said, " To punish the murderers of his son."

If Glyn had looked for some spectacular reply he had got it. Nothing so fantastic as this had passed through his mind.

" But Louis Tessier committed suicide," he exclaimed.

" Oh, he leaped from the Arc de Triomphe. All the world knows that. But he was murdered, monsieur, as surely as though hands lifted him to that height and flung him over. And that his father knew."

" And he came to England to—murder them?"

" I don't know, monsieur. I only know that he had nothing to lose. This film—I tell Julian, who will not believe me, that such a triumph as he planned would have no meaning to M. Tessier. He has not lived in our world since Louis died. Its victories, its fame are nothing to him."

" You think he simply used it as a cover for his own purposes."

" I cannot even say that, monsieur, I know so little. But you must not think of him as one of us, people governed by reasonable laws. He lived by a fire that only burned for himself. And I tell you, monsieur," she came forward, her eyes blazing with passion, " he did not take his own life, with Louis unavenged."

A new thought occurred to Glyn. " Why did he

write to you?" he asked. "Surely he didn't mean to involve you?"

She coloured painfully, but answered him in proud tones. "I was to have married Louis Tessier. Oh, that is no secret. If you turn to the account of the inquest in the Temps or the Midi, you will see my name. Certainly I had told him before he died that the position was changed, I could not fulfil my promise, but the fact remains. I had been affianced to him, and to us it was a serious matter. Rene Tessier considered me almost as part of himself; he should have been my papa."

"And he was going to involve you in these plans for revenge?"

"I don't know what he intended, monsieur. I was to see him at eleven o'clock. When I reached the hotel he was still sleeping. The waiter said he would tell him, but came back to say the door was still fastened. Then that pig, that Pecheron, arrived. If he is not out of his room by twelve o'clock, he said, it will be another day to pay. For myself, I had begun to be afraid. It was not his way to be late for an engagement he had himself made. So Pecheron went up and he rattled on the door and he knocked and shouted—all the street must have heard his shout—and at last he broke in the door."

"You didn't go in?" ejaculated Glyn.

"No, I was downstairs. But they told me. He's dead, they said. Taken poison. There's a letter. Pecheron was greatly disturbed. This is an affair for the police, he said. I knew that ill-favoured one meant trouble. Now it will be an inquest and perhaps the authorities all over my hotel, because he is a foreigner and we must be very formal. Oh, he was angry, that one. Almost you might think I had put a knife in M. Tessier's heart."

"You didn't see him?"

"They would not let me mount. I must remain until the police have arrived. And when they came," she made a comical little gesture with her lifted hands, "they say, Off the premises. Away with you. If we want you we will write."

Lane broke in, "I ought to add that I saw Tessier last night. He was a desperately sick man and, if you'll let me say so, Eve, incapable of realising what he was doing. He'd had no food, he'd been desperately sick, he wouldn't even touch the sandwiches I ordered for him. And he took brandy—a fair quantity of brandy." He was addressing Glyn but his gaze as he said the last words was for the girl.

Eve Dulac stiffened; her eyes were angry, though not a muscle moved. She was like a hooded flame, thought Glyn, watching her, speechless. If once she let that fire free she'd blacken everything within reach.

"I know what you mean, Julian. You mean he had drunk so much that he did not know what he did. That is what you want Mr. Glyn to believe, and what you wish the world to believe. It is not true that he killed himself because he was drunk. But you would like everyone to think so. It is easier so. And what is a man's good name to you?"

"Nothing," agreed Julian Lane, evenly, "nothing at all compared with yours. Mlle. Dulac," he explained, turning to Glyn, "wants to go into the witness-box and tell the world that Tessier didn't kill himself, because he considered it a cowardly thing to do. She can't stand the idea that people will think wrong of him, and she won't listen to me when I tell her it's of no consequence. You remember Hamlet? Be thou chaste as ice thou shalt not escape calumny. What does it matter to Tessier now what people say of him. But it matters to Eve—

to me, then, if not to her, what people will say when they hear she was Louis Tessier's fiancee. They'll rake up the old story, point fingers at her—she doesn't believe it, but perhaps you can make her understand it's true.

"Lane's right," said Glyn, immediately. "Unless you've some concrete proof you'll only stir up all the ancient trouble, without doing Tessier an atom of good. If you were one of my clients I should urge you most strongly not to attempt to go into the witness-box, which, I take it, is what you're anxious to do."

"The world shall not believe this lie," repeated the girl, stubbornly.

"And you think you can prevent it? Without a ha'porth of proof? The shadow of a clue? Another thing. You're making a very serious charge by suggesting that on the face of it the evidence is unreliable. You seem to suggest that someone killed him. You've a story of his obsession about being followed. That's one of the most ordinary of delusions, as any doctor will tell you. Unless you can prove anything, Mademoiselle, I do most strongly urge you to keep out of the case. You may not have had much experience of this kind of action —in fact, I'm sure you haven't, but a coroner can be the veriest jackal. You wouldn't have a shred of privacy left, and you'd have done nothing whatsoever for M. Tessier; indeed, all your subsequent actions would be discredited. If that," he looked anxiously past her to the tall form of Julian Lane, "is why you came to see me to-night, you have my advice. And I hope," he added, in troubled tones, "you won't disregard it."

"If you can persuade her to keep outside the whole affair I shall never be grateful enough," said Lane, and from his voice the lawyer realised that this visit to his rooms was an eleventh hour attempt on the young producer's part. He felt deeply disappointed to realise this; he would have liked to flatter himself that the girl had suggested coming to see him, relying on his judgment.

"But she doesn't," he thought, "and if she'd known you five years it would be the same. She's not the sort to expect support. I should say this chap's had no end of a tussle, with about as much hope of moving her as of shifting the Pyramids," and at once it was of paramount importance that he should succeed in dissuading her from attending the court.

"If I thought you could turn the balance only by a hair I'd say Go on and chance it," Glyn assured her. "But it's simply waste of energy and of—of your own reputation—Lane's right. There's a section of the public that would fasten like gulls on offal on the face of the broken engagement. Oh," he added bitterly, "I know that wouldn't move you, but this attitude of yours is as foolish as that of the fanatic who flings food out of the carriage window when he's starving, not to benefit anyone else but as a gesture."

"I've promised you I'll be at the inquest," Lane urged. "I'll keep my eyes and ears open. If there's a ghost of a loophole we will have the whole story broadcast."

"And there would be none," returned the girl, calmly. "You are an honest man, Julian, but you are in love with me, and so there would be no loophole. Oh, not that you care for yourself," she added, swiftly. "Like Tessier, you can afford to disregard the world. But you would be afraid for me. So for once I dare not trust your judgment."

"Would you trust me?" asked Glyn. "I should be glad to go to the inquest, as your representative, if you wish, on M. Tessier's behalf. If I may say so without appearing conceited, it is more likely that I should discover a flaw than you, since I'm trained to that type of thing. Will you let me do that? I go disinterested. I'm prepared to find some flaw that will prove your case. On the other hand, you have to remember—suppose the verdict is for suicide—that he was exhausted, abnormal, that he was half-stupefied by the brandy he had taken. I only say this to show that you need not lose your faith in him even if, at a time when he could scarcely have been aware what he did, he broke through his own code. My experience has brought me in touch with so many men, fine fellows and full of courage, who've gone under at a moment when only supernatural strength could keep them going; I know how quickly it happens, and that it's not indicative of a contemptible spirit. I think that's what you're afraid of, isn't it?" he added gently.

After his speech there was a long pause. Eve had turned definitely away from Lane, and was facing the lawyer. At last she held out her hand.

"You're very good, monsieur, and I am not gracious. No, I was ungracious last night and still I show you my suspicions. But I know you're right when you say you can serve M. Tessier in the court better than I. You have knowledge and influence, and I have neither. And you have no axe to grind. If you will do this. . . ."

Glyn took her hand. "You honour me," he said. "I shall do everything I can to deserve your trust."

The girl turned at once. "We have taken too much of your time. You are very good. I shall stay away from the court to-morrow and wait to hear from you."

After they had left him alone, Glyn returned to his

chair. The whole interview had a dreamlike quality that perplexed him. Almost he doubted whether it had ever taken place.

" But to-morrow," he exulted, " to-morrow I can prove I'm not quite the useless clod she's regarded me up till now," and he fell into a reverie, brooding with an impatient tenderness on the young fool who was so eager to expose herself to the barbs of public opinion and lay herself open to Heaven knew what scandalous accusations before Tessier was cold in his grave.

CHAPTER IV

PROCEEDING to the inquest next morning, Glyn was obsessed by two visions that were closely connected. The first was of that girl standing, upright and ardent as flame, in his sober bachelor room, turning to him for help; and the second that magnificent, terrible figure he had seen on the screen though never, as it happened, in the flesh, a creature of indomitable impulse, fired by a resolution that no trivial circumstance, such as a wet night, loneliness, a knowledge that he was solitary and unfriended in an alien city, could dismay.

" She's right," he thought. " There's something behind this. You don't extinguish flame so easily."

But though he was excited at the prospect he also disliked it intensely. He knew how the public attention would be caught when what appeared to be an insignificant suicide turned into a mystery linking up with another tragic death, in which the young French girl figured so largely.

" Can't I see 'em?" he groaned. " Like rats going through a warehouse—scrabble, scrabble, scrabble.

Turn up a bit more garbage—there may even be letters she wrote to that spineless young fool, Louis. How do I know?"

It occurred to him that never before had he entered a court knowing so little in a case that so deeply affected him.

Up till the present time the affair had attracted little interest. A fickle public had long ago forgotten Tessier's name and anyway he hadn't been the matinee idol type. He didn't figure in "Films Generally Released"; only those who cared for fine acting took the pains to search him out. The notion that that piece of ancient wreckage might bode harm to anyone would be received with derision. From the outset it was clear that this was the general feeling. Even Glyn, listening acutely for those scraps of evidence that are indirect and often point a road to the truth, began to feel foolish. One part of his mind rejoiced at the simplicity of the solution; but another was disturbed by the thought that Mlle. Dulac would not have sufficient sense to accept the decision of the court without a struggle to establish her own theory.

"What is the story behind Louis Tessier's death?" he wondered. "How much does she know, and how much is there to be known? In any case, two years is a long time to wait."

The evidence unrolled like a ribbon; no knots or doubts anywhere. Pecheron spoke of the dead man's failing condition on arrival and added viciously that when his friend left the old man was in a state of stupefaction. He had himself been a little afraid, because he was sitting so near the fire, but Mr. Lane had hustled him away. His chief concern seemed to be about his account.

"A bottle of my best brandy," he repeated two or three times. But the coroner told him drily that he had no powers to make an order in that connection.

"The door was locked on the inside," Pecheron continued. "I, of course, have a master-key, and when I had coaxed the key from the lock, with a little piece of wire, I opened the door and went in. M. Tessier was dead. I saw that at once."

The coroner interrupted to know how he could be sure. Pecheron shrugged. "I have seen dead men before, monsieur. It leaped to the eye. And so," he continued, "I sent my servant for the police."

"It didn't occur to you to get a doctor?"

"If the police thought it necessary, they have a doctor of their own. No, monsieur, the man was nothing to me; I had never seen him before; I knew nothing of his family and his friends; I came down and said to the young lady, There has been something wrong here, and I have sent for the police. She wished to go upstairs, but this I would not allow. When the police came they also knew he was dead." He glared round the court, as if to enquire why the word of a policeman should be of more value than his own. "The police removed the body, and the young lady was persuaded to go home. I told my story; I knew nothing. Presently the gentleman who had been with monsieur the night before arrived, and asked me this and that. I could tell him nothing, either. I knew nothing. Only that he was very drunk and ill at one o'clock in the morning, and dead, with a letter by his side a few hours later. He was poor, he was old, he was sick; all this I said to Mr. Lane. How he died I did not know. Am I a doctor?"

"You heard no sounds in the night?"

"I went upstairs again to show a gentleman to his room about half an hour after Mr. Lane departed, and I could hear him speaking. He was like a man in a fever."

"You couldn't hear what he said?"

"He was threatening some one; so much I could understand. But do I listen at doors? And is there sense in the ravings of a drunken man? I have my business to attend to. That," he added abruptly, "is all that I know."

In reply to further questions, he said that he had received a letter from Tessier from an address in Paris, asking for accommodation. He had made an especial point of having a room near the fire-escape, and had admitted, when he materialised in the flesh, that he was, in fact, very much afraid of fire.

The coroner asked whether any of the other people spending the night in the hotel were present, but it appeared that they were not. They were birds of passage for the most part, staying for a few hours and then vanishing again. Pecheron produced his visitors' book, but as most of the entries only gave London or some such large city as an address, and as very probably, thought Glyn in gloomy mood, most of the names were false, that contributed little to the solution. But it would be stretching the long arm of coincidence to a questionable extent to suppose that by pure luck Tessier's enemy had found himself under the same roof as his foe.

"Unless Tessier is right, and there was someone on his trail," he added. "Someone who saw him arrive here, and laid his plans accordingly."

Then Lane went on to the stand and told the history of the fatal night in considerable detail. He allowed it to be understood that he had gone to meet the dead man on his own initiative and the court accepted the story naturally enough. Lane said it was obvious the man was ill and exhausted; he refused to eat, though he had taken a good deal of brandy. He had said nothing that would lead any man to suppose that he would take his own life; on the contrary, he had spoken with optimism of his plans for the future, recalling past triumphs.

"He said nothing that gave you the impression he was in an abnormal frame of mind?"

"Only when he spoke of himself as a danger to some person or persons unknown, and said he had been followed. He asked me to look out of the window, and see if I saw anyone loitering in the street below, but of course there was no one."

"You didn't take him seriously?"

Lane hesitated. "I had gone to the station to meet him; all the other passengers had hurried off the train and were disappearing into tubes and taxis as quickly as they could. There was no one near him; even the porters had all been engaged. I would be prepared to swear he wasn't being watched or followed. Besides," he hesitated again, for a longer period this time, "you have to bear in mind that when he made this sudden statement he was— not altogether sober. Brandy, particularly taken on an empty stomach—magnifies men's ideas, distorts them beyond all reason. No, I have to admit I did not take him very seriously."

"And when you saw the news of his death in the papers?"

"When I heard of his death I was appalled. You will remember that I was to produce the play in which he was being starred. I'd banked a great deal on that, and this meant the wreck of all my plans. It's natural, I think, if it does sound a little heartless, that that should be my first thought."

"A very effectual liar," reflected Glyn. "I wonder if he will succeed in keeping Mlle. Dulac's name out of the case."

The coroner, a moment later, asked for the identity of the young lady who had called at the hotel that morning, but Pecheron said she had given no name, and he thought it improbable that he would recognise her again. He was positive that she was not in the court.

"I think," observed the coroner, in tones of heavy forbearance, "it is a pity that no one knows who she was. She might be able to throw a good deal of light on the proceedings."

To the rest of the court, however, the case was dazzling in its brilliance. You couldn't come to more than one conclusion. It would be more exciting if there had been some suspense.

Sergeant Down, of the local police, said he had been called by a man whom he now identified as Pecheron's servant, to come to an hotel where it was supposed a suicide had taken place. He had seen the body and the letter beside it, and it had seemed to him a clear case of self-inflicted death. The letter was then read to the court:

After all, it is too late. I am too tired. And it is better that I take this way before they find me. They might be less kind. I am afraid to sleep because always there is someone watching. . . . I am so tired. . . .

The straggling writing wavered away; the pen had rolled over and over, leaving a weak smear on the dingy paper. Near the foot of the sheet the dead man had scrawled his signature, the last letters being practically invisible. The pen had run dry and he had lacked the energy to dip it again in the pot. Then he had fallen forward over the table, where Pecheron had found him, his mouth open, a stain of violet ink on the index finger of the left hand.

The sergeant had arranged for the body to be

removed to the mortuary, after examination by the police surgeon.

This man, called Barker, gave his evidence briefly. Deceased had died of an overdose of hyoscin; a quantity of the drug had been found on the body. together with a quantity of aspirin tablets. There was no clue as to whence this had been obtained.

Among the dead man's effects was found a letter, without date or address, signed Thomas Bremond, introducing Tessier to a Mr. C. Wilson, of the Charing Cross Road, remarking that the former might require his services in the work he had come to town to do. The police had visited Mr. Wilson, who knew nothing of Tessier, but believed he remembered Bremond, who had bought some second-hand books from him about a couple of years earlier.

"Another avenue blocked," murmured one patient member of the jury to his neighbour, who nodded long-sufferingly. The jury then retired for twelve minutes, for appearances sake, and returned with a verdict of Suicide while of Unsound Mind. The coroner endorsed this with commendable brevity, and there was nothing left to do but speculate who would get the dead man's belongings—the trivial worthless contents of his pockets and bag. A list of these had been made for the benefit of the court, and this list, together with Tessier's last letter, the sheet of yellow blotting-paper, and the wretched hotel pen, had been produced for the benefit of the jury, who pretended to examine these exhibits with a professional eye.

When the court cleared Glyn crossed to Julian Lane, and asked in troubled tones, "What other verdict could they bring in on that evidence? You can't expect miracles in a coroner's court."

"I'm with you," said Lane, gloomily. "It was

practically impossible to suggest foul play. The only more impossible thing I can imagine will be trying to convince Eve this is a true bill. All the same, I can't understand Tessier getting so far and then throwing up the sponge. I could understand it if his nerve had failed him at Calais—the prospect of the crossing and so forth. Even if he had been missing when the boat docked, I could understand that. But to make the journey, to put up with the humiliation and the discomfort, to get so far and then give way—that seems to me utterly out of character. For supposing there is anything in Eve's contention that he had a double purpose in coming over to England, suppose there was something in those letters she was so careful to destroy and that she doesn't choose to confide to us—is it reasonable to suppose he would follow up his plan for two years and then destroy it all in a night?"

"You're unsure about the verdict?" Glyn accused him.

"I shouldn't be if Eve were any other woman. But I've known her for some time. She doesn't walk in the dark, or stab at random. She was very sure before she came to see you last night. I'm not suggesting that any other verdict was possible. I'm only wondering how much there is we shall, probably, never know."

"There's the one chance in a hundred that Wilson might, if he pleased, be able to throw light on the position," Glyn hazarded, but Lane shook his head.

"I doubt if there's much to be learnt in that quarter. I know the place. And I know Tessier's reputation. He once played the part of a banker, involved in some big business transaction, and he sent for a comprehensive book on the subject and ploughed through it in the midst of all his other work, to make sure his details were correct. He was to play the part of a judge in this new film, and Wilson has a name for second-hand legal literature. An unromantic explanation, I'm afraid, and I wish I could suggest something more helpful, but I fancy that disposes of Mr. Wilson. And now," he added on a grim note, "I have to go and try to persuade Eve that we didn't let this verdict go through because we wanted to avoid publicity or trouble for ourselves. That will be enough work to keep me employed the rest of the day."

He went on and Glyn looked round the empty room. There was no one left now but the sergeant collecting the exhibits and an underling trying to tidy the place. A breeze entering through an open window caught the edge of the yellow blotting-paper, and wafted it on to the floor at Glyn's feet. He stooped to pick it up as the sergeant turned to recover it.

"Oh, thank you, sir," he began, but Glyn did not at once yield the paper. Instead he laid it on the table in front of him and said in an abrupt voice, "There's something odd here. Have you got a mirror?"

The sergeant, who knew his reputation, said at once, "I'll send for one. Just a moment, sir. Anything wrong?"

"A whole lot, I fancy. Including the verdict. In fact," he added under his breath, "the only thing that isn't wrong, so far as I can see, is that young woman's conviction that this was less straightforward than we supposed."

When the mirror arrived he held it above the sheet of paper.

"Not that way, sir," said the sergeant quickly. "You want to lay the glass on the table. That's right. Now then." Both men bent over the reflection.

"See anything, sir?" asked the sergeant, after a brief disappointed silence.

"Tessier's signature," returned Glyn, without moving.

"I saw that myself. But then that's only to be expected."

"Perhaps. But unless I'm tight, and I don't think I am, I can see something I shouldn't expect—and that is two signatures, that are no more than second cousins to one another at that, if they do spell the same name."

2

The sergeant straightened himself with a jerk "That's queer," he exclaimed.

"Very queer," agreed Glyn. "So queer it looks as though your department might have to do a bit more work on the case. Perhaps even get the verdict reversed."

"There's no call to think of anything like that," returned the sergeant with spirit. "Most likely there's some simple explanation. Suppose he wrote two letters and tore up the first . . ."

"And ate the pieces?" suggested Glyn, amiably.

"Well, there was a fire—no, that was a gas fire. And they weren't in the basket, because there wasn't a basket. And they weren't in his pocket, because I examined that myself."

"And he didn't write a letter and ask Mr. Lane to post it, because Mr. Lane would have mentioned it, if he had, and most probably the recipient would have come forward. Besides, at no time during the evening did M. Tessier seem capable of anything so lucid as writing a letter."

"He wasn't asked," said the sergeant in obstinate tones.

"Then you can ask him now," returned the

barrister, with malicious satisfaction. "Here he comes."

Wearing an expression of anxiety, Lane came hurrying back into the room. "Anyone seen a wallet lying about?" he asked. "I've dropped mine, and I'm taking a lady out to lunch."

Glyn put his hand cautiously into his pocket, but the gesture was superfluous, for a moment later Lane had stooped and picked up a wallet from the floor.

"That's a bit of luck. Anyone might have collared it. Hullo," seeing for the first time the glum expression on the faces of his companions, "anything wrong?"

"Everything, I believe," returned Glyn, heartily, "including the verdict. Unless you can help us."

"I've done all my helping in the witness-box. I'm not suppressing anything."

"Not the mysterious letter or letters that Tessier wrote after he reached his room?"

"Are you pulling my leg?" demanded Lane, and frowned. "Poor devil, he wasn't in a fit state to write to anyone."

"There was this," suggested Glyn, touching the pitiable scrawl that had been read out to the court.

"If you can call that a letter. It was a broken man's last effort, and even then the signature's barely legible. Sorry if I'm ruining your scheme, but Tessier didn't write to anyone. And if that's all you want me for I may as well get along to my young woman. I have the reputation," he added, with a cheerful laugh, "of always being on time. I won it with much difficulty and stress, and like all things that are hard-won, I value it. Well," he slapped the pocket-book, in his hand, "I was fortunate to find this intact. It looks so bad when you have to borrow the price of your lunch off your companion, or make some transparent excuse and slip out and pop your links in the course of the meal."

"That's right, sir," agreed the sergeant, infected by these good spirits. "Hope for your sake it's got more in it than this poor fellow's had. What he carried a note-case for beats me."

Lane, who was half-way to the door, turned abruptly on his heel, his face extremely grave. "What did you say?"

"Only that I hoped there was more in your pocket-book, sir, than in the dead gentleman's."

"You mean, it was empty?"

"That's right."

"Then so is Mr. Glyn and so are you and so is Eve, but everything else is wrong, including the verdict. Because when I left the room that case was stuffed with notes."

CHAPTER V

He came back across the room and seated himself on the edge of the table. Unquestionably he would be late for his appointment, but for once he was content that his reputation for punctuality should suffer.

"Of course," he offered, producing a cigarette-case, "there's the proprietor. I don't want to make prejudicial suggestions in front of a lawyer, but I must admit I felt sufficiently nervous of the gentleman's honesty to make a note of the numbers of the two bigger notes."

"What size were they?" snapped the sergeant.

"Fifty and a hundred. Here you are." He took out his diary, and Down copied the figures carefully.

"That ought to help. Notes that size aren't passed by a man running a hotel like the Robespierre."

"If you ask me," said Lane, discouragingly, "I should say quite a lot of money goes through that gentleman's hands. I wouldn't be surprised at anything that took place in that hotel, not even murder. Though, mark you," he added quickly, "I've absolutely nothing to go on."

"Still, there's a lot against that theory," Glyn objected. "For one thing, Tessier might have told you about the money, and you might have mentioned it in the court. Then either the notes would be found in Pecheron's possession, or we should be able to trace them. There's another queer thing," he added, stroking his fair moustache. "Why should a man with that much money on him, coming over here to fulfil an engagement that meant quite a deal more," he looked questioningly at Lane, who said, "Don't invite me to betray trade secrets, but—yes, quite a lot." "Why should he," Down continued, "go to a wretched little place like the Robespierre? I'm not suggesting that with his luggage and so forth he should go to the Ritz, but there's plenty of places between the two."

Glyn took a hand. "Suppose there is something in what he says? Suppose, instead of a straightforward and rather sordid affair, this is wildly picturesque and fantastic, and there really was someone on his trail—mightn't he hope to throw them off the scent by going to such a doubtful hostelry?"

"Yes. If there was any truth in that story," agreed Lane. "But was there? For my part it sounds as fantastic as one of the films I refuse to direct. If it weren't for Mademoiselle Dulac, I wouldn't give it an instant's consideration. But I can't dismiss something she takes so seriously without at least an attempt to prove to her that she's been carried away by an illusion. She acts on her instincts, you know, as most women do, and a little, perhaps, on her knowledge of the old man. Of course," he seemed to have forgotten the sergeant who was listening open-mouthed to this colloquy, " she doesn't want to believe that Tessier would betray the resolution of a life-time. He's never had any pity for weaklings. He had a hard time himself at the beginning of his career, and he never went in for self-pity. He's always been an object of great admiration to Eve, and you know how women hate to have their idols broken."

Glyn caught sight of a gleam, malicious and defensive, passing over the face of the sergeant, and he said softly, " How well one understands the feelings of the professional in an affair like this. Why can't these meddlesome amateurs keep out of these things? They only create a lot of unnecessary trouble."

The sergeant said stolidly, " We don't wish to get out of our responsibilities," in so pedantic a tone that Lane began to laugh.

" Spoken like a man and a policeman," he grinned, but Glyn was frowning. After all, the fellow was right. What harm would there have been in allowing this verdict to go through? The subsequent enquiry might elicit any number of awkward facts. Glyn was thoroughly in disfavour of unearthing anything that might be prejudicial to his client, as he chose to regard Mlle. Dulac. He recognised this as a shamefully unprofessional attitude, but, he groaned to himself, the incredible loyalties of women, narrow and intolerant, vastly differing from the comprehensive loyalties of men, how they complicate life. And the fact that this particular young woman had so little appreciation of her own interests increased his own fierce determination to save her from injury in this affair.

The sergeant was frowning also, but for another

reason. "It's a pity you didn't see the blotting-paper earlier, sir," he observed, almost as if it were Glyn's own fault that he had not done so. "Now I daresay that fellow will have cleared every speck of a clue out of the room, and we'll have to start with nothing. So far as I can make out, no one knows anything about the dead gentleman's affairs except the dead gentleman himself, and that's a pity, too."

"Oh, quite," agreed Glyn, gravely, but Lane, still laughing, broke in, "Don't lose heart, sergeant. If I'm any judge of character, Mr. Pecheron won't have touched that room yet, unless the story brought him a sudden influx of curiosity-mongers, those amateurs of the horrible to whom a place where a man committed suicide is of interest in itself. Not that cleaning a room is his strong suit at any time. I didn't urge Tessier to go to bed, not when I'd seen those sheets. God knows who else had slept in them since they last returned from the laundry, and what leprous diseases they may have had. And the whole affair's been handled so discreetly practically no one seems to have heard of it. I shouldn't lose heart yet." He nodded and turned on his heel. "I shall be a case for the police myself if I keep my lunch waiting any longer," he remarked. "You know where to find me, if I'm wanted."

"Let him go," said Glyn to the sergeant, who would have detained him. "There's nothing more he can do for you at the moment. But he's raised an interesting point—I mean, whether Tessier's death was part of a plot or whether it was mere chance, following theft. I'm disinclined to think the last. No one would guess that a man in such a place would have any money, and even if he was surprised by a thief, it doesn't follow the fellow would murder him."

"Might do, sir," said Down drily. "Often does happen that way."

"No," cried the more mercurial Glyn. "You're wrong. It does often happen, but not that way. I can believe a man robbed Tessier—though that still leaves you the problem of the locked door, locked on the inside, remember, and in a moment of rage or terror, or even in cold blood, murdered him. He seems to have had approximately a couple of hundred pounds with him. But I don't believe any thief in the world first poisoned him and then wrote that letter."

"And your solution, sir?"

"Oh, the obvious one that Mr. Lane has already pointed out. That Tessier was speaking no more than the truth when he said to some person or persons he was too dangerous to be allowed to live."

There's something to be said for slovens. With the exception of men who intend to attract notice by the clues they leave to mark the ways they have gone, there are no people so easy to trace. Had M. Pecheron been one of those ideal hotel proprietors who, the instant a guest leaves, strip the bed, fling up the windows and put a vacuum cleaner over the carpet, the police would have been deprived of several invaluable clues. Glyn who, having, as he expressed it, been in at the birth of the affair, had no intention of missing the death, traded shamelessly on the fluke that had brought him so much prominence on the day of the inquest. He was, in any case, persona grata at the Yard, and he had no hesitation in telephoning to his friend, Detective-Inspector Field, and asking for the latest information.

"If it hadn't been for me the whole thing would have passed off as a tame and dreary suicide. I may be giving you the chance of a lifetime," he remarked, boastfully.

"All right," said Field, amiably. "Come over and see the foundations, and tell me what you make of them."

Considering the time Field had spent in the shabby room under the eaves, he seemed to have remarkably little to show. His evidence was spread out before Glyn's discomfited gaze. It consisted of a plate on which were a few crumbs, an envelope containing more crumbs that had been found on the worn rug near the window; a flake of London mud carefully scraped off the tap of the gas fire, and a fragment of rope found on a jutting splinter of window-frame. Glyn looked at this miscellany with respect and asked, "Do they tell you the story?"

"Oh, not the whole of it," said Field easily, "but they're a very good foundation. There are certain obvious deductions taken in conjunction with the facts that emerged at the inquest, that must be as clear to you as they are to me."

Glyn looked a bit harder at the clues and agreed, in what he hoped was an intelligent tone, "Oh, yes," and indeed the significance of one clue could hardly be overlooked.

"It's unquestionably murder now," Field went on. "I'm inclined to think from those," he nodded at the exhibits, "that two men are involved, one of them probably a foreigner. If it was he who wrote the letter, then he knew Tessier personally."

"Do you think Tessier was expecting him?"

"That particular night? I doubt it. He'd hardly have taken all that brandy, made himself practically insensible, if that was so. But I think he knew they were coming to grips soon."

"You don't think he may have let him into the room?"

"I think perhaps he may. I'm sure he didn't let him out."

Glyn frowned at the absurdity of that, but let it pass.

"What do we do next?" he demanded, unconsciously identifying himself with the case.

"First of all we find out who else was staying in the hotel that night—not a very hopeful prospect, as it isn't in the least likely that the man who poisoned Tessier came to the Robespierre in his own name. And secondly, we make a trip to Paris. I always enjoy an investigation that takes me to Paris," he added cheerfully.

"You think your murderer hails from there?"

"I think it's possible. In any case we shall have to pick up Tessier's trail there. We've nothing to work on from this side."

"There's the note for £100. You ought to be able to trace that."

Field shook a wise head. "Don't count on that. I don't. There's every possibility that went up in smoke, not long after Tessier died."

"A note for £100 destroyed?" exclaimed Glyn.

"Most people value their lives more highly than that. The man who took it must know there'll be a watch kept out for it, that is, if this investigation of our leaks out into the press. So far we've kept things quiet; the official verdict is suicide while of unsound mind. But no man who plans a crime so carefully as Tessier's murderer has done is going to take the chance of passing a note whose number can be traced—and you can generally trace these large notes—until all the racket has died down and he's certain he's safe. You see, at present we know so little. He may only have taken the notes as a blind to give the impression that the man was murdered for his money, that is, if the suicide notion failed to pull wool over our eyes. Of course, he'd argue that a man with a couple of hundred pounds doesn't take his own life, so he must remove that as a first step. I shouldn't be surprised if we don't have a long run before we get our fox. Well, it's the hunting that interests me. When it comes to breaking up the body—anyone can have my share of the excitement."

"All the same, that money may be safe somewhere," persisted Glyn. "If he's a criminal of any standing, the fellow must know he doesn't stand an earthly against an organised body like the police, to say nothing of the blundering well-intentioned public that does, every now and again, stumble on something crucial, unless his pockets are well-lined. I remember C—— (he named a famous Chief Inspector, since retired) telling me that to be successful at crime a man must have plenty of money. Half the men who're hanged might have got off— only might, mark you," he added hurriedly, " if they'd been able to get out of the country in time. It's easier for a camel to go through the eye of a needle than for a poor man to be a successful murderer."

It is a phenomenon peculiar to the English race that the prospect of a railway journey brings out the worst in their natures. On the whole a kindly people, the mildest philanthropist assumes for the occasion that anyone who, having purchased a seat, dares to occupy the same carriage as himself, is a person of abominable and probably even criminal tendencies. Men who in their home life are amiable and in their business careers open-handed, become monsters of suspicion the instant they set foot on a platform. Inspector Field was no exception to this rule. Having austerely tipped a porter for finding him an empty carriage, he ostentatiously spread papers, a rug and as much hand luggage as he had brought with him over both seats.

"That may give a false impression," he thought, but without much hope. "I don't want a chattering idiot all the way to Folkestone, who'll probably be sick on the train and expect to be dry-nursed."

But on this occasion all his subterfuges were in vain. The train had actually drawn out of the station, and Field was congratulating himself on his unusual luck when the door of the corridor was slid open and a man came in. Field, normally a polite and helpful man, made no attempt to clear the seat or make any room for the new-comer.

"Aren't there enough carriages?" he thought in exasperation. "How on earth can I do anything with this fellow clearing his throat and chuckling and hissing to himself over the morning news in the opposite corner?" And as some slight mark of his extreme irritation he rustled his paper venomously. The newcomer, a mild and unassuming person, it seemed, gently pushed Field's rug aside, sat down and shook open the *Times*. For about five minutes Field's thinking apparatus was paralysed by his expectation that the other man would break into speech. When he did nothing of the sort, Field grew calmer, and began to return to his original speculations. He was planning what he would do when he got to Paris. First he would go to the Sûreté and hunt up Dupuy for the latest news of Tessier. Then . . .

"Excuse me," said his fellow-passenger in a meek high-pitched voice, "this is the boat-train to Folkestone, isn't it?"

Field wondered spontaneously why the Yard was so merciless to murderers. Come to think of it, they were only men harassed beyond endurance; one might be sympathetic with them. Infernal hypocrites, that's what we are, decided Field, as the man opposite, presumably under the impression that he hadn't been heard the first time put his question again.

"Yes, sir, it is," said Field, not lowering his paper.

"Oh, thank you," returned the other gratefully. "I'm going to Paris," he volunteered an instant later.

Field grunted.

"It always gives me a shock to realise that the outskirts of Paris are quite as sordid as the outskirts of any other large town. Somehow the name conjures up a vision of boulevards and flowering trees and ultra-smart shops and intriguing women . . ." the list sounded as though it might flow along for ever. "And then," continued the stranger with enthusiasm, "with the scene all set in your mind, as it were, you get out at the Gare du Nord and it's as dreary as Kings Cross."

Field, his murderous impulses rapidly heating his normally temperate blood, put down his paper. "Really, sir," he began, in tones of enforced calm, and then, "Why, Mr. Glyn . . ."

"I'm glad you've done that," said Glyn thankfully. "My stock of small-talk was beginning to run short."

Field regarded him with a suspicious eye. "Did you say you were going to Paris, sir?"

"I did. Just running over for a day or two on private affairs," he added airily.

"Ah, it must be pleasant to be your own master," was Field's stolid comment. "I'm over on business."

"The Tessier affair, I suppose?"

"Perhaps." A Dutch doll couldn't have been more wooden than the Inspector.

"Obviously," insisted Glyn. "And I must say, seeing I put you into this from the beginning, I think you're treating me pretty shabbily."

"Shabbily?" Field was startled out of his composure.

"Yes. Slinking off to Paris without a word."

"Well, Mr. Glyn," Field was quick to defend his department, "it isn't usual to tell everyone when we go abroad."

"Not everyone. Only me. I am rather exceptionally connected with the case and expect to be even more so in the future."

"Meaning, sir?"

"When you've arrested someone."

"You're appearing for the defence?"

"I don't say that, precisely. That would depend on whom you decide to arrest."

"Why not wait till the Department's made an arrest?" suggested Field, sensibly.

"It's an idiosyncrasy of mine to follow up my own cases." Glyn smiled blandly at his companion.

Field was forced reluctantly into the open. "You're not suggesting I should take you along with me?"

"Why not?"

"It—it isn't done. I'm not a private detective . . ."

"It has been," remarked Mr. Glyn, disregarding the final plea. "What about Mr. Ricardo whom M. Hanaud dragged half over France? You can't pretend, Inspector, that I shouldn't be more use than Mr. Ricardo."

Field looked at him helplessly. The official mind wasn't armed against this kind of buffoonery.

"And then I was in the case even before you were. And I think I might be able to help you. You'd better take me along, Field. I swear not to be a nuisance. And it's better than having me dogging your footsteps, and as likely as not ruining all the ambushes you spread for your suspects."

The urgency of the man's bearing, that his bantering tone could not altogether conceal, convinced Field that he had practically speaking no choice; and his sound common-sense assured him that he would lose nothing by accepting Glyn as his companion. There is an authenticated belief among the apache groups of Paris that they can always recognise the police—les flics—no matter what their disguise. "They smell," they will say in scornful disgust. While denying any truth to this statement, the police have to admit that something—a sixth sense perhaps—does infallibly warn these wretches of the advent of the law, and even among English criminals a similar position obtains. So that a discreet and observant man, who was willing to take a chance, as Field believed Glyn was, and who clearly had a personal stake in the issues, might prove uncommonly useful.

"And anyhow," decided Field, with characteristic candour. "I can't prevent him, and it's better to have him with me and see the mischief he's plotting than have him blazing fresh trails on his own account, and inadvertently helping the criminal."

Field had the expert's contempt for the amateur developed to the nth degree. He derided mercilessly those fairy-tales in which the authentic police force, helmets jammed over perspiring foreheads, visions of promotion egging them on, blundered painstakingly after the wrong man, while the charming leisured aristocrats, who never did anything so vulgar as sweat, whose loose limbs carried them over the most perilous ground at a speed no policeman would dare to emulate, the Lord Peters and Sir Johns, and commoners like Fortune and Priestley, languidly following obscure trails, always brought home the bacon. Nevertheless, an inferior second string had its uses and, making a virtue of necessity, Field said in complacent tones,

"All right, Mr. Glyn.   So long as it's understood that you don't go off on your own after some hare you imagine you've seen and we're too blind to notice . . ."

"Not without making you clairvoyant, too," Glyn promised kindly.

They were approaching Paris, having left the subject of their journey untouched for more than an hour, when Glyn, coming at last to a painful decision, looked up to say, "Have you thought of connecting Lane with this affair?"

"Of course I have," returned Field in surprise. "He's the obvious person to drop on.   He had the opportunity—he got the old man over here—why he couldn't have murdered him quite as well in Paris I don't quite know, but I daresay he had his reasons—he met him—he gave him his drink.   Oh, he's an easy mark.   There are only one or two things we have to prove—that he had a motive, that he could get hold of the poison—then there's the question of the door locked on the inside, of course— and I don't quite see how he turned out the fire, since Pecheron swears it was full on when Lane left the hotel and, of course, Tessier was heard talking to himself later—but if we can find answers to all those points, he's a very good suspect."

CHAPTER VI

GLYN was right about the sordid appearance of suburban Paris, and the grime of the Gare du Nord, but once away from these Paris itself was like a magazine cover of spring.   A warm sunlight had brought out the reckless leaves in banners of foliage that were like silk against a pale blue sky.   The spirit of irresponsibility and hope found expression in the gay thin frocks of the women, their wide hats and flowered parasols. Field felt his heart lift; he was engaged on the work that most delighted him, a difficult trail with few clues, but the prospect of an exciting, an absorbing chase. Glyn at his side was quieter, more remote. His thoughts were filled with the picture of Eve Dulac, lily-pale, her colourless face rising from her fur collar, her eyes fixed in passionate trust upon himself.

" Field's a good fellow," he reflected, " but he's like all these other professionals. People are simply characters in a story. They don't exist of themselves. He'd as soon arrest one as another. He has no personal stake."

He recognised, of course, how intolerable the existence of a detective would be if he allowed the personal element to influence him. Nevertheless, he experienced a pleasant sense of superiority as of the human being over the machine, without acknowledging the obvious truism that the machine continues to work infallibly long after the man has been pitched on the scrap heap.

" Where are we going?" he asked Field cheerfully.

" Going. To the Sûreté, of course.

" Do you think they'll have Tessier's finger-prints there?"

" They might, though I've no reason to suppose they have. But the French are second to none in their dossiers of people who have ever been in the public eye. And I like to have all the information I can at the start. If he has been living a rather disreputable life for the past year or so they may have kept tabs on him."

Glyn felt the tide of excitement rising within him. It was odd, he reflected, how even a man with a personal bias got swept away on a wave of professional enthusiasm. At the Sûreté Field asked for M. Dupuy, and a minute or two later they found themselves in the presence of that happy little man whose name was a terror to renegade Paris, the tireless, the pitiless, the fearless Armand Dupuy. His round olive-coloured face shone like a billiard ball; his black eyes sparkled with pleasure. He came to meet Field with both hands outstretched.

"I have been reading a book by a Frenchman," he greeted him, "who says that the English are unimaginative. I am hoping you will be able to make me disagree with him."

"We'll do our best," returned Field pleasantly, accustomed to this miniature volcano. "This is Mr. Glyn. He's associated with me—unofficially—in this matter of Réné Tessier's death."

"Réné Tessier," repeated Dupuy musingly. "That was suicide I think?" He looked questioningly at the two men.

"We've reason to think it was murder," said Field.

"Murder! But who would wish to murder a man like that? A street brawl, some quarrel in a tavern, even a disagreement over money, or," he shrugged, "a woman; that might happen to any man. But that he should be deliberately murdered in England—that, messieurs, is difficult to believe. I ask you again, who would have cause?"

"That's what we've come to Paris to learn. And naturally, being in Paris, we come first of all to you."

Dupuy laid his hands on the backs of two chairs; he opened a box of thin black cigars and offered them to his visitors. So ingrained in the man's nature was the desire for pomp and display, so eager was he to shed an air of mystery over the smallest occasion, that he could invest the simplest gesture with all the dignity of ritual.

Glyn, who was at heart as ardent a ceremonialist as his host, delighted in this reception. Field, who took things more coolly, sat down, refused the cigar, lighted one of his own cigarettes and began to explain Glyn's connection with the case.

"Now," he wound up, "we've written in the last chapter for you. We want you to give us the first."

Dupuy spread his hands. "The first is known to everyone," he declared.

"I mean, since the death of his son," Field amended.

"Ah yes. A tragic business. He committed suicide, did he not? A daring leap. We may as well have the official records." He pressed a bell and a clerk arrived to whom he gave an order for a certain file.

"A bad business," he repeated, as the man hurried away. "Murder, eh?" He looked from one to the other with sly smiling eyes. "Regrettable, I agree. But also provocative, intriguing, challenging. It will be interesting to know who cared so much for that miserable life . . ."

The clerk returned with a file of newspaper cuttings. Dupuy's quicksilver manner changed again. Now he was grave and alert.

"Here are the facts, monsieur. This is a report of the inquest. Louis Tessier took his own life by jumping from the Arc de Triomphe on 14th July, 1933. At the inquest it was said that he had been greatly distressed owing to the breaking of his engagement. Friends agreed that he had been strange for several months, but this was put down to the state of his affections. The engagement had been of some months' duration.

"Réné Tessier, giving evidence, said his son was a musician. He had at one time been a successful violinist, but during the past year he had not had so many engagements and had played in the orchestra of a large hotel. Asked if his son had been pressed for money, Tessier said, 'He had enough for everyday needs.' Asked to define every-day needs, witness admitted that the deceased would not be able to go about in the same circle as his friends on his earnings.

"'He had applied to you for help?'

"'He once asked me for money and I gave it him.'

"'You did not help him again?'

"'No. I told him I could do nothing more. I had made my own way and I felt he ought to do the same.'

"'How long before his death did you see him?'

"'About a week.'

"The last person to whom he appeared to have spoken was Mlle. Dulac to whom he had been for several months engaged. He had come to her apartment at about 9 o'clock, clearly in a state of great excitement. She had not seen him previously for some weeks, not since the breaking of the engagement.

"Mlle. Dulac ascended the witness-stand.

"'The break came from your side, Mlle?'

"'Yes.'

"'Did you give Louis Tessier any reason for your act?'

"'I told him I could not marry him.'

"It appeared that there was no other man in the case. Eve Dulac had exercised the age-long female prerogative of changing her mind. On the night of his death, Tessier had come in and begged her to reconsider her decision. She told him it was quite impossible, whereupon he rushed out and destroyed himself.

"René Tessier had been in a state of barely con-trolled fury while he gave evidence. At the verdict of suicide he rose and cried, 'I beg of you to add that he did not know what he did. My son was out of his mind.' The jury, however, refused to be intimidated. The young man had taken his life because the woman he loved had no use for him; the consummation was neither unexpected nor rare; and it would be an insult to the dead to suggest that such an act was the act of a madman. It was an act of homage, fanatical if you like, but comprehensible enough to a beautiful woman."

"There isn't a jury in England that wouldn't have brought in Suicide While of Unsound Mind," remarked Glyn vigorously.

But Dupuy only smiled. "I do not think, monsieur, that I would care to be an Englishwoman," he replied—a comment that admitted of no reply.

After the inquest Tessier seemed to drop out of his world. He broke a contract for a picture he was to have made; abandoned his plans for the production of another; he was heard of in strange places. Unshaven and unkempt he mixed with loafers and ne'er-do-wells; he wore shabby clothes. He left his fine apartment and had apparently no fixed abode. He was seen walking unsteadily through the streets in the most disreputable company and he was suspected of taking drugs; certainly he was seen in the company of addicts and men whose moral sense was completely warped. Other excesses were attributed to him, with how much truth even the police could not be certain. Paris is tolerant but even Paris could not tolerate such vagaries as these. In taking his own life, Louis Tessier had slain his father also.

"What we want to know is, what or who was behind Louis Tessier," remarked Field.

Dupuy shrugged rapidly. "Surely that is obvious. This lady."

"Whoever was behind Louis seems to have been the object of Tessier's revenge," put in Glyn.

"But, monsieur, surely that is obvious. This young lady . . ."

"It doesn't seem to me probable," said Glyn decisively. "Tessier has kept up a correspondence with her. That isn't the act of a man whose mind is full of hate."

"You have seen the letters?"

"No. Mlle. Dulac destroyed them."

"She told you why?"

"She said they were foolish letters."

"That is a word that admits of many interpretations. She may have meant they were threatening. Did she know of M. Tessier's movements?"

"She knew he was coming to London. But then, she's Fleming's secretary. She may have heard through him."

Field put in, "She was afraid, all the same, Mr. Glyn. She wouldn't have sent Mr. Lane rushing up to Victoria if she hadn't known Tessier was planning mischief."

"Unless she was afraid for him?"

"Then why the warning that he was armed?"

"I don't know," Glyn confessed. "But I still think my explanation is at least as tenable as yours. Are we incidentally assuming that Tessier's sole object in coming to England was to be revenged on this mysterious X? What about the agreement with Fleming?"

"Another idea has occurred to me," said Field. "I've been looking up a few dates. You remember at the time of Louis Tessier's death, the father was pretty deeply dipped in a production of his own. He dropped the whole thing and went into the wilds.

The production was taken up by Fleming, who, as you know, made a huge success of it. I'm not suggesting there was anything crooked in Fleming's part in the transaction. It was all perfectly above board. But Tessier's admittedly an unbalanced man. You can see him—can't you?—looking round and perhaps contrasting his position not necessarily with that of Fleming, but with the position he occupied a couple of years ago. It might easily appear to him that Fleming had stepped into his shoes, deliberately stolen his thunder."

"And Mlle. Dulac was so much concerned for her employer that she sends a third party to ensure his safety? And, mark you, she says nothing to M. Fleming of this, shows him none of the letters, gives him no warning. After all, she cannot always be at his side, neither she nor M. Lane speak of this danger to M. Fleming. No, no, monsieur, that cock, as you say, will not fight. If she tells the truth to M. Lane it is because she needs protection for herself, and knows that there she has a right to seek for it."

"There's another point," observed Glyn, speaking more slowly, " Mlle. Dulac came to me to beg me to get the obvious verdict reversed. She knew the court would bring it in suicide; and she was convinced it was murder. If what you say is true, wouldn't she have kept her mouth shut and saved the scandal?"

"Have you heard of that little bird that makes a great commotion and at the same time a great show of moving in a false direction to lead you away from the nest you seek? It is the hen bird that so deceives you, monsieur. It is a practice common to her sex."

"May I ask whether you have met Mlle. Dulac?" enquired Glyn politely.

"Alas, monsieur . . ." Again that indescribable

rapidity of movement, that eloquent gesture more eloquent than any speech.

"I think when you do so you'll agree with me that if she did throw over Louis Tessier, and admittedly she did, she had the best of reasons for doing so."

Dupuy, his eyes bright with a competitive malice, bowed to his protagonist.

"Monsieur, I have the greatest respect for your judgment," he said.

Field turned the subject. "You will be able to help us to find the beginning of the skein?" he asked.

Dupuy's eyes danced in his shining face. "I cannot promise you that, monsieur. Paris is full of these men who have forfeited their identity. You understand?" His gay glance flickered over Glyn's intent face.

"Of course I understand," said Glyn quickly. "It's a miracle to me how the police ever drop on these forgotten men. But they do it—and I don't speak without my book. I've just been involved in the defence for a case that comes on in about a fortnight, where the crucial point was the finding of a particular man for an alibi. Think of it. One man out of the hundreds who throng the Embankment every night; sleep in doorways, crowd into dosshouses, the *Morning Post* Home, the crypt of S. Martin's. All looking alike, all shabby, all hopeless, all trying to escape discovery. But they got him—oh, they got him."

Dupuy was smiling at the Englishman's enthusiasm. "The latest information I can give you, monsieur, is that four months ago he was lodging with the Widow Lemaitre in the Rue Rossignol."

"And is anything known of the Widow Lemaitre?"

Glyn sat in silent and profound admiration of the effect the Frenchman achieved by a change of tone, a complete immobility. "The police know nothing against her," he said, and no active detraction could have more clearly expressed his own attitude of distrust. "She has let lodgings for ten years since her husband . . ." he paused.

"Died?" filled in Field.

"Died to her, monsieur. He was transported to Devil's Island twelve years ago for the murder of a young girl. A big man he was, like a butcher, with a great curling moustache and enormous hands. He was fortunate to escape the knife."

"Did you say he'd been on Devil's Island twelve years?" asked Glyn in a sober voice.

"Yes, monsieur. He is, it seems, of those whom such a climate pleases." Dupuy laughed gaily. "For three years he was in solitary confinement—figure it, monsieur—a stone bed, a stone pillow, a stone cell. Locked in most hours of the twenty-four. And when he is let out he sees—what? The fever swamps of Sierra Leone. He must cling to life, that man. And she—women are incomprehensible. Even when it was proved what he had done she would have saved him. Such affection," he concluded briskly, "is unnatural. It shows a depraved taste."

Glyn looked away. Field said in impersonal tones, "Well, then, we must see how Mme. Lemaitre can help us. Meanwhile," he added pleadingly, seeing that Dupuy was about to end the interview, "there is one more thing. Who is M. Brémond— M. Thomas Brémond?"

The little Frenchman, who had seemed almost uninterested in the case, turned on him with a recrudescence of excitement.

"M. Brémond?" he repeated. "So he is concerned in this?"

"Among the papers on Tessier's body, we found
a letter of introduction, unheaded and undated, from
M. Brémond to a gentleman called Wilson in the
Charing Cross Road. There is, of course, no reason
why M. Brémond should not give a letter of introduction to his friend, M. Tessier—at least—" he
looked questioningly at Dupuy.

"And this Mr. Wilson?"

"Is a book-seller; second hand books and an
occasional valuable first edition."

"In the Charing Cross Road? As we know, they
sell other things besides books in that street. You
have seen Mr. Wilson?"

"He has been seen. He knows nothing of M.
Tessier. M. Brémond he believes he remembers as
buying books from him about two years ago."

Dupuy nodded. "That may be. Our records of
M. Brémond do not go back so far. Well then, I
will tell you. We have been interested in M.
Brémond for a little more than a year. He is the
proprietor of a chemist's shop in the Rue Rossignol.
It is a corner shop with a side door and the rent
cannot be cheap. There is a long-established shop
of the same type nearly opposite. Almost all the
neighbourhood goes to M. Feveral. Nevertheless,
M. Brémond has not only remained open for
fourteen months, he also employs a young man of
perhaps eighteen. When he goes abroad he seems
prosperous; he has apparently no family. He has
occasionally been seen at the tables. He plays for
moderate stakes and he is not noticeably lucky. Of
his past nothing can be learned. He is one of those
strange ones who appear, it seems, out of air. Moreover, he closes his shop unusually early, but it is
open again in the evening when he alone is in attend-

ance.   At that time, customers must use a side-door.
All this, you will agree, monsieur, is very strange."

"What do you suspect?" asked Field, who appreciated a more direct method.

"There has been, as you know, monsieur, a very
great increase in the illicit drug industry during the
past two or three years.   The agents of this terrible
traffic appear in every walk of life and in the least
expected places.   Certain arrests have been made
but we have not yet begun to skim the froth off the
cup.   We have had our suspicions that M. Brémond
was not altogether innocent in this regard.   But he
is clever.   We have laid many traps for him but he
has fallen into none of them.   More than once men
have been apprehended leaving by that so suspicious
side-door in the dark.   But no drug is ever found
upon them.   Brémond must have his spies everywhere.   Nothing escapes him.   We have sent picked
men to buy the stuff from him, but he says he is a
chemist and cannot sell such drugs except by a
doctor's order—a doctor, moreover, known to himself.   Tessier himself was once taken as he left the
house, but nothing incriminating was found.   Yet
we have information that Brémond is bound up
with this traffic.   And so, it seems, was Réné
Tessier.   Perhaps," his eyes brightened, "this Mr.
Wilson can help us."

"It might be a pointer to our people," ruminated
Field.   "We're in much the same boat as your-
selves, monsieur l'inspecteur.   The drug traffic is
assuming vaster and vaster proportions.   At one
time there was a comparatively select circle to whom
you could point as being probable addicts.   Now
the circumstances of life since the war, and particularly these last few years, have led to an incredible
increase in consumption.   The habit of burning the

candle at both ends involves some substitute for natural energy and people find it in drugs. We may have the whole medical force on our side, but they're as powerless as ourselves. The stuff must be coming over in carloads. Oh, we get a distributor every now and again, but, like a better man than I, I ask ' What are they among so many?' "

Dupuy, happily merging the particular in the general, continued warmly. " The position here is outrageous. Men known to be carrying drugs are set upon and robbed. There have been several cases. A young girl who had unhappily contracted the cocaine habit was held up in her car by masked men, and the drug taken from her. In its place she was politely handed a packet of bismuth. With regard to M. Brémond," he continued on a rising tide of disgust, " he has been known even to sell some harmless powder and christen it cocaine."

" I wonder anyone still has any faith in him, then," exclaimed Glyn.

" Faith! What's faith to a drug maniac? He'll take any chance, risk any loss of dignity, so long as there's a hope of getting what he wants."

" You are right, monsieur," said Dupuy gravely.

And suddenly Field cried out, " Of course. What a fool! I ought to be shot."

Dupuy flung up his hands and poured out a spate of ironic Gallic disclaimers, but Field, paying no heed to him, continued, " Those aspirin tablets they found on Tessier's body. Of course! And we never so much as had them analysed! If we could show he was carrying drugs we should have established a definite link. The queer thing is, it didn't come out at the inquest that he was given to taking them."

CHAPTER VII

THE Rue Rossignol was an obscure street of tall
houses whose windows were veiled in curtains, and
decorated from within by vases of gold and silver
artificial flowers. Coloured parakeets screamed and
scolded in a gilt cage in the ground floor window of
No. 5, the house they had come to visit, and when
the door had been opened to them by an enormous
woman with an overwhelming bosom they saw in
the hall other testimonies of a zoological bias. A
moulting white seal in a case made a convenient
table for letters and walking-sticks, while a stuffed
little puffin leered with its single eye from its glass
cage across the passage. Mme. Lemaitre fascinated
Glyn. She was so huge and ugly, with her great
bony nose and out-thrust chin, her green eyes sunk
so deep in fat that they seemed smaller than actually
they were, her incredible transformation of ginger-
coloured hair that she had bound with a green
ribbon.

"You are wondering why we invade you like this,"
suggested Dupuy cheerfully, and, indeed, they
seemed a formidable gathering in that narrow hall.

The landlady chuckled with her whole body, her
great bosom as broad as a shelf, her voluminous
hips, the magnificent curves of her thighs, were all
agitated by her laughter.

"I think perhaps I can guess, messieurs," she said,
"but you have come to the wrong house if that is
what you want." She looked at them with frank
good-humour. The two Englishmen's faces
remained staid, even embarrassed, but Dupuy cried
gaily, "You are wrong, Madame. All that we wish

of you is a little news about our regretted friend,
M. Réné Tessier."

She looked at him in sharp astonishment. "You
are his friends?" Then her face grew dark with
anger. "You come late, messieurs. Why did you
not come before?"

"Well, you see, he didn't need us before."

"Need you? Does a man with friends take his
own life? I tell you, it made my heart wring when
I thought of him dying there, without hope—."

"You were shocked at the news. You didn't
expect him to take his own life?" He looked round
him enquiringly, as if to suggest that some more
private place might be found for this conversation.
Mme. Lemaitre took the hint and led them into a
room on the right of the hall. This was packed
with furniture, the walls covered with badly executed
water-colour paintings, shelves full of undusted bric-
a-brac, a soiled cloth scattered with crumbs on a
round table near the window, a cat the colour of
gunmetal on a pot-bellied chair by the fireplace.

Glyn, the imaginative man to whom thought was
more natural than action, decided that the room was
very like its owner. On the surface it was slovenly,
good-natured, rich in a superficial manner with velvet
tablecloths and elaborately embroidered curtains
round the tarnished gilt mirrors but underneath
put to innumerable sly shifts and devices. He saw
that the leg of the handsome circular table was
propped up by a piece of firewood; the writing-desk
was ink-stained and the flap cracked right across; the
seats of the velvet chairs were worn to threads. He
thought with dismay of the once elegant Réné
Tessier flying from this soiled and discredited
splendour to a refuge that was no refuge in a sordid
London lodging.

Field, his experienced eyes examining the room

and its owner in dispassionate detail, decided that, in spite of Madame's disclaimers, it was the sort of house that in England is distinguished by the label "No Petty Restrictions."

Dupuy had no eyes for the room; his sole concern was for the woman it framed.

"Madame, you asked us just now why we did not come sooner. We could not. We had not the right. His life belonged to himself. Now that he is dead . . ."

She broke in tumultuously, "He did not require to go to England to die."

"Precisely, madame. If he had wished to take his life it would be as convenient here as anywhere."

She laughed. Glyn was suddenly reminded of the ogress in his childhood's fairy-tale. "Oho, monsieur, not convenient to me."

Dupuy joined in her amusement. "But Paris offers so many opportunities to the suicide," he urged. "And a man who suffers torment on the water does not make a bad crossing in order to die at the other end. Did he tell you, ma mère, why he wished to go to England, he who belonged to Paris?"

"He said, 'Life takes us to strange places, sets us strange tasks!' You must remember he was artiste, monsieur. They are not the same as others."

"He said that when he was leaving you?"

"When he spoke of going to England, when he said goodbye."

"He wasn't coming back then? He took all his possessions with him?"

"All his possessions? La, la! That would not incommode even so small a man too much. I tell you, he carried them all in one case."

"He was, then, very poor?"

She nodded at him, her bright eyes glittering with

a derisive malice. It seemed to Field that in some way she despised the little French detective and wished him to realise it. Before she attempted to reply she patted her tremendous bosom, releasing a quantity of wind.

"Monsieur," she said, leaning back in her chair and clasping her hands on her stomach, "when you came here this evening I did not think you desired an apartment here. I know that a monsieur like yourself does not look for accommodation in the Rue de Rossignol. And do you think that Réné Tessier, accustomed to rich living and fine silver and an elegant house, would be more at home here than yourself?"

"You have intelligence, madame," Dupuy approved. "I take it then that M. Tessier remained here because he could afford nothing better. Did he have many friends?"

"He was in so little, monsieur. Early in the morning he would go out and even though he might come back at night it was as if he could not rest. This is a quiet house, monsieur, too quiet he sometimes thought. I am used to being among people, he would say. It becomes a habit. And out he would go, wandering Heaven knows where."

Dupuy asked a rather sudden question. "Should you say he was a happy man?"

"Happy? What a word! He was *artiste*. He was not one man, but a dozen, a hundred. I think more than anything he regretted the work he did not choose to do any more."

"Choose!"

"Yes, monsieur," retorted the woman definitely. "I am sure it was his own choice. For, mark you, he still had the power. I have seen him in this room, repeating some story, mimicking some droll fellow till I had a stitch with laughing. Yes," she repeats more slowly, " he had the power, but I think he had not the will."

" Because of his son?"

She nodded; life flashed in all her limbs. Glyn saw suddenly how Tessier must have delighted in her. How that flame of living must have merged with his own!

" How he loved that one! And how he hated the one that ruined him?"

Glyn stiffened. Dupuy attached no particular significance into the words, but the lawyer thought he perceived, in the C.I.D. man's attentive immobility, a hostile attitude to Eve Dulac, whom he regarded as the root of so much evil.

" He would talk to you of her?"

" But I had known the son, monsieur. I had a lodger here, a young man called Barras, who went afterwards to America, and this M. Louis was a friend to him. Often has he sat in my *parloir* playing on his fiddle."

Dupuy leaned forward. " And talking, too, perhaps."

She laughed heartily. " Talking, too, of a certainty. He would talk of his fiancée, how sweet she was, how good, how they would soon be married and once that happened his friend would give him all the money he needed."

" He could not afford to marry?"

" Not then. But he thought his fortune would change."

" And did you know that before his death, his engagement was broken off?"

" Yes. She grew tired of waiting for a poor man. She had engaged to marry the son of the rich, the famous Réné Tessier, not a poor violinist living in the Rue Rossignol."

As she spat out the contemptuous words Glyn had

a sudden feeling that everything she said was untrustworthy, that she was incurably prejudiced, that she wanted to damage this girl in the eyes of them all.

He broke in in a swift, soft voice, " Might she not have felt he would prefer to be—unhampered—until he had won a place for himself?"

Mme. Lemaitre turned squarely round and impaled him with her derisive gaze. " You would not say that if you had seen him, monsieur. He was like a monster—a madman—a ghost. At first he could not believe it. He became violent—he shouted. He laughed. He said, 'It is a trick.' But it was no trick."

" And you told M. Tessier this?"

" He knew it all. He said, 'I live only to pay my son's debt.' "

Glyn broke in again. " But that, of course, was only a *façon de parler*. You cannot take a desperate man too seriously."

Mme. Lemaitre shrugged. " You did not perhaps know M. Tessier. His son was his life."

" There was his work. I know he abandoned it for a time, but at the end he came back to it. He came to England not to commit suicide, not to be revenged on his son, but to regain the place he had once occupied in the world of the film."

The woman shook her head : one end of the green velvet ribbon had become unfastened and flapped ridiculously above her ear. " He could not do it," she declared. " He was burnt out; when a fire is extinguished, who can warm his hands at the ashes?"

" Then why do you suppose he left France?"

" To be revenged. That girl was in England. He knew it. He had written to her."

Dupuy's eyes, swift and glittering as those of a

snake, moved from the woman to Glyn. "He will be of use later perhaps," he decided, "but not now. At this moment he has forgotten all his legal training. He can remember only that this girl is in peril." And he chuckled inwardly to think how easily logic and reason may be overthrown by a purely instinctive emotion with no backing other than that of desire. The same process had taken place in Réné Tessier and behold, the lamentable result.

Field broke the long silence, speaking for the first time since he had entered the house.

"There are one or two things I should like to know," he remarked. "When M. Tessier was here, did he have many visitors?"

"He couldn't rest. He was always out, as I told you. He had friends, some of them friends before catastrophe overtook him. He went out in elegant clothes—I used to press them for him afterwards—he would come back in the early hours of the morning—"

"Sometimes not quite steady on his feet, eh?"

"He was not a complete man," she defended him hotly. "He was often in pain. He could not sleep."

"He took sleeping-draughts, perhaps," suggested Dupuy.

"There's no harm in a sleeping-draught. There are times when I've been glad of one myself."

"But he did take them?" Dupuy insisted.

"Sometimes."

"You know what they were?"

"You had better ask the chemist that. How should I be able to tell you?"

"Perhaps," suggested Dupuy, "you have a bottle here that belonged to him?"

"If there is one in his room, and I don't say there is, it'll be empty. That won't tell you much."

"Except perhaps the name of the chemist."

"I could tell you that well enough. It is M. Brémond of the Rue Félice."

"The Rue Félice? But surely that is some distance from here. It's a long way to go each time you want some shaving cream or—perhaps—chloroform for an aching tooth."

"Perhaps he went to him in more prosperous days."

But Dupuy shook his head. "That was careless, madame. Brémond is a new name this last twelve months or so. But perhaps you don't know the shop."

"M. Tessier would sometimes execute commissions for me at Brémond and other places. I do not think I have entered the shop myself. Oh la, it is sad to think I shall see no more of him."

"But he had told you he would not return," expostulated Dupuy.

"No. It was not precisely that. It was a strange thing he said. 'I am going away and this is farewell.' I said, 'And what of Paris? You will not stay long in London with Paris waiting.' And he said, 'I may return but I do not think we shall meet again.'"

"And that seemed to you strange?"

"Well, monsieur." Her eloquent gesture was a revelation of economy. Glyn had a second vision of the pair in a new relationship. This time with the woman as the stronger, for all her lack of culture and charm. "There were times when he was strange, the little monsieur." There was an indulgence, a tenderness almost, that should have increased his admiration for her, but instead, he was aware of a sudden nausea, a revulsion of anger springing from his own respect for the dead man. It was as though she said, "He was so weak, that little one. He was poor, he was feeble. He might have wit and genius, but what use were they? It was on me that he leaned." The detestable note of patronage, in short, and instantly he resented it on the dead man's behalf. He was reminded of an occasion when he had seen a middle-aged scholar, unaccustomed to wine, inadvertently intoxicated at somebody's cocktail party, one of those inane affairs that begin at seven in the evening, whose last stragglers, rather the worse for wear, droop hollowly down the steps in search of taxi-cabs at four a.m. next day. He could recall still the passion of shame and rage that had flushed him, and he felt a recrudescence of that feeling now. René Tessier might have died white-faced, ruined and bereft in an attic in a fourth-rate London hotel, but nothing could rob him of the dignity of his own achievement. And now this woman, sly and coarsely familiar, would tarnish his memories of that magnificent defeated man.

Field looked at him sideways, but Glyn remained unaware of the glance. Dupuy did not look at him at all. He was leaning towards the window saying confidentially, "And at such times, madame, he looked to you for comfort?"

"And if he did, monsieur?" Glyn received the impression that she would like to toss her head at him, but it was so huge under its heavy embellishment and her neck so short and stout, that the gesture was an impossibility to her. Nevertheless, he could see that she trembled on the verge of displeasure.

"You were kind, I am sure."

Now she made no attempt to conceal her feelings. "Monsieur, when you came to-night I told you mine was not that kind of a house. Can I help it if everywhere there are scandalous ones who would point the finger at *la Sainte Vierge* herself, were she living in the Rue Rossignol?"

"The owner of a kind heart is always at its mercy," agreed Dupuy diplomatically. "You have then, even had to endure that?"

"There was one that tried to make scenes, to put me out of countenance, as one says. He was behind with his rent and I told him I could not afford to keep lodgers for charity. You know my story, monsieur, perhaps. I am a widow in all but name. And he said—he said—that ugly one . . ." she seemed as though she might have an apoplectic fit. Her fat ringed hands were extended, shaking with passion, the bright stones of her many trinkets filling the clear evening air with colour. "And all, monsieur, because once—once, mark you,—he saw that poor one coming from my room, and at a time when I was not so much as in the house."

"Infamous!" agreed Dupuy warmly. "But surely, madame, you pay no heed to such scoundrels."

Her rage quieted. "He thought that a new way to settle his rent," she admitted. "But indeed, there was so little one could do for him. Let him talk of the beloved son." She heaved a vast sigh. She could do nothing discreetly, Glyn thought. Every gesture involved her whole enormous body.

Field had listened to this monologue dispassionately enough, but now he said, "Perhaps, madame, we might see his room, that is, if it is not yet occupied."

Madame admitted that it was not. "But if it is keepsakes you desire, monsieur, there were none. Never was such a tidy man. He left no trace."

She led them up several flights of stairs, with mustard-coloured paper peeling from the walls, into a barn of a room, with a long window looking over the roofs of Paris. The furniture was of the barest —a bed, a table, a press—and all swept as clean as Mother Hubbard's cupboard.

"He liked being high, didn't he? Did he choose to be at the top of the house?"

"He said he could not bear to feel people above him. And then there was the view," she added proudly, moving across to the great expanse of window. "Do you know that on a clear day one can even see . . ."

"The Arc de Triomphe," broke in Dupuy's voice behind them.

Madame Lemaitre turned in surly amazement. "That is so, monsieur. He had sentiment, you understand . . ."

Dupuy answered in a rapid flow of French that was wasted on Glyn who, standing with his back to the room, let his attention wander to other considerations.

He was suddenly obsessed by thoughts of the dead. Though this room had been empty of him for a week and although there now remained in it no possession or hint of his residence there, the air seemed impregnated by that dominant personality. It seemed to him that only a man of compelling strength could have left so powerful an imprint on such insignificance. Standing there, his fingers drumming idly on the sill, he gave his imagination free rein. Here night by night had Tessier stood, looking over the great playground of Paris, detached, like a spectator watching some amazing pageant, seeing himself not as part of it but in some manner its possessor. A sense of his own tininess oppressed the lawyer as he thought of the thousands of lives sheltered beneath those clustering roofs, lives in which he had no part, that were as secret to him as were the movements of those beyond the grave or the convent grille. Diminutive as toys from that great height, Glyn beheld the minute green squares, the miniature vehicles rolling along beneath him, and he wondered, over-mastered for the first time by a sense of passionate pity for the dead, "What were *his* thoughts as he stood here, looking over the Paris that was once his slave?" So strong was this feeling that for an instant he forgot his own identity, and was that lonely figure, deserted of hope. And he knew that Dupuy was right, that Tessier had stood here seeing only one thing—a tiny human form poised for an instant on that mighty arch, and then falling, falling, small as a fluttering sheet of paper, into space. It was no wonder that he had no heart left for his work, no ambition that he cared any longer to pursue . . .

A hand was laid on Glyn's arm. A voice said anxiously, "You are feeling faint? Come and sit down," and there was Field, his face touched by a genuine concern, yet in his manner just a hint of pleasure that it should be the amateur who betrayed weakness.

"It's nothing," cried Glyn, hurriedly turning away from that glittering city under the glow of sunset. He was surprised, indeed, to see that the clouds above the roofs were now capped with gold, like an irregular mountain range against which the sloping Paris roofs stood out in sharp relief. His mind, during the moment or two that he had been unconscious of himself, had been strained to a tension so acute that he now perceived everything about him in meticulous detail. A small bird had perched itself on the window-sill and was twittering there with its head on one side.

"*Quelque moineau,*" said Lemaitre indulgently, seeing his eyes fixed upon it.

He put one hand to his forehead. "I must apologise," he answered. And then in a wondering tone he turned on Dupuy, exclaiming, "It was you, then, who spoke of the Arc de Triomphe."

Dupuy nodded. "I was saying that from this window on a clear day a man with good sight might even see that."

He was standing with his back against the mantel-shelf, his hands in his pockets, his face, with its engaging smile, turned innocently towards his companions. That new quality of imagination suggested to Glyn a grim parallel. Such a position must be most uncomfortable for so small a man, and the notion sprang into his mind that this sharp edge of the mantel was not unlike the edge of the guillotine, pressing against the little Frenchman's neck. He was himself intimidated again by the woman's manner, her suggestion that it was her own virtue rather than Tessier's fastidious taste that had prevented a situation between them, from which the dead man surely would have shrunk in disgust.

"I think that was why he chose this room," Dupuy continued, nodding sagely. The widow seemed awe-struck by his insight. She also began to nod as though the infection were irresistible and this strange exhibition continued until Dupuy stopped it by striding forward and clapping his hands together.

"They think we are mad, these serious English-men," he cried, catching the widow by her elbows. "Nodding like two mandarins in a bazaar. But now, there is one more thing you shall tell me. If you had been this enemy of M. Tessier, would you not have been afraid? Would you not have cried out for the rocks to fall down and cover you? For the lightning to destroy him? He was a terrible fellow, this Tessier, was he not?"

Behind the bantering tone, the extravagant gesture, Glyn discerned a burning, an insatiable desire to have the point answered accurately. The mind of this man moved so quickly and in directions so unexpected to the lawyer that he found himself bewildered, but he had a feeling that this question and its reply were the crux of the position.

"Of course," he reasoned within himself, "he's trying to prove that someone was so terrified of Tessier that he—or she—had to put him out of the way before ruin overtook the opposition." The sentence thus framed in his mind was obscure, but its meaning was clear enough. What he was less certain about was whether Dupuy's quarry was still Eve Dulac or whether, since his arrival at this house, he had pounced on a fresh scapegoat.

Madame Lemaitre looked unwontedly grave. Her good-humoured chuckling ceased as though some-one had turned a handle and cut it off short. She said, "Monsieur, if I were that man or woman I would not sleep for fear. He is not the kind that forgets and he would never forgive."

Glyn shivered. He thought, turning to observe Madame Lemaitre, still held in that familiar grasp by the little Parisian, "What is it she is hiding from us? There's something she is concealing, something she doesn't mean to tell. Something," his mind insisted, "it is essential that I should know." He had no doubt that his deductions were right. These others—they were officials. The affair was a matter of bread and butter to them, only to him was it something personal. To him, therefore, belonged the right of knowing every detail, no matter how irrelevant it might appear.

"I will come again, alone," he decided. "To me alone she may be persuaded to tell what she would shrink to repeat to the police." It was evident that Tessier had often talked to her, and there was a wealth of detail, any scrap of which might be of supreme importance to a man intent on solving a riddle, and she must divulge it to him. He decided that money might unseal her lips, and money, he resolved recklessly, he would offer her if that were the only solution. Could he have stood back and observed himself and his conduct from an impersonal standpoint, he would have been shocked and amazed at his attitude. He had no thought to spare for the claims these two colleagues might have on his loyalty. His natural discretion, hitherto powerfully reinforced by the demands of his profession, he flung to the winds. No echo of the scores of times he had solemnly warned harassed men and women against putting themselves in the power of scoundrels by paying away money, troubled his ears. His pulses throbbed, his eyes were shining, his mouth opened in sudden laughter.

"I've made a fool of myself," he cried candidly. "It's you, madame, who must accept the responsibility. Your descriptions of M. Tessier were so vivid for the moment, I almost forgot I was myself."

Field, whose upbringing had been extremely pious, was reminded for the first time in years of the psalm his father had always read aloud, before breakfast, on his mother's birthday.

". . . Then were we like to them that dream. Then was our mouth filled with laughter and our tongue with joy . . ."

"He thinks he's discovered something," he thought, "and he's pretty sure both Dupuy and I have missed it. Oh well." He didn't feel anxious. It was improbable that the police of two countries could be easily deceived while an amateur in crime, his nose to the trail, outstripped them both with scarcely an access of breath. Glancing across the room he saw that Dupuy had come to the same conclusion as himself. A faint gesture of recognition, unperceived by the self-satisfied Glyn, passed between them. The lawyer, meanwhile, his resolve taken, knew an instant's lightening of heart. He was prepared now to leave the stage to the professionals. For himself, he could wait. To-morrow would be his hour . . .

Dupuy approached Lemaitre, saying guilefully, "Madame, we take up a great deal of your time but, as you have said yourself, M. Tessier is an important man. Now there is perhaps one other thing you can tell us. I will confide to you that we have our suspicions of this M. Brémond, the innocent chemist of the Rue Félice. Tell me, he is a tall fair man, is he not?"

"You are hunting the wrong fox, monsieur." Her baying laugh filled the room. "He's a little fellow with a dark beard and a paunch—so," she patted her own large stomach complacently.

"She said she had never seen him," reflected Glyn, and he saw that the same thought had occurred to Field.

"M. Tessier has often described him to me," continued the widow cheerfully, and Dupuy began to laugh at the lawyer's crestfallen appearance. "He would strut and caper—oh, he had a wit that one. But I," she added more gravely, "what should I know of him? He was a chemist like any other."

"And you had no reason to suspect that he supplied M. Tessier with mixtures that are perhaps not to be so easily bought elsewhere. Remember," his face hardened and his eyes flashed, "this is a serious question I ask you."

But she turned on him in sudden anger, exclaiming, "I don't pretend to misunderstand you, monsieur. I've read the papers and I've heard people talk. I know the things they whispered about him. He was addicted to this vice and that. He was a debauchee, drunkard, a human monster who had to hide his crimes in an obscure street. There is nothing too bad, monsieur, to be said of a man who drops out of the race. The truth is never enough. Réné Tessier had lost his son and he had lost him in a terrible way. Would you expect him to be the same as other men? But no, that explanation is too simple. There must be something behind it, something dark and wicked. And so they whisper and they invent. I tell you, monsieur," her face worked with a rage that astounded them all, " if M. Tessier did take his life as they say, he was driven to it by the lies they told of him here. There comes a breaking-point beyond which a man cannot go."

Watching her, listening to the violent spate of her speech, Glyn once again forgot his companions. He was speculating on the improbability that relations had existed between this woman and the dead man. She must be very certain of herself to speak with so much assurance: yet he found it difficult to believe that the fastidious Réné Tessier had so easily found a confidante. " Most surely I shall come again," he told himself, and he nodded as though to say, " Soon I shall have the key that will unlock the whole of this puzzle."

Coming down the stairs he tried to isolate himself and this woman for the time necessary to fix the appointment. The three men had passed out of the house and turned to the right when suddenly Glyn stopped, clapping his hands to his sides. " My glove," he said. " I must have dropped it in that room. And yet I swear I had it at the head of the stairs."

" Perhaps monsieur dropped it before he reached the hall," said Dupuy, not altogether pleasantly, Glyn thought.

Field said, " Don't trouble yourself, Mr. Glyn," and turned, but Glyn, saying sharply, " No, no, you wouldn't know it if you saw it," pushed past him and hurried back to the house. The sitting-room into which Madame Lemaitre had taken the three men was evidently the one she used herself in the evenings, for, as he mounted the steps, the sound of her voice came clearly to Glyn's ears as she opened the window.

" He was asking about M. Brémond," Lemaitre was saying, and a stranger's voice replied quickly, " I wonder what he will find out there. The truth perhaps. I should be glad to know . . ."

Then Glyn pressed the bell. The widow came out of the sitting-room, leaving the door ajar, so that Glyn, entering the hall, saw her companion quite clearly. He was a young man, with fair hair cut *en brosse,* clean-shaven, with the pale complexion of one who spends most of his time indoors. Unquestionably he was sprung from the small shopkeeper class. Glyn put him down as a clerk or counterhand in one of the local shops, earning a small wage and unable to afford a better lodging.

To his surprise the lawyer found that he was extraordinarily excited by what he had just heard. It seemed to him that Dupuy was beyond all doubt right in suspecting a mystery about the chemist, and he wondered what part the young man would play in that drama.

" I dropped my glove," he explained to the attentive woman, " on the stairs perhaps." As they ascended together, he suggested an appointment for the next day.

" There is much that could not interest the police," he explained. " And then I have for so long been an admirer of his—and I know the lady who was to have been his daughter-in-law."

Her eyes turned on him with a strange fiery look. " That, monsieur, is most interesting," she said. " Come to-morrow at eleven. There is much that I can tell you. Ah, and here is the glove." She stooped and picked it up from a corner of the dusty stairs. He took it, making some formal remarks in a voice loud enough to be heard by the young man in the sitting-room. Then he went out and rejoined his companions, who waited patiently by a little faded blue pillar-box. He showed them the glove and they smiled and congratulated him on his good fortune.

"You can't lose a thing if you know where you dropped it," remarked Glyn, thinking their enthusiasm rather misplaced.

Dupuy turned with exaggerated humility. "Indeed, monsieur, it is well to know that. Your hear, mon cher Field. If you know where you have left a thing, then it cannot be lost. Alas, monsieur, if only we could agree with you. But some things are more securely hidden than a glove in a corner of the stairs. Eh, Field?"

But Field frowned and said nothing. Dupuy broke into a cackle of malicious laughter. "I am not being kind," he acknowledged, "but you must not be permitted to think that the police are all fools. You wished for a few more words with the widow. Is it not so? Well, well, that is not perhaps so strange. The good Tessier found her companion-ship encouraging, if we listen to what she tells us. But—a word in your ear, monsieur." He leaned close and spoke in an exaggerated whisper. "You cannot always believe what these widows say. You will remember that." He drew back and looked at him comically. "You think me interfering, pre-suming? And so I am. That is our work, monsieur. All the time we interfere in the lives of others and presently we must meddle even in simple affairs. And so we offend our companions. But you must not be offended, monsieur, for believe me," and now all trace of mockery died out of his expressive face, "this trouble, this mischief is greater than we dreamed. We need all our wits."

And in an access of solemnity he marched them back to their hotel.

CHAPTER VIII

THE following morning Glyn woke with a faint sense of apprehension. He thought for a time of his coming interview, and wondered with a little distaste what the two detectives would say when they heard of it. For he had no hope of keeping it a secret from them for long.

"And yet," he told himself energetically, turning over on to his back, and staring at the ceiling, splashed with the light of the morning sun, "I'm not an official investigator, as they are. I'm in Paris —as I've made it clear to them from the outset—on Mlle. Dulac's behalf. Once they rule her out of their suspicions I can go placidly back to London."

He reinforced his determination by a remembrance of her standing against a cream-panelled wall in her frock of white ruffles and the little short brown coat that presented so piquant a contrast. And, unbidden, the frightful thought sped through his mind that the next time he saw her she might be wearing, not the trappings of innocent enjoyment, but an altogether more sober and ominous garb— and he might see her, not in a ballroom, but in the dock, fighting desperately for her life. And after that? People wouldn't be kind to a girl who had already driven one man to his death and cold-bloodedly arranged for the murder of another.

"Oh, it isn't true," he told himself passionately. "It's absurd on the face of it. That girl isn't entangled in such a net of intrigue. As for Réné Tessier, how do we know what his activities were, who were his enemies, how he spent these last two years? No, no. I shall learn more of that at eleven o'clock."

Now, instead of that undercurrent of dismay at the thought of the coming interview, he experienced only a sense of excitement, even of importance, that indefinable, slightly ridiculous delight known to all men since Perseus rescued Andromeda from her rock, or Galahad rode out to champion nameless ladies in distress. The cheerful sunlight pouring through the open windows encouraged his mood. Hitherto, from the very outset of his career, he had been the cool-headed impersonal lawyer to whom situations were more than people, and facts vastly more important than personalities. Now, however, more than his head was involved: it was absurd that he should be so enthralled for he was no longer a young man and his interests were mainly academic, but the sensation was delicious—it was intoxicating and new. Perhaps it was the air of Paris that lent it a covering of reason: certainly in London he might have blushed for such ingenuous enthusiasm.

He was astonished out of his reverie by a sharp knock on the door and Field came in. He was already fully dressed and the brightness of the morning found no reflection in his sombre face.

He said, " Good morning, Mr. Glyn. I'm sorry to intrude on you like this, but something serious has happened."

Instantly, as the snapping off of a light will plunge a room into absolute darkness, all its happy assurance crumbled from Glyn's mind. He had no notion what was coming but he felt that they were now faced by unparalleled disaster. That sense of inferiority engendered by being on his back in bed, under the watchful regard of a man fully clothed and on his feet, increased his discomfort. Whatever it was, the thing that had happened, that had made Field look so grave and brought him to this room at so early an hour, it was clear that he held Glyn responsible.

"What is it?" the lawyer asked, sitting up briskly, as though to suggest that any tragedy could be put right now he, Glyn, was on the scene.

Field answered with another question. "Mr. Glyn, what was it that you went back to say to Mme. Lemaitre last night?"

Whatever answer Glyn had expected it hadn't been this. He sat bolt unright, staring at the Inspector.

"You mean——"

"I mean, sir, that it would have been obvious to a blind man you dropped that glove there on purpose, because you wanted to speak to the woman alone. I want to know what you said to her."

"I asked her if I might go round again this morning—I wanted to hear more about the son, Louis. That's all."

"And she agreed?"

"Yes. She told me to come at eleven."

"Were you alone when you made the appointment—nobody could possibly have overheard you? Think well, sir, before you answer."

"There was no one in the hall."

"And no one who could have heard?"

"There was the young man— " hesitated Glyn and Field pounced without any hesitation at all.

"Which young man was that?"

"I took him to be one of her lodgers who had arrived home while we were talking upstairs. She was telling him of our visit. I could hear her while I was waiting for the door to open."

"Yes? And did you hear what she said?"

"She said M. Dupuy had been asking about Brémond, and he, the stranger, replied, 'I wonder whether he will learn the truth there. I should be glad to know.'"

"And was that before you had spoken to Lemaitre?"

"Yes. Why? Is it of any importance?"

"I don't know," said Field reflectively. "Perhaps on M. Dupuy's return I may be able to answer you better. All I can say now is that Madame Lemaitre was found in her bed this morning—dead."

Glyn sprang to the floor with a startled cry. "Dead! But how? Do you suspect foul play?"

Field shrugged. "How can I tell? It's very strange anyway."

"Dupuy's down there now?" Glyn had rung for his shaving water and was now hurriedly lathering his chin.

"Yes. He's making the inquiry."

"You're not with him?"

"No. This is a French crime and he does as he pleases. But he'll tell us the position when we meet him."

"And when will that be?"

"At the café on the corner of the Rue Mont St. Michel. This morning we have to see M. Brémond."

It was a very chastened Glyn who presently joined the Inspector in the lounge, despite his feeling that it was ridiculous to hold him responsible for this fresh death—even though it should prove to be murder. As for whether there was any such proof, they would have to wait. Nevertheless that faint apprehension had increased to a fever of dread.

"At least," he told himself, "they can't link up Mlle. Dulac with this," and then a realisation of his own ignorance rose up to confound him, and he had to admit himself baffled. He didn't know what link they might find between the two deaths. And he could do nothing but wait.

When they reached the café at the corner of the Rue Mont St. Michel they were surprised to find Dupuy waiting for them. And instead of the dark looks Glyn had anticipated, his face wore a cheerful and eager expression.

"Bonjour, monsieur," he greeted Glyn, drawing out a chair in welcome. "I have been watching for you." And the examination began again.

"Brémond," repeated Dupuy. "Yes, I think he may be the key to the whole situation. And that young man—we must find him. He left the house early this morning as he does always. No one seems to know where he comes from."

"And you're afraid he won't return," suggested Glyn.

"Oh, I didn't say that. A man who leaves his room unlocked and all his possessions scattered about is not usually planning an escape."

Glyn felt he had been snubbed but Dupuy went on in the cheerful friendliness with which he had begun the conversation. "We shall find him there this evening, I think. Meanwhile it might be of use to learn something about him."

Field asked, "Does he know of Lemaitre's death?"

Dupuy shot him a queer look. "How little satisfaction I can give," he deplored. "When I know why—how—Lemaitre died I may be able to answer all these questions. But now," he added gaily, "let me do what I can to make amends. I will tell you all I know myself about Madame's death."

It appeared that the alarm had been given by Marthe Leblanc, Mme. Lemaitre's *bonne*, who came in each day at seven o'clock, leaving at about two in the afternoon.

"Mme. Lemaitre had not many guests in that big house of hers. There was this young man, about whom we know so little, there was a woman, no longer young, very pious, who had two rooms on the first floor. She was out a great deal. She was *dévouée*: she made pilgrimages to all the Churches, St. Michel, St. Gabrielle, Notre Dame de Sept Douleurs—oh, there is a number of Churches tucked away among these little crooked streets. And in all these at all times you might find Mlle. Martin on her knees. She lived very much with her saints and her own soul. Those in the house saw little of her. She took her meals alone—even prepared them for herself. She was the kind that hotels find fatiguing: always keeping a fast or a novena—having her meals at strange hours. She found that house in the Rue Rossignol convenient and not too dear."

"It's a bit out of the way," suggested Field dubiously.

"Out of the way for what? For the theatres—for the big shops—yes. But Mlle. Martin had nothing to say to theatres or big shops. No, no, all she needed she found there. Then, besides her, is a young lady who has been away for two weeks with a sick mother. There was a letter this morning to say she will be returning in a few days. There was, of course, M. Tessier, and there are two or three empty rooms. *Voilà.*" He snapped his fingers. "Now we go on. Last night, as we know, Mme. Lemaitre was well and healthy. She did not expect to die this morning—no, for she made her engagement with M. Glyn. What she would have told him at that engagement we cannot tell. But there is someone else who knows of it—not M. Dupuy, of the Sûreté, not Inspector Field, of Scotland Yard—no, but an insignificant young man living in the house. And the next thing we know is that Mme. Lemaitre has died. She was found by Marthe Leblanc at eight o'clock. Generally she is dressed before Marthe arrives, but to-day the house is quite still. The young man is still asleep. Mlle. Martin has gone to Mass as is her daily custom. Marthe sets the breakfast, lays the fire, sweeps the floor. Then she calls the young man. She is rather deaf, this good woman, and she cannot tell us the young man's name. He has not, she says, been there very long. At eight o'clock, with Lemaitre still unheard, she goes to her room. She taps on the door and there is no reply. She taps again and still there is no answer. That, of course, may be because she is deaf. But you must not say so to Marthe. She knows her hearing is as good as your own, but some of these naughty people will take no notice when she taps on a door. At last she goes in and there is Madame asleep on the bed. She approaches, she touches her, but Madame does not stir. She shakes her: Madame's head rolls slowly over. Marthe sees the open eyes, the dropped jaw—she knows at once that Madame is dead. She was not afraid—French peasants, you know, teach their children when they are quite young to live with their dead. See the processions at the cemetery where grand-père or grande-mère, in life perhaps no more than a gruff voice, a withered face, lie buried. Week after week the children come to pay their respects to les anciens. So then Marthe has no fear. 'The old pig,' she says. 'One might tell she would end like this—always stuffing,' and indeed," he added with an absence of respect for the dead that shocked Glyn, "if you had seen her, monsieur, the mountain that she was under all those blankets in that little dark room, with the shutters drawn and the candle guttered down to a mess of dirty wax in its stick, you would have said the same."

"And the doctor?" asked Glyn rather coldly. "What theories has he on the subject?"

"He is a police doctor, monsieur," retorted Dupuy in a voice of ice. "He will not have theories—he will give us facts. But for that he must have a little time. Theories—oh, they are like the coloured bubbles children blow from soapsuds: they are pretty, I know, but touch them and where are they? No, we shall need something more solid than that to satisfy the Sûreté."

Smiling at Glyn's discomfiture he continued his story. "On a small table beside the bed stood a round box containing three white pills. The full box would contain perhaps a dozen and the directions order her to take one each night at bedtime. So she has had the pills a little more than a week. They were supplied by M. Brémond of the Rue Félice."

"So he can tell us what went into them?"

"Certainly he can, monsieur, if he wishes to do so."

Glyn stared. "But why should he mind? He must know you'll have the remaining pills analysed."

"Ah, the remaining pills?" With a fine gesture M. Dupuy consigned them to the Seine. "I do not expect, my friend, to learn anything from them. Oh yes—the prescription perhaps—so much rhubarb —this and that—a stomachic purge no doubt for an old woman who will eat too much—but the pill she took last night—now an analysis of that might be of interest. However," he added, uncrossing his legs and standing up, "this is all conjecture. We do not yet know why she died. To-night—ah, that will be another matter. And now let us go and see M. Brémond and learn what he has to tell us."

They set off for the Rue Félice which was not far distant. M. Brémond's shop stood at the corner of the street, with a glass central door and a smaller wooden door set in the wall round the corner. This was clearly the door through which M. Brémond admitted his secret clients, those who came to him after dark when the shop itself was shut. An elderly woman was buying some cough candy as the three men entered: she was being served by M. Brémond's assistant and as they waited near the doorway Glyn's hand stole out and caught Dupuy's arm by the elbow. Dupuy made no sign that he felt the touch, but Glyn knew that he was attentive. "That is the young man to whom Madame was speaking last night," he whispered.

When the woman had gone out of the shop Dupuy stepped smartly up to the counter and said, "I should like to speak to M. Brémond, if you please."

"I'm sorry, monsieur," said the young man, "he isn't in."

"What time does he generally come in?"

"Oh, in the ordinary way he's here at half-past nine but he isn't here to-day at all."

"Can you tell me where I could reach him? The matter is very urgent." And he took out a card and displayed his identity to the young man. Goriot looked suitably grave but his manner did not appreciably change.

"I'm afraid I can't, monsieur l'inspecteur. I've no idea where he is."

Dupuy drummed his fingers with annoyance on the counter. "What is his private address?" he asked presently.

"He just has two rooms over the shop."

"And he went off this morning?"

"He didn't sleep here last night, monsieur. In fact," he added in desperation, "he has been away for more than a week."

Dupuy's eyebrows lifted. "So? And he leaves no address?"

"None."

"And he writes no letters?"

"No. Not to me, that is."

"He asks for no account, he gives no instructions. But that is, surely, very strange."

"He's never done it before."

"Have you spoken of his absence to anyone?"

"Some of his customers have asked. I have said he is abroad."

"What made you say that?"

"Well, monsieur," the young man's fair face flushed in miserable embarrassment, "a man does not like to say he has no notion where his employer has gone."

"No doubt." Dupuy's tone was very dry. "But did he say nothing as to how long he would be away when he went?"

"He told me he expected to be away a day or two, but I should hear. And that was more than a week ago."

"You have done nothing about it? Made no enquiries?"

"What could I do? M. Brémond is not a child. If he chooses to prolong his absence—— "

"Without writing?"

The young man's chin went up. "That shows his trust in me."

Dupuy nodded. "And that is flattering? Of course. Though I suppose it is only the simple remedies that are required here. All the same, I would like to see M. Brémond's rooms."

The young man still appeared to hesitate, but with a sudden gesture Dupuy swept him out of the way. Glyn had the impression that the youth had been scooped up and flung aside, as you toss a weed out of a garden bed, so forceful was the French detective's personality.

There were two storeys above the little shop. Brémond lived on the first floor, where he had an austere suite of rooms, furnished very barely.

All the same, Glyn decided, he's a man of taste. These things may be severe, the chairs may not be comfortable, but they're finely made, first-class of their kind.

In the first room was a narrow bed, covered by a handsome silk quilt. But beneath that the blankets were cheap and thin and the sheets a harsh cotton. There was a single pillow and a short, hard woollen bolster. The remainder of the furniture consisted of a large press standing against the wall, a table, a shaving-stand, two chairs and a small cupboard with a polished top. The linen on the bed was clean and unused: a fresh pyjama-suit was folded on the pillow. A pair of bedroom slippers, scarcely worn, stood in one corner. A dressing-gown of coloured towelling hung on the door.

Dupuy crossed to the press and opened it. It contained one or two suits, a spare pair of sheets, pillow-cases and a little linen. In the dressing-chest he found underclothing and a pile of large plain white handkerchiefs. There were no photographs on the mantelpiece and no books in the room.

" Who looked after M. Brémond?" asked Dupuy of the young man, who replied hurriedly that he always looked after himself.

" Did he prepare his own meals? Clean his own plates?"

" Yes, monsieur. He used to say men were much handier at such work than women."

" Did he have many friends here? Or entertain?"

" I was only here during shop hours. He didn't talk much."

"Was he always in the shop?"

"He would make up the prescriptions, and serve particular customers. And of course he was always at the counter when I was out."

"Were you often out?"

"Sometimes there was delivering to be done. But at other times he would be invisible."

"Quite." It was Dupuy who was puzzled. He walked across to the bed, stared down at it, came back to the dressing-table.

"Let us go into the next room," he said suddenly. This was as barely furnished as the first. A table, a secretaire, a few chairs, a wooden lamp, one or two reproductions of modern French paintings on the walls. Dupuy stood looking round him in bewilderment.

"Oh," he cried, "there is something here I do not understand," and he dashed back to the bedroom; Glyn following an instant later found him standing in the middle of the room.

In the drawer of the secretaire was a bundle of bills that Dupuy examined. "I wish my gas bills were as low as these," he murmured ruefully. "But then he has no wife nor children."

With a particularity that Glyn thought exaggerated he examined every account. Then he returned to the bedroom and his glance ran along the wainscot: he shook his head, doubled agilely and searched underneath the bed.

"It is abundantly proved that M. Brémond employed no bonne," he told them, exhibiting his hands, that were streaked and stained with dust. "Ah well," he shrugged comically, "a little grime is no matter. It washes off." In spite of his smile there was something in his voice that made Glyn stiffen. It was as if, while he spoke of dust, in his mind he was thinking of something more perilous,

119

something that, even washed off, would leave traces.

"I wish one knew what he was driving at," Glyn told himself. "He's clearly got some idea in his mind." He looked speculatively at Field, but as usual Field looked quite unperturbed and Glyn didn't like to put any direct questions. He felt that Dupuy blamed him for Mme. Lemaitre's death, though as yet they had no proof that it was anything but natural. Dupuy hadn't said a word, but he of course was only waiting for the analyst's report. Let him learn that there was a suspicion of foul play and Glyn's position at the English bar wouldn't weigh with him for an instant. Meanwhile he was on another trail now. He had climbed nimbly on to a chair and was examining the flat top of the press. But whatever he was looking for, he didn't find it. Down he came again, his cheerfulness quite unimpaired, and went upstairs to the attics. Here was a silence and a degree of desolation only to be found in places that are unoccupied and uncared for. No one ever came up here. That was obvious. Dust lay thick on the floor, and no foot had disturbed it. There was a large cupboard at the end of one of the rooms, but this also was empty. Dupuy continued his tiresomely meticulous examination, though it must have been obvious to anyone that there was nothing to be found here. At last he permitted them all to return to the sitting-room. The assistant was still in the shop, serving insignificant customers with cheap remedies—corn plaster and lipsalve and aspirins.

"You thought I would never be done," Dupuy accused them. "You thought this and that. You wondered why I asked no questions of that obliging young man down below. Well, I will tell you. It is because first of all I ask questions of myself and

I like to find my own answers. Now I have found my answer."

"And that is?"

"That I think that young man was right when he said M. Brémond had resolved to go away."

Though he did not move as he said the words, his manner had all the effect of a grand gesture. His glance flashed from one to the other as if he expected them to be enormously impressed by his reply. To Glyn it came with all the sense of an anti-climax until he remembered that Dupuy was connecting the assistant, whose name was Goriot, with Lemaitre's sudden death.

"Does he think Brémond is a party to this murder? Or does he think Brémond also has been murdered?" And he began to work out that theory. Suppose Goriot had some guilty secret connected with Brémond's disappearance, a secret that Lemaitre shared? Then at all costs Goriot would wish to prevent the widow's keeping her second engagement with the police: perhaps she had threatened him that last night of her life, made demands he could not meet, blackmailing till her victim struck out in self-defence and silenced that insinuating tongue for ever. Glyn's mind grew dizzy at contemplation of these inward ramifications of crime. And still he couldn't link up these scattered events with the death of Réné Tessier in London.

"Let us," continued Dupuy cheerfully, "hear exactly what M. Goriot has to say about his employer's plans. We know so far only that he purposed being away for a day or two. I think we can learn more than that."

Goriot came into the room behind the shop at Dupuy's summons, leaving the door ajar so that he could see any customer who came in. In reply to Dupuy's invitation, he said, "I can't tell you more

than I did at first. A week or ten days ago it
would be," he considered, " the 9th May—M.
Brémond said to me: 'I am going to leave you in
charge of the shop for a day or two. I have to go
out of Paris on important business. But you know
where all the stores are kept, including the drugs.
Remember the stringent laws governing the sale of
drugs. We want no trouble with the police.' He
meant, of course, the regulations regarding doctors'
prescriptions and the necessity for signing the poison
book. The police," he added gravely, " are always
on the watch for irregularities of this kind."

" They have their reasons," responded Dupuy
equally gravely, and Goriot continued: " It was his
custom to close the shop one afternoon a week.
That, I believe, was for my benefit. It was on such a
day that he left. I saw nothing of him after I
myself departed at midday, that is to say, a little
after one o'clock. On these afternoons he would
open the shop again at night for anyone who wished
to buy."

" And you would return? "

" No, monsieur. He would serve his customers
himself."

" You have no notion, therefore, of any particular
persons who may have made a point of coming on
that evening when they knew they would find him
in charge? Or indeed they may have come in the
afternoon—to the side-door, perhaps."

" Naturally not, monsieur, since I was never here."

Dupuy looked profound. " That," he remarked,
" is a pity." Then his face brightened. " Ah, but
what is that but one more mystery to be solved?
And why else are we here? " He began to laugh
gaily, but Goriot's face retained its severity, as he
went on:

" I asked if he would leave his address, but he

said he would be writing in a day or two and would send an address. If anyone asked for him particularly I was to say they should hear very shortly."

" And when no letter came?"

" He was a temperamental man. He would be moody and gay in turns, but more often moody than gay. I thought, perhaps he is busy—he has forgotten —he has written and the letter is lost. I did think— perhaps an accident. But what could I do, monsieur? I had no idea where he was—no one wrote. I have been waiting for news."

" You didn't think of going to the police?"

" I thought of it, monsieur, but no." He shook his round fair head. " Perhaps M. Brémond would not wish the police to be consulted."

" Why should you think that?"

Goriot spread his hands. " How should I know? I know nothing of M. Brémond, his private life, what he does in the evenings when I am not here— who uses that side-door——"

Dupuy broke in sharply. " What has the side-door to do with it?"

" Indeed, monsieur, I don't know. But once or twice at night when I have been here late—it has not happened often—I have seen shadows flit in through that door."

Dupuy leaned forward. " Were you ever close enough to see any of their faces?"

" Never, monsieur. That side-door leads to a staircase and the staircase leads straight to M. Brémond's quarters. And once, passing the shop late in the evening, I saw two shadows on the blind."

Dupuy nodded. " And have there been letters perhaps?"

" There was one, monsieur."

" And that is where?"

"It is in a drawer in the shop, monsieur. I have been expecting to hear."

"I should like to see it."

Goriot fetched the envelope, which was addressed in a weak sprawling hand and marked "Personal." He slit it open. It was signed "Pierre Lecontre," and said: "I came last night but I could get no reply. You have cheated me again. How will you like it if I go to the police and denounce you for what you are? They won't be very easy on you. You had better take care."

"Do you know this M. Lecontre?" Dupuy asked, folding up the letter and returning it to its envelope.

"There is no such name on our books," returned the young man.

"Ah, that's a pity. I thought you might know him by sight."

"I'm sorry, monsieur. Perhaps he is one of those that came to the side-door."

"Uncommonly likely," muttered Field, and Dupuy agreed.

"Has there been anyone in the shop asking for M. Brémond personally?"

"No, there hasn't, but I'll tell you this, monsieur. Three times since M. Brémond has been away someone's telephoned to him. Very urgent, he said."

"It was a man? You're sure?"

"Perfectly sure. And the same man each time. I could not mistake that voice."

"And he said?"

"He must speak to M. Brémond. He must. He must. And if he is not there then I am to tell him at once where he can be found."

Dupuy nodded as if this confirmed a suspicion he already harboured. "And now," he said, "this unhappy death of Madame Lemaitre. That is a tragedy, is it not? And unexpected?" He looked questioningly at his companion.

Goriot assumed a comically professional air. " With a woman like that—a veritable mountain, monsieur —one should never be too greatly surprised. They have a stroke—their hearts cannot endure the strain of those vast bodies—a blood-vessel breaks— I tell you, monsieur, I once saw such a case. It is as if they choked themselves in their sleep."

" But you hadn't expected anything of the kind? Madame Lemaitre did not seem ill last night? You saw her, no doubt?"

" Yes, monsieur. I encountered her on the stairs on my way to bed. She was cheerful enough then. I could scaarcely believe it when Marthe told me this morning that she was dead."

" You saw the body?"

" Marthe insisted. She said I was not a doctor, I might not be even a chemist, but I was the next best thing."

" You—passed a verdict, monsieur?"

" I thought it must be her heart. But you are making fun of me, monsieur l'inspecteur," he added warmly. " You know I can diagnose nothing. One learns a little with M. Brémond perhaps, but he is not one that talks much. The action of certain drugs—— "

" Ah, you do know about that?" said Dupuy keenly. " Did it seem to you that perhaps a drug had played any part in Madame Lemaitre's death?"

Goriot looked startled. " You suspect that, monsieur? But why should she? Madame was not an unhappy woman."

" She had no troubles of which she ever spoke to you?"

" She was sad—angry, too—for M. Tessier's death. She was fond of that one. She would do little services for him that she would not perform for anyone else. When he went she said, ' I will keep his room for a little. He may return.' "

" Ah yes. Now I think M. Brémond had made up prescriptions for her?"

Goriot shook a dubious head. " No, monsieur. You are misinformed. She was never inside the shop that I can recall."

" Ah, but M. Tessier acted as her messenger. M. Brémond would make up her prescriptions. Is it not so?"

But Goriot clung to his original denial. " Not to my knowledge, monsieur. I do not even remember seeing M. Tessier here. Unless, of course," he added grimly, " he was one of those secret customers who used the side-door."

" I think, monsieur, you do not share madame's opinion of her late guest," Dupuy teased him softly.

" He was nothing to me," declared Goriot, " less than nothing. He never so much as spoke to me, monsieur. A chemist's assistant was too small beer for such as he. But tell me," he continued hurriedly, " of what did Madame Lemaitre die?"

" I am all attention to hear. I had hoped you might be able to help me. Now I must wait for the official report. Aha! That is an ill-fated house, monsieur. First one dies, then another. I think," he laughed gaily into the young man's dumb face, " I think I am glad I am not living there. I think perhaps I might be afraid."

Goriot threw back his head. " That's absurd, monsieur," he said loudly. " An old man takes poison in an hotel in England—an old woman dies —perhaps of a strained heart in her own bed—and you, monsieur—you of the Sûreté—you say you are afraid."

" You are a brave man," said Dupuy, nodding at

him in a friendly manner. "And now," his hand slashed through the air as though he swept away an ugly curtain obscuring their view, "let us forget our danger and continue to look for this naughty M. Brémond, who gives us so much trouble. You will tell me the date of his departure?"

"May the ninth."

"You yourself saw him go?"

"No. He was putting up special prescriptions that night. He said he'd be at the work until late. Certainly he was at work when I left at seven o'clock."

"Had he any appointments for that evening—here? I mean, after the shop was shut."

"I would not know, monsieur. He never spoke to me of these visitors, and, as I say, I never saw any of them."

"But he may have had such an appointment? Did he keep no diary?"

"He had one in his own pocket, I believe."

"But not one that he kept in the shop?"

Apparently there was no way of checking his movements. Dupuy could find no trace of an engagement block. The missing man had left no more personal notes than a record of certain prescriptions in the prescription book. His large formless hand sprawled across the pages: and Glyn, who had theories about caligraphy, thought: "That's the writing of a helpless man; not necessarily uneducated, but uncharacteristic, weak, nothing definite about the letters," and he visualised him, the little dark-bearded creature, not the villain of Dupuy's imagination, but a creature, exuberant and easy-going, for whom circumstances were too strong. Dupuy, who perhaps had theories about handwriting, too, shut up the book and continued his questions.

"Then you have no actual proof that he ever set out?"

"Well, monsieur," protested Goriot, "he is not here."

"How true!" agreed Dupuy unkindly. "Unless, of course, one has contrived to overlook him. You think the police suspicious, eager to make a scandal. And perhaps you are right. It is by finding sinister interpretations for a gentleman's silence, by suggesting that a man who took his own life was really murdered, that we rise to fame. And consider how eager is the public to create scandals if by any mishap a gentleman who has been poisoned is buried as a suicide. We do well to be suspicious, M. Goriot. Then the people believe we are earning our salt: they believe in us: they feel more safe when they know we are active. So, you see," he concluded with a spectacular flourish, "I build up an ugly case on no grounds at all, and you destroy it immediately, you show me that I have no case. M. Goriot, I thank you. And now I trust you if you hear of or from M. Brémond to let me know at once. And meanwhile if we require your help we shall find you either here or in the Rue Rossignol."

"Yes, monsieur," agreed Goriot, hesitating. "But of course now that Madame is dead I daresay I shall be changing my lodging."

"But not for a day or two," Dupuy besought him. "I may need your help again at the enquiry into Madame's death."

Goriot's large pale eyes almost popped out of his head. "You don't think," he began, "monsieur, surely you don't think——"

"Ah, the suspicious policeman again! I begin to frighten you, do I not? But have no fear," he clapped the agitated young man on the shoulder, "the innocent are safe with the police, always, utterly safe."

They came out into the glare of the afternoon sun. Dupuy turned politely to Glyn. "I am afraid I have made you very late for your déjeuner, monsieur, but there is a capital little place here of which I think you will be glad to know. I only recommend it," he added proudly, " to my friends."

Glyn murmured something appropriate and the three men walked up the road together. The lawyer felt as though he had been assisting at a play. He had no notion in which direction Dupuy's mind was working: he hoped that Field was similarly baffled, but there was nothing to be read in that alert inexpressive countenance. Glyn felt that this affair was becoming more and more abstruse, and he himself was increasingly in the dark. He was unaccustomed to cases of this kind: indeed, it was his first experience of murder. For the most part he dealt with quarrels over wills and property and an occasional libel action. But then his facts ranged within a small compass, negotiable practically from the outset. Here they seemed plunging deeper and deeper into the wood. There was all the difference between these two types of case that there was between a short story and a novel. The one was a clear-cut incident with a defined outline: the other knew no limits; it could include half a dozen countries and as many generations between the same covers. This story, which had begun with Tessier's death, was spreading and spreading until he could see no end to it at all. To Glyn, Tessier had been the peg on which all enquiries should hang: to Dupuy he was one of a row of nails, all or any of which might serve the Sûreté's purpose. For Tessier the man he didn't care a jot: for Tessier as a power in a game that might uncover the greatest drug scandal for years he cared tremendously. Glyn was astonished, even a little ashamed, to find that this chase left him unmoved. His admiration for Tessier, his original desire that the man's death should be avenged, had been destroyed—temporarily at all events—by this welter of police activity. Let him be assured that no harm threatened Eve Dulac and he would return to England at once. He tried to excuse this unadventurous spirit in lofty ways—for instance, he had other interests, clients of his own—but recklessly he shattered all his illusions by admitting to himself that he would probably experience a far keener throb of interest if he himself were cast for an heroic part. He felt that both the detectives, when they weren't actually laughing at him, remembered him only as a nuisance they didn't quite like to dismiss. An echo of an old rhyme rang disagreeably in his mind:

> The engine-driver took his spade
> And scraped him off the wheel.

It seemed to him singularly appropriate.

After a déjeuner that justified all Dupuy's praise, the Frenchman suggested that they should accompany him and learn whether the post-mortem on Mme. Lemaitre was concluded.

" So much will depend on that," he said, and Field agreed. " Meanwhile," Dupuy continued, " there are enquiries to be made. This mysterious M. Brémond, for instance. Who saw him leave? Where is he now? Why has he not written? There is something strange there."

" I think when you've answered the puzzle of M. Brémond you'll find the rest will fall automatically into place," remarked Field. " There are a number of things I, too, want to know about M. Brémond."

CHAPTER IX

THEY returned to find that Robinet, the police surgeon in charge of the post-mortem, was not ready for them. Dupuy resolved to 'remain at headquarters where he had various enquiries to make, while waiting for the medical analysis: and Field, accompanied by his faithful shadow, departed to interview M. Pierre Lecontre. This young gentleman had a suite in a tall white house in a street out of the Champs Elysées. Field interviewed him in a long narrow room painted in silver. M. Lecontre wore a silver-grey suit and suede shoes. His face was a white so deathly that Glyn's brows jumped at sight of him: and his manner alternated between a great haughtiness and approximate hysteria. Field shook hands with him, retaining his hand longer than Glyn thought necessary. At the first mention of Brémond's name he jumped like a nervous horse.

"He is back in Paris?" he said. "They told me he was away, and his address was unknown. You see," he explained elaborately, "it is important that I should find him. I am not very strong. I have a tonic M. Brémond makes up for me. He is the only man in Paris who has my prescription. And there has been a mistake. Last time he gave me the wrong medicine."

"You have it in a powder, I suppose?" said Field, intelligently.

"An ordinary white powder," the young man agreed.

"And you say there was a mistake about it?"

"Yes. It was most careless. Brémond knows how much I rely on this tonic of mine."

"I wonder if you have by you the powder that you got from him last time?"

"Yes. I could fetch it. It's a mere stomachic, I assure you."

When he had gone out of the room Field surprised Glyn by turning to him saying, "What do you make of this, sir? Did Brémond give him that powder by accident? Or did he do it deliberately? And why? Does this M. Lecontre owe him money? There's no account in the book but if it's what I expect there wouldn't be."

"You mean is Brémond such a scoundrel he'd deliberately cheat him, knowing he won't dare bring the case into court?" Glyn's voice lifted suddenly. "Would anything so paltry be worth his while? These big drug dealers are enormously wealthy men as a rule. And even a rat like Lecontre might make trouble. He might in a storm of rage go to the police, denounce the man."

Field said quickly: "Here he comes," and Lecontre re-entered the room. He carried a little white packet in his hand.

Field tasted it and laughed. "Bismuth," he said. "How long have you been getting this stuff from him?"

"Oh, not very long. There was another man before that. He died, I think. His name was Laurier. You can't get it everywhere."

"I can quite believe that. What or who started you on it?"

"I hadn't been well—I was overdone—and I couldn't sleep. I had some trouble, you understand, and a man I knew called Tessier told me what marvellous stuff this was. That would be nearly three years ago. And he's quite right. It is marvellous. Only once you've got accustomed to it you can't do without it."

"It isn't always easy to get it, though," said Field.
"No, that's just it. But Brémond isn't so good as Laurier. Not so certain, I mean. Sometimes when you go round there at night he hasn't got it."

He went on chattering nervously. Glyn felt sick. There was nothing behind all this nervous spate of words, nothing but a dandified appearance, an incurable lust for self-satisfaction in the only mean way known to the man, and a neurotic mind as eaten away as a cabbage leaf destroyed by caterpillars. He wasn't so much accustomed to this kind of encounter as Field, whose face showed no expression at all. The detective was leading the young man on to talk, though a good deal of what he said was irrelevant. And at the end of the conversation he had difficulty in persuading the young man that the authorities had no more idea where the missing man was than had M. Lecontre himself.

"Though that's not strictly accurate," he added, as they turned into the Champs Elysées. "Still, we've no proof of anything. And we know how far it's safe to rely on guess-work."

Glyn, baffled by that last reference, yet not liking to ask questions, possibly shrinking from the notion of displaying his denseness of perception, was suddenly struck by another thought. "How forgetful I am," he cried, angry at his inferiority in apparently every direction. "There's something I've been meaning to ask you since we arrived. The aspirins in M. Tessier's pocket—they were analysed?"

"They were—and I've just heard the result. There was enough cocaine in each tablet to kill a giant."

Glyn nodded thoughtfully. "So Tessier was mixed up in the hideous traffic." He remembered the young ruined face on which they had just turned their backs, and felt sick again.

"Yes," said Field. "That throws a lot of light on the position. Eases your mind a bit, I should think." And he flashed an unexpected smile at his companion.

The medical report was still delayed and Glyn talked to Dupuy while Field wrote out his notes of the interview. When he had read them Dupuy rumpled his hair and exclaimed comically:

"But what a mystery he is, this M. Brémond. Still," he added reassuringly. "I think we may not have to wait long for news of him."

"You don't think he's dead?" asked Glyn.

Dupuy looked grave. "If my suspicions are right, monsieur, yes."

"And—murdered?"

"I'm afraid of it, monsieur."

"And you connect his death with that of M. Tessier?"

"I think the hand that slew the one slew the other also."

At last Robinet bustled in: an enormous man with the figure of a butcher and the face of a pugilist. Glyn wondered for a moment of whom he was reminded and recalled a famous bishop of the Anglican Communion. But when Robinet spread his hands in graphic gesture all doubt of the wisdom of his vocation faded out of the watcher's mind. They were miracle-working hands, as many a sick man could testify. "He has a brain in each finger." Who had said that and of whom? At all events it was true of this great lively police surgeon, who leaned against the table and talked to Dupuy in a rumbling bass voice.

"My full report," he said, "you shall have later. But the cause of death—obvious, my dear fellow. The woman died of poison."

"What poison?"

"Cocaine. There was enough in the body to kill three women."

"And administered—how?"

"Oh, unquestionably, through the mouth. There is another point. So much cocaine must have taken very speedy effect. For instance, she could not have taken such a dose and gone on with her usual round. The stomach shows that she had had a heavy meal shortly before death. Therefore I should say the cocaine was taken some time after that meal and after it she would be unconscious."

"If, for instance, she took a pill in which cocaine had been inserted, on going to bed, that would tally with the facts?"

"Most excellently."

Dupuy nodded.

"You suspect suicide, M. l'Inspecteur?"

"I have no reason to do so, monsieur. I think perhaps a few questions in another quarter may aid us. For the moment—ah!" The telephone bell rang sharply. Dupuy jerked the instrument from its stand.

"At the Gare du Nord Station? The rogue was daring. M. Field will come down. You will oblige me this far," he appealed to his English colleague. "I sent out this afternoon an enquiry concerning a gentleman wearing a thick black beard and moustache who travelled—presumably from the Gare du Nord—about ten days ago. First of all I tried the taxi-drivers. Had anyone driven M. Brémond from his address in the Rue Félice? These things are learned quickly; here in Paris we have a system." He said it as though this were true of no other city in the world. "Monsieur, no taxi-cab called for M. Brémond at his lodging that afternoon. But there was a private car standing in the alley facing the side-door for certainly more than twenty minutes. This was observed by a *sergent-de-ville* who was passing through that neighbourhood at two o'clock. Shortly before half-past, as he was returning from his errand, he saw the car crank up and depart. Unhappily he cannot recall the number: but he recalls the initial letters. It was a Parisian car: but there are, of course, a great number of big dark red cars in Paris. Nor, of course, have we proof that M. Brémond has any connection with this car. A driver might leave it there for a little while during which business took him elsewhere. That, perhaps, we shall learn—for the moment, then, we are faced with the question of how M. Brémond left Paris. And believe me, monsieur, we have not been idle."

"Did he leave Paris?" asked Glyn tensely.

"You shall judge, monsieur. There was nothing to distinguish this little chemist—this man who is apparently so friendless, so insignificant, that he is missed by no one except a disappointed drug addict—except perhaps his very luxuriant beard and moustache. We have during the day traced a number of men and women who have met him; from each we have asked for a description of the man. Each description, monsieur, begins with that beard and moustache. So then, if we wish to track him down, we must seek a man whose beard is—not prodigious but at all events extravagant. This is not like your country, monsieur, where to say you know the man from No. 28, the one with a beard, is to identify him immediately. No, here in France we still cherish the beard. And yet, mark you, each person who knows this M. Brémond, speaks of that feature first. So we start to search for a man whose beard and moustache attract attention. And quite soon we hear of him. He is boarding a tram in the Rue de Cent Fleurs. And he is carrying a rather bulky suitcase that he wishes to take inside the tram with him. The conductor remonstrates: there is plenty of room on the platform. Our friend strikes an attitude. He says, No. Paris is full of thieves. The contents of his case are valuable, though the case itself may be poor. At last the conductor threatens to throw him off: a gendarme intervenes: our friend returns to the kerb with his case. This is half-past two."

"Then, if he's carrying a case, the car in the alley can have no connection with him."

Dupuy shrugged. "Who can say, monsieur? We do not suggest that he travelled to his destination, that is, to the Gare du Nord, in this car. But to resume. After that we hear of him in a café at about half-past three. He is complaining of the food. The coffee is execrable. There is a scene, he refuses to pay, and does not do so. He arrives at the Gare du Nord and books a ticket for Dijon. He names an hour at which there is no train. He becomes abusive, speaks of connections. He demands a time-table. There is no mention of his train. He flings the time-table down. He asks if he is expected to parade the platform for an hour and receives an impolite reply. He is then seen entering the gentlemen's cloak-room and he is not seen again. He is vanished like the conjurer's rabbit."

"And where does he reappear?"

"Monsieur," replied Dupuy solemnly, leaning forward until his head almost touched that of his companion, "he has not yet re-appeared."

"And that's the last you heard of him?"

"Not quite the last. You see, we of the Sûreté begin to think, here is something strange. Believe me, monsieur, we do not like things to be strange. We like them to be ordinary, dull, safe. Now there is an English detective, perhaps the second most famous detective you have ever had. There is, of course, no one to equal your Mr. Holmes. But the Reverend Brown was a great man too. And he has pointed out that when a man blazes a trail, as you say, makes himself noticeable in place after place, then you may begin to make enquiries, for you may know there is something wrong. Figure to yourself. This M. Brémond is not a fool. He knows that he is suspect by the police. But he is careful. He has, I think, spies to guard his interests: he does not fall into traps that are laid for him. He wishes to remain the little chemist of the Rue Félice. But now, on this last journey, at every stage he does something to render himself conspicuous. Now, monsieur, a man may attract attention once in an evening: that may be a misfortune. But when again and again you see him in the centre of the picture, then you begin to seek for an explanation."

"And the explanation is that he wishes to be noticed."

"Precisely. And then we begin to ask ourselves, why? And why did he suddenly cease to wish to attract notice? Why did he disappear into the cloak-room?"

"Because he had done what he set out to do," commented Field, quietly.

"Meaning that he had established M. Brémond's movements?" added Glyn.

"You understand what you say? Here is a man who knows that questions will be asked. The police even may wish to know where this M. Brémond was on the afternoon of May 9th, so someone arranges that, when they ask, the police shall learn precisely how M. Brémond spent that afternoon. For if he is quarrelling with a tram conductor, complaining of his coffee, arguing about a non-existent train, why, then, he must be alive and well at such an hour."

He looked at Glyn as though to say, " There, monsieur, is your mystery," · for all the world as though he offered an enterprising child an elaborate mechanical toy and stood back to see what he would do with it.

" And after half-past three? " asked Glyn.

" Exactly, monsieur. A living man does not vanish into thin air. But this is what M. Brémond seems to have done. He is not on the train, for there is no train. No one sees him on the platform—no one recollects him at all. He is gone—pouf! like that . . ." and he snapped his fingers in the air. " Monsieur, I ask you, where did he go?"

" Out of the cloak-room, I suppose," said Glyn drily. " It's where is he now that's of consequence. How will you learn that?"

" There was one thing I could do and that I have done. It has not been altogether without fruit. I had been seeking a man wearing a black beard. The man had vanished. But there was still the beard."

" You have found that?"

" I believe so."

" And where?"

" In a shabby suitcase in the cloakroom at the Gare du Nord."

Whatever reply Glyn had anticipated it had not been this. Dupuy was delighted with the sensation he had created.

" You did not credit it, monsieur? And yet it is simple enough. Even in Paris there are accidents on trains, luggage is lost, such a disguise might be difficult to explain away. Besides, arrived at his next destination, will not people be curious? No, no, his was far the better plan."

" Then—do you think Brémond never reached the station?"

" I believe, monsieur, that he started on his

journey. And he got just as far as those interested in him intended he should go."

"And—where do you expect to find him?"

"That, monsieur, I cannot tell you—yet. But I will say this: that it will be in some place so strange that only a madman would dream of searching for him there."

CHAPTER X

THEOLOGIANS declare that humility is the rock foundation of the virtues, without which no man shall enter into the Kingdom of Heaven. Glyn brooded on this discouraging article of faith after Dupuy's departure, leaving the two Englishmen alone together. Even if the barrister had been foolish or optimistic enough to ask the French detective to explain his last sentence, he had no opportunity. Dupuy had picked up his black hat with a melodramatic gesture and disappeared.

"I never saw anyone who looked and behaved so much like a detective on the films," exclaimed Glyn, impulsively, watching the little man swagger down the street. "How he loves to mystify you: and how much pleasure he gets from his own bizarre effect. Not," he added with a polite smile, "that I suggest he's mystifying you, but he's got me on toast and he knows it and is revelling in it. He wouldn't have unbent the official mind to the extent of letting me see the wheels go round if he wasn't certain I should be hopelessly bewildered by the mechanism."

Field laughed in a friendly fashion. "We all have our little ways," he said. "And there's no denying it helps to be a bit queer. Helps to fix your name in people's minds, I mean. Look at Mr. Bruce, for instance. I'm not saying he isn't a first class lawyer. Look at the way he got Mr. Paget out of a tight corner last summer, when the odds on him being hanged started at 40 to 1. But what folk will remember about him isn't the cases he's won, but his habit of drawing the Judge and the prosecution and all the witnesses in turn as fish—yes, and doing it so you can't help recognising them. Dupuy may be as brilliant as Bertillon, but it isn't his brilliance you'll remember when you're away from him, but his funny ways."

"Quite the philosopher," grinned his companion. "Do we wait here for the fellow?"

"I'm expecting a message from England at any minute," returned Field coolly. "They're after the man who got into Tessier's room after Lane left it."

"What, the murderer?"

"Give us a chance. We haven't even got our hands on the man yet. He'll not find it very easy to explain what he was doing there. Anyhow, what we do know about him will justify our keeping him in custody till we've unravelled this affair."

Glyn had a sudden inspiration. He looked at Field, he hesitated a moment as if unsure of his wisdom in putting his suspicion into words, then apparently decided to take the plunge.

"Inspector, you think perhaps Brémond, our man of mystery, was in that room on the night Tessier died?"

"I think he was there at the very moment that Tessier died. Presently I'll tell you why."

2.

The group of women standing round the doorway of No. 5 in the Rue Rossignol made no attempt to lower their voices as the stranger came round the corner of the street. They were talking of a neighbour with more candour than discretion and the stranger paused to hear what they said.

"The old miser! " exclaimed the first. "Serves her right, is what I say."

"If she was clever enough to have all that money she deserved it," shrieked a second.

"If it's come by honest, yes."

"Maybe it was," sighed the third, a thin, downtrodden woman in a shabby blue overall, with wisps of black hair straggling over a sallow face. "Some folk are clever."

"Honest?" jeered the first. "I ask you, neighbours, is it likely Marie Lemaitre came by all that money honest? Didn't she live in the Rue Rossignol the same as ourselves? Didn't she let rooms the same as ourselves? And have we got money stored away? You know it's all we can do to get food for ourselves and our children. One thing, when she came here ten years ago she was poor enough."

The stranger came closer, approached the group hesitantly.

"The Widow Lemaitre?" he said.

They stared at him.

"She lives in this street?"

For answer they pointed to a house just across the road at which all the blinds were drawn.

"Then— " he looked at them blankly.

"You'll find her in the mortuary," said the woman who had spoken first. And she laughed. "All that money she was so fond of counting couldn't buy her a better bed."

"She wasn't a rich woman," Dupuy told them seriously. "She let lodgings in this street. It's not too easy for a woman to make a living in times as hard as these."

"We'd none of us complain if we could make as good a living as her."

"But there's not all that money in letting lodgings," Dupuy objected.

"But there's other ways of making money," they told him, derisively, standing round him in a half-circle. "Who were the men who came to see her at night?"

"How should I know?" returned Dupuy defensively. "They were her friends, I suppose."

"And it was her friends that gave her her fine clothes, I suppose."

"Had she fine clothes?" asked Dupuy, in genuine amazement.

"I can only say," the big swarthy woman with the sly narrow eyes was the speaker now, "I saw her in the Champs Elysées one Sunday. The clothes she wore then weren't the clothes a woman wears that gets a living letting rooms in the Rue Rossignol." ·

"But when was this?"

"Oh, some time back. Besides, what about the money?"

"But has anyone seen this money you speak of?"

"Seen it? A hundred times I've sat at my window there after lamplight—after the house was asleep—and there she'd be bowed over her table, counting the notes into piles. And then she'd gather it up and carry it off—don't ask me where. I couldn't see more than just the table. She'd have a lamp lighted and there she'd sit like a great black mountain with just her hands moving and clutching in and out of the circle of light. And at last she'd stand up and gather all the money together and she'd move away beyond the light till she was just a part of the blackness."

Dupuy was aware that all the women were staring

at him curiously. They made a subject that might have attracted an artist, their intent vitality—even the sallow drab seemed warmed as by a flame—contrasting with the dingy curve of the terrace that was their background. The big woman was the obvious leader of the group; the dead woman was like a figure she moulded with her words, and the passion of spite that possessed her to recall the two pictures—first brooding and triumphant in that semi-circle of light, and then mysterious and anonymous in the encroaching dark, as she carried away her treasure to hide it once again: on one side of her stood a sharp little woman with a voice bitter as vinegar and on the other the unassuming wife of a lorry-driver, alternating between long periods of fear when her husband was out of work and ill-treated her and the children, and bouts of jealousy when he kept his money to himself, sometimes stayed out all night.

"A double life, eh?" he said. "You remember the saying—an English saying, of course—'In the dining-room Dr. Jekyll, in the kitchen Mr. Hyde—in the basement God knows what.' And now she is dead!"

"Poisoned, they say. And what's the good of all that money to her now? It'll shrivel up quick enough where she's gone."

Dupuy left them and crossed the street. It was amazing how quickly rumour got about. This story about Lemaitre being poisoned, for example—He rapped on the door of No. 5 and it was opened, not by the French *bonne* as he had hoped, but by the religious spinster whom he had not hitherto seen. He asked for Marthe but was told she had not come that morning.

"She asked me yesterday who would pay her?" Miss Martin told him. "I said I didn't know, so she said she would not come unless her wages were promised."

"And who is managing the housework?"

"I'm sure none of us felt like eating much last night, after such a tragedy. That young Goriot didn't come back at all—" Dupuy started, but relaxed as she continued—"I heard him come in quite late and he went straight to his room. I got some sort of breakfast tray for him this morning and of course he's gone to his work now. I've been expecting someone to come over since yesterday morning."

"Who, precisely?"

"She must have had friends—or relations, anyhow. Everyone has relations."

"None have come forward. I represent the police. Perhaps you may be able to help me. When did you last see Madame Lemaitre alive?"

Miss Martin considered. "I suppose some time that evening. Yes, I remember meeting her on the stairs. I didn't see a great deal of her, you know, because I prepared my own food. Not," she added, hurriedly, in the interests of Christian charity, "that I wish to say anything against Madame's food, only when you've been accustomed to rather dainty feeding—one shouldn't depend on luxury, of course, and the more detached one can become—"

"Quite," agreed Dupuy, expressively, feeling the conversation was becoming completely detached from the subject under review. "Can you remember what time that would be?"

"About seven o'clock, I think."

"And that is the last you saw of her?"

"Yes. Quite the last."

"You heard nothing unusual?"

"No. Ah!" she looked at him brightly with a finger to her lip and her head cocked, resembling a lunatic bird. "Now I come to think of it that isn't quite the last glimpse I had of her, but the detail had quite escaped me for the moment. No. I remember now. I was told many years ago by a doctor—a most highly-spoken of physician—his name was Montrose—but he has been dead for more than two years now—I saw a notice in the ' Times '— I have the weekly ' Times ' sent out here, you see— with a photograph that certainly did not do him justice—he told me to take a glass of hot water every night before going to bed. I don't like to say I am suspicious or fussy, but I must say I am particular. One knows what foreign water is like. And though Marthe is quite a nice woman and has, I believe, had a very hard life—a bad husband—so trying for her—"

"Quite, Madame," interrupted Dupuy, keeping his temper with difficulty. (Sometimes, *mon ami*, he would say to his friends, I think I must look like a priest, so many ladies wish to confide in me). "I understand that the servant, Marthe, has been unfortunate in her marriage, and I know that a woman who has been badly treated by a man acquires a peculiar virtue in the eyes of other members of her sex, who are themselves unmarried. It is not obvious to a man why this should be so, but the fact remains." This anomaly, indeed, had always perplexed and interested him, and he would have liked to continue the point. For all its gripping capacity, there was a corner of his mind that was like an attic, stored with quite valueless pieces of information, and questions whose answers, if indeed they existed, bore no relation to his work. Now, however, controlling a whimsical impulse to exploit the moment to its utmost capacity, he said in austere tones, "And that night, madame, something unusual happened in connection with the hot

water?" But even as he said the words his eyes
began to gleam and his face creased with amusement at the very absurdity of them. "The hot
water," he repeated softly.

Miss Martin, who distrusted men of all nationali-
ties, but Frenchmen in particular, looked
embarrassed, alarmed and insulted. She said in a
hurried voice, horribly conscious of the fact that
she was alone in the house, and knowing, less from
her experience than from assurances in her fictional
and devotional reading, that it is the privilege of
virtue to be perpetually assailed, "This was what
happened: quite insignificant, I've no doubt. I
always go into the bathroom last thing to fill my
little kettle. I'm very careful what I drink and I
don't like water that has stood at all. I had just
filled my kettle and was coming out into the passage
when I heard the sound of voices just outside. So of
course I stayed where I was."

"And perhaps you were able to hear what was
said?" Dupuy encouraged her.

She turned on him, scandalised. "Certainly not
for that reason, officer." He grinned at the appella-
tion. "But I couldn't help myself, I was—well, as
I've explained, I was just going to bed."

"I understand perfectly, Mademoiselle," Dupuy
assured her, wondering why she found dressing-
gown such a compromising word. "So you waited
till the passage was clear?"

"Yes. And I heard M. Goriot's voice. I
couldn't be mistaken; he's got one of those high-
pitched voices that carry a very long way."

Dupuy nodded: "I also had noticed that. And
he said?"

"He sounded rather upset. He said, 'What
about the police? Do you think they . . .?' and then
Madame broke in, 'Why do you trouble so? Can

you not believe me when I say it is all right?' And he said, moving away, as you could hear because of his voice being a bit fainter, 'I hope you are right, but I confess I am a little afraid' . . ."

"And that's absolutely all you heard, Mademoiselle?"

"Absolutely all. The next minute I heard his door close and I came out and went to my own room. This would be about half-past eleven."

"I see. Thank you very much. Now, this M. Goriot sleeps on the same floor as yourself?"

"Yes, but at the end of the passage. All the lodgers sleep on the same floor. Upstairs there is an empty room where that M. Tessier used to sleep . . ."

"Ah, yes, M. Tessier. You knew him?"

"I only knew who he had been. I don't go to the cinema myself, though, of course, I say nothing about those that do. I really didn't know him at all. And he was a quiet sort of man."

"Not really friendly with anyone, I understand?"

"He used to talk quite a lot to Madame. I always thought—mind you I've nothing to go on, and I may be quite, quite wrong—but he had apparently been immensely rich—not, of course, that I believe all they tell you: if half of it's true it's a good proportion—but he used to do errands for her sometimes. I remember hearing him say once: 'I'm going round to the chemist. Is there anything I can bring you?' and that did seem to me a little strange." She had lost sight of the beginning of the sentence.

Dupuy strove to recall her with a suave: "Why strange, Mademoiselle?"

"Well, a man like that, to be running her errands —I thought perhaps— "

"Perhaps they were better friends than one expects as a rule between landlady and lodger?"

The outraged spinster's face turned a deep unbecoming pink. Women with sallow skins should learn not to blush, decided Dupuy. "I—I never even thought of such a thing. I—what I meant was that perhaps she accepted him on reduced terms— "

"In return for which he was obliging enough to go as far as the Rue Félice?" suggested Dupuy silkily.

"It is a long way, isn't it?" agreed Miss Martin, innocently.

"But perhaps M. Brémond is a particularly recommended chemist? Perhaps there are none so good any nearer the Rue Rossignol."

"Oh, but there are," cried Miss Martin at once. "There are several. And there's a much better one in the Rue Félice, almost opposite Brémond. He's quite a cheapjack little shop, only the sort quite poor people would go to."

"But I understand that both M. Tessier and Mme. Lemaitre are quite poor people."

"Yes, but if they only want the kinds of things you can buy at Brémonds' such as Epsom salts and sticking-plaster—there are two or three shops much nearer and quite as good and exactly the same price."

Dupuy decided that the moment had come to strike one of his exaggerated attitudes. "Then, Mademoiselle, we can only assume that M. Tessier is a man of character. Human nature is as full of strange turns and twists as a maze. You seem to progress straight along a path and behold, a moment later you are walking backwards on your own feet. And it pleases M. Tessier's sense of character to go a mile from his lodging to buy his shaving cream." He was watching her closely as he spoke and now he discovered a new look on her face, a look of manifest disapproval that all her intentions in favour of Christian charity could not repress.

"I think," said Dupuy suavely, "there is something else you could tell me about M. Tessier."

"It was your saying he was a man of character," explained Miss Martin, a little flustered. "He was a very queer person to be living here. I mean, if he had been very poor, that was one thing. There's no disgrace in poverty—not if it's honest—but you don't expect a poor man to go about in dress clothes as he often did."

"Perhaps he eked out his living by waiting," suggested Dupuy.

"I hardly think it was that. They've a very low standard for waiters in this city, if that's so. Why, there was one night, I remember," her voice became more assured, "when I couldn't sleep. I often don't sleep very well and then I like to get up and sit at my window—I say night but really it was early morning. It was one of my worst bouts of insomnia. I was sitting in my little basket-chair, with the blind drawn up, watching the street. I saw the light deepen and presently one or two blinds went up and the first early morning workers came to their windows and stood looking out at the new day. Perhaps," she went on hurriedly, imagining a smile on the detective's face, "it seems strange to you, but it gave me a feeling that women of my kind often miss, women, that is, who have no tangible connection with life as it goes on all round us, the material world that is, a feeling as though we had a place. Anyhow, there's no harm to sit at your window and watch people going down the street. And this particular morning—it's no use asking me which day it was, I've no head for dates: if I didn't keep a calendar I wouldn't even know the big feast days—I saw M. Tessier come round the corner of the street. He had two or three men with him and they were all clearly the worse for drink. They laughed and made the most terrible noise. It was shocking and all the rest of the world so quiet. That seemed to make it worse. At last they separated and M. Tessier came down the road. Almost opposite, as you can see, is a telephone box. He reeled across—really he couldn't walk straight, and went into the box. He stayed there quite a long time talking and then he came into the house. I heard him creep up the stairs like a cat as if he didn't want to be heard, not a sound. I must admit I don't like that kind of thing. It's never happened in any house where I've been before. I had serious thoughts of moving, but otherwise this has always seemed such a respectable house—and of course the terms are reasonable."

" Was he often out at night?"

" Well, really, I couldn't say. He was a most mysterious person. What he did with himself all day I've no idea, but I've always understood he had the most peculiar friends."

" You never saw any of them?"

" I? Oh no. I don't think he brought them here. Madame Lemaitre was very particular in the ordinary way. I think that man must simply have bewitched her. I spoke about it once. I felt it was my duty. There was a young girl here and it wouldn't be very pleasant for her if she'd met him when he was in that condition."

" Still, if he kept such irregular hours, it's hardly likely they would meet," suggested Dupuy briskly.

" Oh, perhaps not. But drunken men are scarcely responsible for what they do. Anyway, it wasn't at all pleasant to think of his being in the house in that condition."

" Well, Mademoiselle," Dupuy consoled her,

drily, "you need have no more fear of M. Tessier's drunken footsteps disturbing your peace. Where he goes now he will have no such opportunities and, indeed, if what you believe of him is true, he might be thankful even for water. And now, Mademoiselle, since you are good enough to remain in the house, I must warn you, you will not any longer be alone. A *sergent-de-ville* will be on guard: he will see to it that you are not annoyed by strangers or the merely curious."

Miss Martin said breathlessly: "You're going away?"

"I have so much to do," deprecated Dupuy. "And I have a theory that when there is more than one man can manage, the wise man chooses the personal rather than the impersonal, that which calls for tact rather than for mere knowledge, which may be any man's possession. And so I will leave the routine to my colleagues and myself will undertake the difficult, the delicate share of the work."

Miss Martin stood looking at him oddly, as if she couldn't make up her mind about him. And indeed this was the truth. He might be no more than a pretentious fool, or he might be sly, be tricking her, though into what admission she could not have said. She knew nothing, she even cared nothing for the mystery that made Dupuy's eyes shine so brilliantly, set all his restless energies aflame. And so she said nothing, but stood there pleating her dark skirt in her foolish fingers.

"You think me arrogant," Dupuy accused her, suddenly, "conceited, a fool. But I will tell you a secret." He stepped up to her, light as a cat. "This house is full of secrets, but I will tell you one more. It is this"—he put on his most important expression, he nodded his head, his voice sank to a whisper. "It is this. One day I shall be head at the Sûreté.

Oh, no one has said so but I know it. The man with that future ahead of him has the right, has he not, to be a little conceited?"

He moved away again, passing into the room on the right of the hall where Madame Lemaitre had taken him and his companions on the occasion of their visit here. It was in the same state of shabby magnificence, a rather squalid disorder, yet a sense of richness that could not be gainsaid. He walked over to the window where the birds in their gilt cage hung from the ceiling.

" You extend your charity to them?" he suggested, to the wondering and slightly alarmed Miss Martin, who had followed as far as the threshold and now stood staring about her as though she had never seen the room before.

"I—I clean the cage. I give them fresh water. I don't know what will happen to them now. I couldn't undertake permanent responsibility."

Dupuy put up his hand and thoughtfully scratched his head. Miss Martin averted her eyes. An instant later she nearly jumped out of her skin as someone thundered on the front door.

" Oh dear!" she whispered, but Dupuy had slipped past her into the hall before she had recovered from her shock. He opened the door with a flourish to disclose Field and Glyn on the step.

" Aha!" said Dupuy, stepping aside. " Now I will tell you what I have learned. She is without. doubt an interesting woman. Listen." He laid an impulsive hand on the arm of each. " Here is something—one of those additional touches—that we of ourselves could not supply. This widow Lemaitre is not only a widow of exciting proportions, she is more, she is a mystery. More than that," his pressure on their arms tightened, his voice dropped, " she is a miser."

" And you've found the secret store?" asked Glyn.
" No, monsieur. That I am leaving to you, while
I go to visit that so dull M. Goriot. I have something I must ask him to explain. Meanwhile, I
leave you to find the buried treasure. This is what
I have learned." Vividly, with an economy of gesture
that surprised his audience, accustomed as they were
to his flamboyances, he sketched for them a picture
of that enormous, secretive figure, bent over its hoard,
within the golden circle of light. " You will, I
think," he wound up, " find your quarry in that room
under the eaves where Lemaitre would creep up in
the evening. Miss Martin tells us that she was
creeping upstairs, the old woman, that last night of
her life. The other room on that floor, overlooking
the street, belonged to M. Tessier. Oh, there was
some secret between them. Be sure of that." He
caught up his soft-brimmed black hat and hurried
out.

Goriot was selling a much-advertised make of
gripe water to a mother with an unfinished-looking
baby when a dapper little man with a curled and
perfumed moustache came briskly in, turned an
astonished glance at the woman and barely waiting
for her to leave the counter stepped up and asked
for a little packet of Epsom Salts. Goriot took it
down from a shelf and began to wrap it up. " It is
chilly to-day, monsieur," he observed pedantically.

The new-comer said with such total irrelevance
that Goriot dropped the little parcel. " I am a brave
man, monsieur."

" A—brave man?" Goriot's pale face was at once
haggard and vacant, as he seemed to grope for a
connection between courage and Epsom salts.

" There are other things—less innocent—that can
be made up to resemble Epsom salts," said the

customer, blandly, "and it is known, M. Goriot, that you do not love the police."

"What have the police to do with it?" demanded Goriot, angrily.

"That was what Madame asked, wasn't it?"

Goriot clutched the counter and leaned forward. "Who are you?"

"You haven't recognised me? Oh, my dear Goriot, I think I may plume myself on my success here."

"M. Dupuy?"

"You must forgive me," said Dupuy in a deprecating voice. "I am experimenting—and at your expense. But it was important. I do not lightly make a fool of a man. But if you see me and do not know me— " he spread his hands.

"I see." But Goriot was still breathing fast.

"I believe that I alarmed you," remarked Dupuy, leaning across the glass case of face creams and powders, purges and foot salts. "I wonder why?"

The other hesitated. Then—" As a matter of fact, I thought you were enquiring into the disappearance of M. Brémond. I don't mind confessing that I'm a bit anxious."

"About M. Brémond? Or the police?"

"M. Brémond. It's all very well for Madame Lemaitre to say he's met a pretty lady and gone off for a week, but he wasn't like that. He was a quiet sort of man and anyway he'd have written to say he wasn't coming back for a few days. I'm afraid something worse has happened."

"There are many things worse than spending a few days with a pretty lady," Dupuy agreed. "What do you think has happened to him, M. Goriot?"

"I think he may have had an accident. I think we ought to start enquiring. He can't blame me after so long, when he hasn't even troubled to let me know. This is his shop and although I'm not afraid of responsibility, I'm not easy in my mind."

"We are indeed overwhelmed with mysteries. There is this sudden death of Madame, for instance. She was not what you would call an hysterical woman?"

"Certainly not, monsieur. She was always most cool-headed."

"Not the sort of woman to commit suicide?"

Goriot started up, his face frightful in its pallor. "What's that you say?"

"Madame died of cocaine poisoning."

"Then—oh, it must be an accident."

"Accidents with cocaine do not occur very often, particularly in the case of a woman who is not being treated by a doctor. Now, Madame took pills in the evening—one each night. Quite harmless and made up to an easily analysed prescription. No amount of search has revealed cocaine on the premises, and the jury, I think, may ask awkward questions about the pill she took that night. Accidents do happen—and when they do they are very regrettable. I was speaking a moment ago of the ease with which a deadly poison may be substituted for Epsom salts. It would not be difficult for a dispenser to insert cocaine into one of these pills. I understand that the prescription was in M. Brémond's hands."

"But Brémond wouldn't want to put poison in her pills. Besides, they didn't even know one another."

"The pills, nevertheless, came from here."

"But monsieur,—pardon me—that is not possible. I am in the shop all day and Madame has never so much as entered it."

"I told you—M. Tessier used to bring them for her."

"But we have no prescription. I am sure of it."

He took down the prescription book. Madame's name does not appear in it—nor that of M. Tessier. There has been some mistake."

Dupuy took a little box from his pocket. " Here are the remainder of the pills. You observe M. Brémond's name on the label."

" I know these quite well, monsieur," returned Goriot in a puzzled voice. " There is no need to have a prescription for them. You can buy them over the counter. I could have taken them back to Madame at any time."

" But she never asked you?"

" Never."

" There is then only one avenue left to us. M. Tessier must have been among those who pay calls by night at M. Brémond's side-door."

" I don't know anything of that," said Goriot swiftly. " I was never here. I don't know anything about Tessier."

" You've heard the rumours, though. You admit that?"

" People talk. I never pay any attention. I can't tell you anything."

" Very wise, monsieur. And now, you can perhaps help me with regard to the death of Madame. You were, I believe, the last to speak to her on the night before she died. She said nothing —it is essential that I stress this point—that would make you think she might even contemplate self-destruction."

Goriot shook his head, with a strange eagerness. " No, monsieur. I am sure of it. Why should she?"

" You were speaking of the police just before you separated. Please recollect most carefully before you answer me. She showed no sign of agitation whatsoever?"

"Absolutely none. And why should she? What had she to fear?"

"One can never be sure, M. Goriot. If I did tell you one-hundredth of the strange things I have learned about these respectable old women, your eyes would come popping out of your head."

"I think you are mistaken about Madame Lemaitre. I am sure she feared no one."

"Not even the police?"

"Why on earth should she be afraid of the police? I don't think I ever heard her mention them."

"Think again, monsieur. The last night of her life the police were mentioned between you."

Goriot stared at him uncomprehendingly. "I don't know what you mean."

"You don't remember, perhaps. You were discussing this strange affair of M. Brémond and you wondered what the police might or might not do, if they were informed. You were perhaps trying to shield your employer."

"I wasn't doing anything of the kind," cried Goriot, indignantly. "Even you, monsieur l'inspecteur, can't get a criminal pact out of that conversation. I had spoken already to Madame of my anxiety regarding M. Brémond and I was suggesting that, as so many days had passed, we should perhaps inform the police."

"And Madame said, No?"

"Madame said he was all right and he would not be pleased to have the police dragged into his private affairs."

"You did not think that perhaps Madame knew where he was?"

"I thought Madame was a woman of the world. She did not know M. Brémond, but she believed that she knew men. A man disappears for a week—well, that is his affair, is it not? Be assured he does not wish to be followed, like a child escaping from a nursery."

"And if I tell you, M. Goriot, that the Widow Lemaitre was by no means what you believe, that she lived a double life— "

Goriot leaned his hands heavily on the counter. "It isn't true," he said, contemptuously. And then, in less assured tones, "It can't be true."

Dupuy's eyes were like a toad's, bright and motionless. "And if to that I add that there is reason to believe she had knowledge of Brémond that she did not choose to share with the police, that it was not only out of consideration for his feelings that she was desirous the police should not be approached, but because she knew that it might be dangerous to her that the police should hear?"

He had by this time fulfilled his threat of making the young man's eyes pop out of his head. "You are serious, monsieur? You mean that? She had some hand in the disappearance?"

"Oh, I don't say that, M. Goriot. The wise policeman does not speak without his book, and that I have not yet to my hand. But—that surprises you?"

There was no need for him to put the question. "That young fool knows nothing," decided Dupuy. "If he did he would be incapable of concealing it. Now we will see what the good Marthe can tell us."

Marthe occupied a single room in a house not far from the Rue de Rossignol. She had just returned from a two-hour cleaning engagement when Dupuy came rapping on her door. She opened it at once, a short pale woman in a torn blue apron. She looked at the new-comer with a natural suspicion born of a difficult life and years of stringent poverty. Dupuy found her slow of speech and always on the defensive. At first he thought she was going to refuse to answer any of his questions. She seemed to resent his very presence there, and to believe that his most powerful motive in making the enquiry at all was to catch her tripping. She knew nothing —but nothing at all—of Madame's affairs, she told him emphatically. She arrived at the house at eight and left at three. The house had the most respectable reputation. Otherwise, she assured Dupuy, she herself would never have consented to work there.

"I have already told my story to the police, monsieur, on the day that I found Madame. I have no more to say now. I am not a teller of tales."

"You never went into Madame's room?"

"No, monsieur. I was occupied almost completely downstairs. I did not speak much with Madame and then only about the things of the house."

"Did you know that she took pills?"

"I have sometimes found little pill-boxes in her basket to be thrown away. They were, of course, always empty."

"Madame never mentioned them to you?"

"There was once," admitted Marthe, grudgingly. "But it was nothing. She dropped a pill-box into a basket of rubbish I was about to empty, and she said: 'Another box finished. How jealous I am of women who do not need such things to make them sleep.'"

There was little to be learnt in this quarter, though Dupuy approached the problem from every angle: and presently he was walking away from the house, saying for the second time in an hour, "She knows nothing. We are wasting our time in this direction. And how can we prove a word of anything they say?" he asked himself with a fine show of resentment. "As my friend, M. Field, would say, we must put all our shirts in one basket. I wonder what treasure they have found?"

Walking back in the direction of the hotel where Field was staying, he brooded over the question of this money the dead woman had so scrupulously hoarded. On his way—and he came by a devious route that brought him quite near the Rue Rossignol —he stopped at some of the shops to make certain enquiries before rejoining his English colleague.

The answers in each case were precisely what he anticipated.

CHAPTER XI

THERE is a fascination in searching for hidden treasure that has its source deep in the springs of the human heart. The games of the nursery—Hide and Seek, Hunt the Thimble and the rest—testify to this. Even Glyn, who was known in London as a cold logician rather than a man of enthusiasm and eloquence, felt his pulses beat faster. The circumstances of the search added to the charm of the situation: this tall, badly-lighted house, the pale gleam of the drab morning stealing through skylights and narrow heavily-curtained windows, the scared face of Miss Martin seen through the dark banisters, the long, deliberate closing of a door as she escaped their possible scrutiny, the sense of the emptiness of the place, as though the full tide of urgent life had ebbed, leaving it bare and void, all these contributed to the sum of his pleasure. They went steadily up to the top floor to the room where the dead woman had come by stealth, unaware of the eyes that watched so secretively across the road. When Field tried the handle, however, he found the door was locked.

"It looks as though Dupuy's right and the money is hidden here," he observed. "The rest of the house seems open enough."

They found the key in the dead woman's room, and opened the door.

"Not many hiding-places here," remarked Glyn. "Besides, so far as she knew no one suspected she had the money. There'd be no need to hide it very cunningly."

Field walked across to the window and looked out. "The house with the blue curtains, Dupuy said, didn't he? That must be No. 2. To see the picture at all the woman must have been on the top floor, which is on a level with this one. The house is situated to the right of this one, so a woman sitting at that window across the road wouldn't be able to see more than a part of the room. How strange it is," he added, "that with all the precautions Lemaitre took, keeping this room locked and creeping up here at night when all the house was asleep, having that heavy curtain over the door so that not a hint of lamplight should escape, she should overlook the possibility of being seen by neighbours. Now," he drew a chair up to the table, "stand by the window, will you, Mr. Glyn, and try and give me an impression of how much of the room you could see if you were standing behind those blue curtains. You have to remember the room was in darkness, except for the patch lighted by the lamp."

They divided off as much as could obviously be seen: and then settled down to their search. The room contained few obvious hiding-places. The walls were drably papered; there was a rusty fireguard round the great black stove in which a fire of sticks and paper had been laid: the only furniture was a big shabby cupboard and a couple of old leather-seated chairs, the stuffing protruding. The two men examined the chairs and the shelves of the cupboard, took up some of the loose linoleum and removed the torn rug in front of the hearth.

"No sense in tearing down the walls," remarked Field. "If she came here fairly often, it must be in some reasonably accessible place. And she must have kept it here or why have the door perpetually locked?" He put his hands behind his back and looked carefully about him, presently going round the walls, sounding them cautiously for a hidden panel.

"Up the chimney," suggested Glyn. "It doesn't look as though there's been a fire in that hearth for years."

Field nodded. "It's difficult to see a woman of her build getting behind that stove," he observed pleasantly.

"There's one other thing we haven't considered," continued Glyn in the same equable tones. "It's just on the cards that Madame did commit suicide, and, resolved that no one should benefit by her death —she was a venomous old creature—made a bonfire of her fortune first, perhaps in this very room."

He stooped down and pulled open the door of the rusty iron stove. "No luck," he began, "no ashes here." Then he sat back on his heels, chuckling softly. "We come back to Poe again and again," he told Field. "That wretched purloined letter theme has been exploited almost beyond endurance, in fiction, and Poe himself is being discredited. I heard a young man arguing the other day that the Murders in the Rue Morgue was a thoroughly bad detective record on the ground that various essential facts had been concealed—or rather, overlooked. For instance, no one is told if the window was open or shut. I needn't go into voluminous detail: the young man may have been right, but the fact remains we still have a good deal to learn from **Poe**," and he plunged his hands into the grate. Lightly covered by newspapers, and resting upon a bed of sticks, lay piles of notes, secured by rubber bands.

"A good place," commented Field briefly.

Glyn was frowning. "Scarcely wise, was it? Suppose by some mischance someone broke in here and put a match to the fire?"

"No one would be likely to come in except Madame Lemaitre, and—well, Mr. Glyn, you know as well as I do that it can't be easy to make so much money by letting lodgings. Dupuy's informant, the lady with the blue curtains, is right. If this money was honestly come by, why not bank it? And why go on living in this squalid neighbourhood? I know there's a popular superstition that French people distrust banks, but a woman like Lemaitre would be even more likely to mistrust her lodgers. Besides, it's wonderful how these things get about. If—I only say if—the police were making erquiries in this neighbourhood and they chanced to learn about Madame's hoard, they might, don't you think, be justified in being rather curious. And it might not suit Madame's book to have too many questions asked."

"Meaning the source of Madame's fortune is not above suspicion."

"Perhaps not. And then suppose her to be suddenly surprised. It might not be quite convenient for her to answer questions about this money. The large notes could, perhaps, be traced. This way—a match—and the whole fortune goes crackling up, and with it all the evidence of the police against her."

"You're thinking of blackmail?" hazarded Glyn.

"Perhaps. Who knows? There are other crimes visited with heavy penalties by the police. Now we must wait for Dupuy's evidence. He may have learnt something from Goriot."

"You think he's involved in this tangle?"

"Oh, not of necessity. That's another point on which it isn't safe to speculate. But there's some underground connection between the Rue Félice and this house and Dupuy's the man to ferret it out."

They had arranged to meet the French detective at the Café Michel and he came towards them smiling with obvious delight in his own activities and waving a slip of paper in his hand. Glyn didn't recognise him in his disguise, at first.

"And nor did M. Goriot," said Dupuy, gaily. "I gave that one a shock, I can tell you."

"You told him afterwards who you were?" speculated Glyn.

"Of course. Otherwise he would not have answered my questions. I could not have expected it."

"Then—what was the point?"

"Oh monsieur," pleaded Dupuy, "do not, I beseech you, grudge us our little pleasures, our relaxations. You think, perhaps, that the life of a policeman is one long chase after excitement and romance. Believe me, that is not so. There is much drab routine, much disappointment, even. So when the opportunity for romance offers we leap for it. It is understandable, is it not?" He smiled in a reassuring manner and continued, importantly: "I have here a note of Madame Lemaitre's house-keeping orders. Butcher so many francs: grocer—fruiterer—dairy. She is a clever manager, monsieur. It is not surprising to me that Frenchwomen should afford to dress so well. They save so much on their housekeeping accounts. I have also a note of the rent that she charged her lodgers—all except M. Tessier. Now, be she as clever as any woman in

France, she could not profit rolls of notes out of such a transaction. Her rooms do not let high. I don't know what rent M. Tessier paid but Madame spoke —to Miss Martin—as though she gave him reduced terms, and certainly he had a room very high up in the house. No, Madame had another activity but of its nature we have no proof as yet."

"You suspect, though," remarked Glyn, shrewdly.

"Monsieur, you are perceptive. I suspect. But what I suspect I will not tell you, no, not even Monsieur Field, who is my colleague in this affair. For, believe me, we are not yet at the end of this case. There is much to be done, much," he added, his brow creasing to an unwonted gravity, "that may be grievous. You, monsieur," he bent his dark gaze on the attentive Glyn, "you have, I think, much at stake. I beseech you to keep a calm mind and to remember, as I said before, that human nature is inexplicable."

Glyn, a little disturbed by these warnings, said drily, "I have had ample opportunity for discovering that, M. Dupuy."

"But, of course," cried Dupuy in penitent tones. "I had forgotten. You are likely to know it at least as well as I. Only," he touched Glyn gently on the sleeve, "we are accustomed, we men, to—to back our fancy as your racegoers say. And we do not like it if our fancy does not win. We think it is our fancy's fault. But that is not always true. Sometimes it is the fault of our own judgment. And now," he added briskly, "let us consider the case of this poor woman. How she died is undoubted. Of cocaine poisoning. How then was it administered? I have consulted with the doctor. I have drawn from my own experience. I have talked it over with M. Field. We believe that one poison pill had been inserted in place of the innocent one she should have taken."

"A point arises there," Glyn interrupted, eagerly.

Dupuy turned to Field with an expression of mock dismay. "Your friend here," he said, comically, "he rides always in front of the dogs. Yes, M. Glyn, there is a point. And the point is—how could a murderer be sure that the pill would be taken that particular night? I answer—he could not be sure. No. I do not see how he could be sure. But there was one thing on which he could with all reasonableness count—within twelve days his enemy would be dead."

"Enemy?" ejaculated Glyn.

"Men do not as a rule poison their friends."

"And he would not be suspected?"

"I think he would make provision for that."

A light broke over Glyn. "You mean Brémond. Brémond who made them up for her? Oh, no wonder he's disappeared."

"Yes," agreed Dupuy. "I did not expect him to send us his address. That we must learn for ourselves. And indeed I hope to have news for you soon."

Glyn was frowning. "Short of the fellow's own confession I don't see how you could bring a case against him in court. He's only got to swear that the pills weren't mixed and the prosecution wouldn't have a leg to stand on."

"If you could prove motive you'd have gone a long way," broke in Field.

Dupuy watched them both with a sly smile. "Come, monsieur," he rallied Glyn, "this is not like you. I have had the greatest admiration for your memory up till the present."

Glyn felt himself colouring. "What have I forgotten? Ah!"

Dupuy smiled, and put his hand on the lawyer's shoulder. "That is all right, monsieur. I knew it was only for a moment. Now perhaps you see light again."

Leaving the café, they walked back to the Englishman's hotel and Field invited his colleague to come in. "I had word yesterday that our people believe they are on the track of the missing notes. You will realise, of course, that information regarding them was supplied at once to every *bourse* and station and bureau de change, both here and on the Continent. Our theory was that our gentleman would not change those notes on this side of the Channel if he could help it. But he might be hard pressed——"

When they got into the private sitting-room reserved for the two men they found a cablegram propped against the ornate clock.

Field ripped it open, then glanced at his watch. "They've traced him," he said, "but he's slipped between their fingers. He's on his way to Calais now on the Dover Queen. She's due in thirty minutes. Apparently the fellow changed the fifty pound note at Dover and the clerk who changed it didn't realise it was the one we were after. Luckily there was a more enterprising fellow on the premises, but unfortunately by the time he happened along the boat had sailed. We shall have to detain the fellow at Calais."

"We have some description?" asked Dupuy, anxiously.

"We've got his finger-prints. They took them from the banknote and cabled them over."

Dupuy nodded, with a satisfied smile. "I take off my bowler to your policemen," he said, in grave tones. "But, oh Field, how angry all the innocent passengers on that boat are going to be when they find they are to be held up, like sheep in a pen, because there is a suspected criminal on board." He bustled away to telephone instructions to the Calais police, and Field looked up the Calais trains.

" No luck," he commented, briefly. " There isn't a train for an hour. I wonder if it would be quicker to go by road." But when Dupuy heard the news he only said :

" That is excellent. I can now take these finger-prints to the Sûreté, and see whether we have any record of them there. When you are hunting foxes it is as well to stop up all your—holes?" he looked questioningly at Glyn.

" Earths," supplied Glyn. " You're keen on fox-hunting, M. Dupuy?"

" Alas, monsieur, it is an English sport, and my temperament ties me to Paris. But if it did not, if I could be a rich English gentleman, yes, then I think I would live in the country and shoot foxes." Glyn maintained an admirable gravity, and Dupuy con-tinued unabashed : " As it is, I am a poor man and a Parisian, so for my living I must hunt men. And perhaps, after all," he concluded, cheerfully, " it is the better sport of the two. You agree, *mon ami?*"

Glyn was aware of a disagreeable sensation : he took a serious, even an elevated view of the respon-sibilities of his profession, and this calm linking of himself with a man of Dupuy's admitted outlook was no compliment to himself. He thought such an attitude had a regrettable amount in common with the tendency of urchins to torment stray cats and pull the wings off flies.

Dupuy, however, was in no mood to notice any slight aloofness on the part of the lawyer, for on reaching the Sûreté he discovered that he had indeed netted a prize. The man now being held by the Calais police was no other than Jacques Rentoul, a well-known cat burglar, wanted on two well-defined charges of theft. The police had been skilfully decoyed into believing he was still on the outskirts of Paris and had laid many subtle lures to entrap him.

"He's no good," said Dupuy, briefly, as the three men sat in a first-class carriage discussing the position. "He had escaped from Paris—so far, so good. And now he cannot remain in England and he must return to put his head in the lion's mouth. A man so clumsy or so unlucky should not take to crime."

"So unlucky?" Glyn was surprised at the adjective.

"It is like that for some men—nothing goes right. There are some men who should not play cards, who should not gamble. There is a fate against them. Some have beginner's luck. But I think this time it is the cards that are against Rentoul. When he entered M. Tessier's rooms that night he could not guess he would presently have the police of two countries after him, in a murder mystery."

As Dupuy had prophesied, the passengers of the Dover Queen were on tiptoe with rage at being held up for nearly four hours. There was one American in particular, clean-shaven and bow-windowed, who was telling the world this was the last time, by heck, he ever came to this lousy God-damned country.

"They're all out for our cash," he stormed, "and they treat us like a lot of criminals."

The police had further enraged the passengers by insisting on taking records of the finger-prints of everyone on board.

"Rather a high-handed thing to do," suggested Field, following Dupuy up the gangway.

"Our police do not like to be held up to ridicule any more than the police of other countries," said Dupuy more curtly than usual. "And if Rentoul makes his escape now we shall be a laughing-stock in Europe. We have our feelings like other men."

Dupuy was inclined to revise his opinion of his prisoner when he saw the manner in which he accepted the inevitable. He was a small man, with a body like whipcord, very slender and beautifully trained. He might have been a professional dancer, he admitted later, "but," he added, scornfully, "I would as soon be in hell. The pay is bad, the work is degrading: it becomes agony to move the feet after a time. There is not much choice for such a man. He must work honestly for the short time that he is able to work before he is finished and flung on the scrapheap: or he must become the property of some rich woman who buys him as she would buy her car or her dog: or he seeks something better to do."

In his case he had chosen a life of crime. He told Dupuy that nothing he could conceive gave him a more exquisite sense of delight than the danger and the success of his vocation. Such a life, devoid of dangers, would probably not appeal to him. He enjoyed matching his wits against the police and when he lost, as on this occasion, he accepted defeat as a good gambler accepts heavy losses. He had been betrayed in Paris by a man who hoped to win the favour of the authorities by denouncing him. He had successfully bamboozled the police and, but for Tessier's unexpected death, he doubted whether they would have taken him now. But with the net drawn tight everywhere he had been desperate. In London he had happened to see a French detective, and had assumed that the fellow was over on his, Rentoul's, account.

" So I felt London was no longer healthy for me," he told Dupuy. " And indeed, London brought me no fortune." He had, though he refrained from saying so, successfully broken into two houses, only to find that in the first the owners were away and the jewels had been sent to the Bank for safety, and in the second, the hard times had persuaded the lady to have her valuables replaced by paste, not worth the trouble of stealing.

His account of the night of May 9th was as follows: Owing to his persistent ill-luck he had been reduced to a negligible amount of money. Only that morning he had seen the French detective and had decided to leave town immediately. His first concern was to provide himself with enough money to show a clean pair of heels. It was not only the police, he demonstrated, who understood the help-lessness of the pursued man without money. He had that day—May 9th—changed his lodging, fearing the French detective was on his track. He knew the Robespierre well by name, a slatternly house of dubious reputation. Throughout his successful criminal career he had put up only at luxurious and ostentatious hotels: it was unlikely that the police would search for him in so mean a lodging. He did not, in any case, intend to remain there. Since the French police knew that he was in England he must leave that country at once. It only remained to obtain money.

"I resolved," he told Dupuy, "to break my London luck. In any event, I must be caught, I told myself, if I had no funds. One takes these chances, it is necessary. For three years I have been winning—now it is your turn. Well," he shrugged his shoulders, "to be a dancing-partner is to be always in prison, instead of just for a little time."

So he had waited until evening and had slipped out of his window, working his way over the roof to the fire escape. One could picture him, now crouching against the chimney-stack, now spreadeagled against those gleaming slates, like a great shadowy bat, working his cautious clever way towards the steps. He had just reached these and was about to descend when he saw the light between the inadequately-drawn curtains of Tessier's room.

"I peered in," he said, "and there was that old man, leaning back in his chair, helpless, unconscious. I saw at once that I should have no trouble with him. There was a bottle of brandy three-parts empty, there were dirty glasses—and on the table was a wallet full of money. I could see that it was full even from my place by the window. This was not even bolted. It was easy for me to make an entrance. And once in the room I lost all sense of fear. It was like being in a little cell of quiet. I helped myself to the money; there were sandwiches on the table and I ate these, prowling about the room. I moved like a cat. The night had been so wet and the roof was smooth like glass: I dared not wear my ordinary shoes. I put on, instead, a pair of espadrilles—" (When Glyn heard this, he started, remembering the scrap of rope found in the window-frame. It had never occurred to him that it might come from the sole of a shoe.) "I stayed there for perhaps a quarter of an hour. I did not touch the old man's clothes. Only a fool takes clothes unless he is forced. But I had been cold and hungry and without money. Now my pockets were full of notes and I was fed and had warmed myself at the fire. I wanted no more adventure that night. And still unobserved I left as I had come. A few hours later I paid my bill and went away."

Luck, however, still failed him: a slip on the wet pavements had resulted in a sprained ankle and it was several days before he could walk. His money was stolen from him while he lay in bed, and he was compelled to change the fifty pound note that had brought him to ruin.

"And even then," he added ruefully, "I believed that I had won. And now—" his eyes were bright and alert as he met his captor's gaze.

"And now," Dupuy completed for him, "you have quite an amount of travelling to accomplish. I hope for your own sake you are a good sailor, M. Rentoul."

Rentoul's eyelids flickered. "So?" he said, dispassionately.

"Indeed, yes," nodded Dupuy, energetically. "For you must return to London in connection with the death of M. Tessier. You are the last person to admit to seeing him alive."

Rentoul said: "I don't know much about the English police, M. l'Inspecteur. This is my first encounter with them, but even they can hardly suggest that I should trouble to murder a man too drunk to resist me."

"No doubt they will make you an opportunity to explain that," returned Dupuy, politely. "And then," he continued, "Paris will be eagerly awaiting you in connection with two charges of robbery."

This was the story that Dupuy told his English colleagues in the evening of that day.

"There are some puzzling points there," suggested Glyn.

"There are, indeed. And there is one that puzzles me above the rest." He paused, but Glyn said nothing. "You do not ask which that is, monsieur," observed the Frenchman in a disappointed voice.

Glyn laughed. "I have enough experience of you by this time to realise that that's no way to get my information."

After an instant Dupuy laughed, too. "Then, monsieur, I will tell you. I cannot—no, I cannot for the life of me conceive how so simple a story can take

so long to extract. One reads in reports of trials—
So-and-So was three hours in the box, and you think
' But this is ridiculous. It cannot be.' Yet there is
the fact—in print."

"And no judge worth his salt lets counsel waste
his time putting unnecessary questions. He pulls
him up without ceremony. I'm often amazed
myself to see how long I have kept some poor wretch
on the rack."

Dupuy nodded. "One should not be surprised.
But to-day—these hours—to extract that one little
story. And he was not what you would call a difficult witness—no, he was a good sportsman. He did
not try to make things hard. But, ah well. Now,
my dear Field, I think we have accomplished all
there is to be done in Paris. London must be our
next stop."

"You think we'll find Brémond there?" demanded
Glyn.

"I am hoping for it," said Dupuy, gravely.

"Tell me something," urged the lawyer, yielding
to a sudden impulse. "Do you think—yourself—
that Rentoul had anything to do with Tessier's
death?"

"You have a saying in England," returned Dupuy,
with one of his customary flourishes, "that every
man is innocent until he is proved guilty. Over here
—I speak for myself, of course—all men are guilty
until they can show they are innocent. You think
that harsh? But, believe me, monsieur, it is most
effective. And now," he added, "I think we have
earned a little recreation. To-morrow—London.
To-night—pleasure. There is an entertainment,
monsieur, that I think you would appreciate. A
new dancer—like a swan, veritably—" he flung out
his arms. "Come, to-night you shall be my guest.
To-morrow we shall be back at the treadmill."

CHAPTER XII

LONDON greeted them next morning with a brown wall of rain, with a fog hanging six inches above the pavement, with cold, squalor and dismay. Field put back his head. "Nice to be home," he remarked simply.

Glyn looked at him in admiring amazement. "That's the type that keeps a climate like ours going," he decided. "A more temperamental race would have abandoned this country ages ago. Field likes this stink and grime. I believe," thought Glyn, "he likes it better than the airy charm of the Boulevard." He decided that this was due to a lack of romantic imagination, and on impulse he said so.

"Romantic imagination," scoffed Field, "and what's that when it's at home but the thing that makes ladies buy sixpenny and shilling magazines to read about people whose lives are exciting and unreal? Imagination's all right for criminals. They need it if they're to have a chance. Cold facts are enough for us."

In London the party separated, Field and Dupuy going to Scotland Yard, and Glyn being free to follow his fancy.

"We shall meet again soon enough," Dupuy assured him. "We shall not forget what we owe you, monsieur." Glyn looked at him hard, but came to the surprising conclusion that the little Frenchman was sincere. And he was a little shocked to find that this implied compliment pleased him more than many a congratulation he had had from the High Bench.

"You're going to solve the Brémond mystery on this side of the water?" he asked, and Dupuy, looking for the moment almost sad, said, "I believe it, monsieur. Yes, I think so. But you shall be with us for that."

Then they were off in one direction, and Glyn hailed one of the new luxury taxis that were delighting the hearts of Londoners. and was driven to his club. It was pleasant, he discovered, to find himself in familiar surroundings, with faces he could recognise, and whose owners recognised him. Life had been so bizarre lately, with Dupuy and his rapid changes of identity to add the final touch of unreality to the unusual, that he appreciated the commonplace. Yet how quickly his mood changed. Instead of feeling at home, it was not long before he felt as though, with his arrival in England, he had stepped on to a stage where people behaved according to certain codes that were not those of everyday life.

"That fellow must be a wizard," he reflected uneasily. "My reaction ought to be absolutely dissimilar. I ought to feel I've escaped from pantomime into normality. Instead of which that Parisian adventure seemed actual and this seems no more than a play."

This fantastic frame of mind persisted even while he talked to fellow-clubmen and drank the famous club sherry before lunch. At length, impatient of the absurdity, he returned to his own chambers, where a number of letters were awaiting him. Some of these needed instant dealing with, and he was almost at the foot of the pile when he came upon one in Eve Dulac's handwriting. At once he felt himself at home. The letter was short and urgent and was already two days' old. It ran:

> I took the liberty of telephoning to your house, but I was informed you were abroad. If you have anything fresh to

> tell us in connection with M. Tessier's
> death, I beg you will let me see you on
> your return.

Instantly all Glyn's blood began to sing in his
ears. "Can that mean she has something fresh to
tell us?" he surmised, and, at the notion of bringing
Dupuy some detail of which he was at present
ignorant, a sense of pleasure assailed him. Even to
himself he would not as yet acknowledge the true
cause of his exulation.

Eve Dulac was out when he telephoned, and he
was unreasonably cast down at this information,
until he remembered that she was Fleming's secretary and would, of course, be at work. Discretion
warned him not to try and get in touch with her
until her duties were over; never get in touch with
a man on alien territory; it is apt to tie his tongue.
The rest of the day passed slowly, and at six o'clock
he rang up the flat again, and was invited to come
in at nine that evening. Mlle. Dulac was engaged
until then. Glyn wasted some further time brooding
over the possibilities of the girl's private life. He
knew nothing of her beyond what Lady Hunter had
told him, and that was little and unsatisfactory
enough. He disliked the part that Louis Tessier had
played in her life, and he still was considerably in
the dark as to the actual position between her and
Louis's father.

At a quarter to nine he found himself in the
neighbourhood of the flat, and it required all his
self-control not to turn in at the big double doors.
As the church clocks began striking the hour he set
foot on the first of the seventy-two steps that led to
her apartment. The building was old and
unfashionably constructed; there was no lift and the
stairs were covered with a cheap carpet in a jazz

pattern that made his eyes ache. Eve lived at the top, right under the roof, with a compensating view over square gardens. She opened her door to her visitor herself and over her shoulder Glyn was disappointed to see the tall cool figure of Julian Lane.

"I have asked him to come also," Eve told him tranquilly, "because he is as anxious as myself to learn anything you may be free to tell us. And also," here she stretched an impulsive hand towards the young man, in a gesture that Glyn found irresistible, "because we hope to be married very soon."

Glyn found himself saying over and over again in his heart, "I knew it. Of course I knew it. It's natural and it's right," and then uncontrollably: "What a fool I've been! What a lunatic! Of course, she's never even thought of me as a human being. Why should she? I probably seem old enough to be her father."

And all the while he was taking the young man's hand, saying, "I congratulate you," and listening to Eve telling him, as though he were accepted as a friend of the family, that Fleming had definitely decided to abandon his film of "The Judge." "He is immovable," she said, but it wasn't really of so much consequence, since Lane was already involved in another enterprise.

He spoke of it for a minute or two with enthusiasm and expectation. Glyn found himself humiliatingly jealous of the other's youth and superior height, though he only said pleasantly, "You're full of ideas," at which Eve laughed, saying, "We shall need them, monsieur. I have no *dot* with which to enrich my husband," and she smiled at the young man with a tenderness that made Glyn savage, and for the first time scornful of his own success, because it couldn't get him the one thing he now desired. "I am fortunate to be marrying an Englishman," she continued.

"In my country, a man does not care for a dowerless wife. But that," she added the next moment, "is enough of ourselves. We hope, monsieur, you may have something to tell us."

Glyn looked disappointed. "I had hoped you might have something fresh to tell me," he said. "We have still a good many gaps to fill in."

The words were scarely spoken before he was aware of a change in the girl's bearing. It was—so he put it to himself—as if she turned a key in a lock, a definite gesture of defiance and—he hesitated over the word but finally accepted it—of fortitude and he was conscious of a twofold stab of disappointment and of fear.

"So after all there is something she won't tell us," he decided. And remembered, with an odd sensation of dismay, that he had had the same certainty in the company of the ill-fated Madame Lemaitre. Well, he reminded himself, he had been right there. And the secret, which was not yet revealed to him, had proved dark enough in her case. So before the girl could speak, he said very gravely, "Mademoiselle, if there is anything you are keeping back, I beseech you to trust me. This is a very ugly case, uglier perhaps than you have any idea of. Its consequences are wide-spread. Believe me, nothing is more dangerous than secrecy at this juncture."

As though his sudden warmth had cooled her mood, Eve looked at him with an inscrutable smile, and said, "I have nothing more to tell you, monsieur. But surely you can reassure us to some degree."

"I'm not free to tell you a great deal," returned Glyn, accepting defeat for the moment. "You'll realise that. But at least the stigma of suicide seems likely to be lifted from M. Tessier's name which was, I think, your chief consideration."

It was impossible to tell from her manner whether

she were disappointed or pleased. She only said in quiet tones:

"You must tell us all that is possible. But first we must entertain you."

She had preceded both men into the living-room of her flat, a long rather narrow apartment, widening at one end. This bulge was, of course, invisible from the door, and one came upon it with a sense of agreeable surprise. Rooms, Glyn had been told, reflect the character of their owners. This one was comfortable and cool, with deep chairs in striped tweed covers, with a coal fire burning, and squat standing lamps on small tables, with shades of rose and silver. A coffee-table in veined walnut wood was drawn up near the fire, and Mademoiselle now proceeded to make them French coffee that she served in tall thin cups of Sèvres china.

"This is the last of the china from my mother's house," she told them serenely, seating herself, the firelight touching her pale frock with dull red stains, and throwing its shadow across her colourless throat. Watching her, a frightful premonition seized Glyn, as though that shadow were indeed blood.

"Who would dream of cutting that lovely throat?" he thought, enraged at his own wild dreaming. And in reply to that came an answer so incredible, so dreadful that instantly he thrust it out of his mind. Later it was to return and he was to find it less easy to dispose of it. But to-night it was only one of those absurd fancies that fasten on a man's imagination and are lightly dismissed.

Before he had set his cup aside the girl began to thank him for what he had done, with an earnestness that embarrassed him.

"I think you cannot guess what this means to me. M. Tessier was—very dear to me. I loved and admired him, and I think I could not endure that he should be dishonoured in the eyes of the world by a crime—for so, monsieur, he regarded it—that seemed to him the final, the unforgivable event."

"I've done little enough," Glyn protested. "It was pure chance that made me notice the blotting-paper. Thank yourself that I was in the court at all . . ."

"If there is anything," she repeated, and suddenly Glyn found a thing to ask her. Even so, he hesitated before he put his thought into words. It seemed to him intolerable that he should make this girl suffer afresh, or remind the young man at her side of an attachment, a devotion even, that had preceded her engagement to himself. But the lively curiosity that had placed him in his present position made him turn to her and say, " There is still one thing that puzzles us, one thing that may be the clue to all this misery."

"If I can tell it you, monsieur, the information is already yours."

"Then—why did Louis Tessier take his own life?"

There was an appalling silence after his words. Lane sprang up, standing close beside the trembling girl in an attitude of protection. Eve had moved and now the firelight no longer lay on her throat and frock; like a ghost she was, like a great pale moth in that shaded light. He thought she even shrank from his presence, and to his amazement, instead of instantly retracting the question, assuring her that it didn't matter, that he had never intended to hurt or to alarm her, he found himself saying more sternly, " Mademoiselle, I don't wish to recall too many wretched memories, but I must have your answer. Why did Tessier die?"

She said in a low voice, " I can't tell, you that, monsieur. Of that I have sworn never to speak to a soul. But this I will say: that Réné Tessier died because his son, Louis, had died first."

Glyn turned the words over and over in his mind. So Louis Tessier was driven to his death, he thought, and this girl knows who drove him. And because of that Réné was ruined, and subsequently murdered. Why? Presumably because he'd discovered the truth and the truth spelt ruin to someone else. Problem—who is X?

Again he leaned forward. "Mademoiselle, I can't impress upon you too strongly the need for candour now. The police of two countries have made tremendous efforts and great progress in this enquiry. If you have any information that would assist them you have no right to withhold it. If you suspect a particular person you should voice those suspicions—oh, not in public, but Scotland Yard is discreet. You may not know English law, but here the subject is compelled to render the police every possible assistance. To withhold information that may be of value is to be an accessory after the fact, a very grave offence. Mademoiselle, you are compelled to come forward if you can help us at all."

He had unconsciously resumed his legal manner, and his voice and the way in which he used it were mightily impressive. Lane said at once, "I hope if I'm ever in the dock, sir, I shan't have you prosecuting. I'd never do myself justice."

Glyn knew he only said this to give the girl time to pull herself together, and disregarding the interruption he went on, "Mademoiselle, I believe you to be concealing essential facts. If, as you say, the death of M. Tessier is linked with the death of his son, you are in honour bound to come forward."

She lifted her eyes to his, and now he saw in them a resolution no argument of his could hope to shake.

"Monsieur," she said steadily, "I have nothing to tell you, nothing, nothing, nothing."

Glyn stood up; he was angry; now he had forgotten he had been in love with her like any callow youth. He saw her in the light of a reluctant witness, who persists in concealing a piece of vital information.

"If you refuse to tell me that, mademoiselle, I can do nothing to force you," he said coldly, coming to his feet.

She also rose; she was so small she was scarcely higher than his shoulder, but he thought he had never beheld such dignity.

"You are going to the police, monsieur?"

"I am conceited enough to suppose that what you will not give me you will also refuse to the police. But the time will come," he added, "when you'll be compelled to yield up that information."

"I shall never do that," said the girl simply. "I have promised."

"Whom did you promise?"

"M. Tessier, for one."

"Death absolves from vows," Glyn told her, but she shook her head.

"And I promised Louis and I promised myself. You can't break your word to three people."

He saw that she was fanatic on this point and understood that no amount of argument would move her; in an access of generosity, over-mastering his natural chagrin at this obstacle and his own failure to overcome it, he said, "Your friendship's worth having, mademoiselle. I congratulate you again, Lane."

They asked him to stay a little longer, but he refused. He had hopes that Field would give him his confidence as to developments on his side, and he hurried away. Besides, they must want to be alone.

A sense of overwhelming hunger for the common things of life, companionship, friendliness, love such as these two now enjoyed, gave him a curious feeling of despair as he walked with Lane into the little hall. Mlle. Dulac did not move; she was sitting in a low chair, the wings of her pale frock gleaming against its dark material. She seemed so tired she could scarcely smile.

"She's an angel," said the young man with unexpected fervour as he stopped by the front-door. "I can hardly believe my own luck."

"Tell me one thing," said Glyn abruptly. "Do you know what killed Louis Tessier?"

He saw the young man hesitate and believed he knew the reason. Naturally, a lover would like to assume that his beloved kept no secrets from him, but after an instant honesty prevailed and Lane replied, "I don't. If I did I suppose I'd consider myself bound by the vow that holds Eve silent. Naturally she doesn't want to talk about the fellow much, and naturally I don't want her to. That isn't pure selfishness," he added. "It upsets her tremendously. I know she broke off the engagement, but there was some story behind that we've never been privileged to hear. If it hadn't been for this second death she might have got over it well enough, but some people seem to be pursued by fate. That's no figure of speech. It's true. I remember an old woman we had to work for us when I was a boy. Her life had been one long succession of tragedies, pointless and brutal, for which she certainly couldn't be blamed. Eventually she developed cataract and went blind. It begins to look to me as though Eve were being involved in a similar process. She had a bad time in Paris making a living after Louis Tessier died; as I say, I don't know the whole story, but I believe it was pretty grim. And now this."

"Tell me something," said Glyn. "She sent you to meet the old man. They were on quite good terms?"

"I believe she was the only person he knew with any intimacy in the whole of London."

"I suppose she sent you because . . ."

"She couldn't meet him herself. For one thing it would be too painful, though as a matter of fact she did suggest it. But she agreed finally to let me take her place. She spoke of him with a very real affection, and a very real fear."

"For herself?"

"For his enemy, whoever he was."

"The man responsible for Louis' death?"

"I think so."

"You've no notion who he is? Ah, but you said not. But from all the evidence it sounds as if he were in England."

"That, I think, is what no one knows. Mind you, I won't vouch for the fact that Eve knows who this fellow is. She may suspect, or it may simply be that she knew that Tessier knew, and when he came to England she thought there was a second motive behind his decision. A lot of people, you know, were surprised to hear that he was coming back to the screen. Anyway, she wanted to make sure he was safe for that night. In the morning she was to see him. I don't think she had any further plans. But as it happened all her forethought was wasted." He passed a hand, the long nervous hand of the artist, over his expressive face. "You didn't see him in that room, did you? Slumped back anyhow in his chair, with the overturned glass and the empty plate —a magnificent subject for a painter."

Glyn made a faint instinctive gesture of distaste, that his companion was quick to interpret.

"You're disgusted?" he asked. "You think it's

a low commercial sense prompting me? Do you remember the story of the actor who adored his wife and was given a telegram as he came into the wings, telling him of her death in an accident? For an instant grief deformed him; and then he shouted for a mirror so that he could see his own expression, for one day, he said, I may need to act such a man."

The subject intrigued Glyn and they remained for a few minutes discussing the normal attitude of the artist to the everyday world, Glyn suggesting that a man's profession came second to his humanity, and Lane demurring.

"Take your own profession, sir," he urged. "Do you mean to tell me that you aren't automatically a lawyer first and a man afterwards?"

"If that's true it's only because of the humanity of my clients," Glyn defended himself. "I can't base a case wholly on facts as the police do, as Field himself assures me he does. Of course, lots of lawyers are like that. Take Bruce, for example. Facts are meat and drink to him; he likes to play with them, to fit them together into a perfect pattern. That's what he cares about. He has the usual professional desire to get a verdict for his man, but when he fails, and if he's convinced that the fellow was guilty, he's not only satisfied, he's pleased. I couldn't be like that; I might acknowledge the justice of the verdict, but, irrationally perhaps, I'd still wish my man had got it. And that's not pure vanity, either," he added, parodying his young companion, as he shook hands for the last time and prepared to descend the seventy-two steps.

But with an odd expression on his mobile face, Lane stopped him.

"There's something I'd like to ask you, sir, if you feel free to tell me. You're in this case up to the neck. We—Eve and I—only glean what we can

from the wrong side of the shop-window. Do they—
to put it bluntly—suspect me of having a hand in
it?"

"No," said Glyn. "Why should they?"

"I had the opportunity. I brought the old man
over from Paris—it was Eve's suggestion, as a matter
of fact, but I was instrumental in getting him here—
I poured out his drink . . ."

"And motive?" smiled Glyn. "Don't tell me that
the English law doesn't insist on proven motive for
murder. I know it doesn't. But, after all, it's the
jury you have to convince, and a jury of ordinary
men isn't going to accept a statement out of the air,
as if murder were an indoor sport to which you'd
turned in an idle moment. In spite of the fact that
we're becoming daily more accustomed to accept
murder as a comparatively normal occurrence, and
people aren't shocked as they were a generation ago—
they talk of psychology and glands and all the rest
of it—no one yet believes that a man commits a
haphazard murder without either motive or some
brain-storm that renders him unaccountable for his
actions."

"I've been in Paris," Lane said. "I might have
had some tiff with the old fellow. I daresay I'm
being absurd," he added, recovering himself with a
quick laugh, "but I don't want Eve dragged any
deeper into this. Her luck hasn't been up to standard
as it is."

2.

Glyn was greeted on his return by his man who
told him that a gentleman had been waiting for the
past half-hour to see him. Glyn went in and found
Field standing by the window doing the cross-word
in the "Times."

"I hope you don't mind, Mr. Glyn," he said, and

Glyn, who invariably did the cross-word at night with his extremely dilute whisky and water before retiring, said inaccurately that he didn't.

"It's good of you to come round to-night," he remarked politely, and Field grinned at his ingenuousness.

"It was thought that perhaps you'd have something to tell us, Mr. Glyn," he said.

Glyn, taken unawares, felt his face go as red as fire.

"How should I . . .?" he began.

"Perhaps Mlle. Dulac could help you," returned the Inspector blandly.

Glyn smiled with an effort. "I found a note among my letters asking me to go round and see her," he admitted, "but she wanted to learn the position."

"And you told her?"

"You can trust my discretion," snapped Glyn. But nothing moved the Inspector. "I'm sure of that," he murmured. "But she told you nothing else?"

"Presumably she'd nothing to tell."

Field still continued to smile. And on impulse Glyn exclaimed, "I don't know whether this will interest you, but there was some mystery about Louis Tessier's death, and Mlle. Dulac knows what is it."

To his chagrin Field's smile did not waver. "So do we," he said. Glyn's surprise was such that he could make no effort to conceal it.

"You knew?"

"Of course. That's what we've been building our case on all along."

It was obvious that he would say no more on this head. "We've had no more information than yourself," he said good-humouredly, "but it's our job to make out a case and then hand it on to you."

Glyn realised he was bound to get the worst of any argument on these lines and, yielding the point with as good a grace as he could muster, he said pleasantly, " You didn't come round just to crow over me, I'm sure."

" No, Mr. Glyn. I came to tell you that to-morrow we expect to get our hands on Brémond."

" You know where he is?"

" I fancy so."

Glyn looked puzzled. " He's under lock and key then?"

A curious expression changed Field's face. " Yes," he said at last, " in a manner of speaking."

Glyn suddenly lost patience. " Not my manner of speaking," he exclaimed.

But Field was imperturbable as always. " You'll know better what I mean to-morrow," he said, and with that Glyn had to be content.

CHAPTER XIII

GLYN had allowed this Tessier affair to bulk so large on his horizon, effectually dislodging every other consideration from his mind, that he could scarcely at first accept the implications of the piled correspondence he found at his chambers the morning following his return. To say " This is one case among many in which I chance to be involved " was beyond him. He could only think, " This is the sole affair that concerns anything beyond my pocket." The fact that in other homes and other hearts similar passions and terrors were reigning, that other men, perplexed and alarmed, sought from him official advice regarding their rights or their revenge, had no sense of reality for him. His clerk couldn't make him out.

" There's this brief from Mr. Prothero, sir," he

said, and was shocked at his employer's casual manner as he replied, " Well, put it down there. I'll look at it presently."

This process of readjustment to a normal sphere took some time, and during the early part of the morning he was constantly expecting to hear Field's voice. But though the telephone seemed to ring interminably, and sometimes he would snatch it impetuously from the stand, it was always shop and more shop. Réné Tessier, Eve and Julian Lane, that enormous swollen old woman from the Rue Rossignol, regarding whose death Dupuy was maintaining so unusual a silence, these people might never have existed. And presently his natural delight in his work began to re-absorb his attention. He began to forget his own affairs in intricate argument and delicate riposte. When Sullivan telephoned that he had a new client, who was bringing a case of attempted murder against her husband and he thought this might be in Glyn's line, Glyn so far forgot his private affairs as to glow with excitement. Probably the old fool was all wrong, but a case like that gave one any amount of scope. His clerk saw the familiar expression return to his face and sighed with relief.

" If this is what a trip to Paris does to him, the less often he goes the better," he confided to a friend of his during lunch.

" That kind, is he?" said the friend. " Never guess it to look at him. Still, stands to reason you can't trust bachelors. Bound to be trouble one way or another, and p'r'aps it's best this way. More natural, anyhow."

It was late afternoon when Field telephoned, briefly making an appointment for that night. He gave Glyn no hint of what they were going to do or what development he anticipated, and Glyn asked no questions. The meeting was fixed for eight o'clock, but when Glyn arrived at the rendezvous he found, not Field, but Dupuy waiting for him. The little Frenchman was in a more restrained and silent mood than Glyn had ever seen him. He said, "We are to join Field and the others at the place," and looked disconsolately up at the sky, where the clouds were gathering for rain.

"You have a raincoat, monsieur? It would be advisable;" he saw Glyn was carrying a light mackintosh, for all day the weather had been sullen and uncertain. Dupuy made a solitary remark about the coldness and general colourlessness of the city. "Sometimes, monsieur, I think the only streets of London where I feel warm are in the districts marked E.C." Glyn knew what he meant; there was activity there; the tall stone offices betokened a myriad vocations; behind those walls the business of the world was being transacted. Elsewhere the town was too prim and restrained for anyone so volatile; he missed the open-air cafés, the general air of bustle, the rows of prudent housewives doing their morning shopping from booths in the market. And then Dupuy also was quiet. A police car was to convey them to their destination and no sooner were they settled in it than the storm broke.

As though the clouds had actually opened to disgorge tons of water, the streets seemed flooded in a moment. The car in which they were travelling swerved, as though this sudden onslaught caught it unawares. Water, as if flung from a bucket, dashed against the closed windows; the outside world was blotted out; all that could be seen was a miserable huddle of humanity bent double against the deluge, making what pace it could for shelter at all costs.

Glyn by this time had lost all sense of directions; nor had he heard Dupuy give any instructions to the driver. He glanced once at his companion, who sat wrapped in his own thoughts; Glyn said, with an extraordinary sense of being divorced from reality, swept into a nightmare maelstrom from which he might eventually emerge, but only to a strange and inimical world, " Where are we going?" and Dupuy, huddled like a small unhappy captive bird, his black hair like a plume across his creased forehead, only said, " To join the others."

This sense of horror was beginning to infect Glyn also. He struggled against it, but it was overwhelming. He stared round him at the little unlighted box in which he was travelling at a fair pace over the drenching roadway. No, he couldn't believe any of this; no such sense of unreality had attacked him during that fantastic experience in Paris. But now he abandoned himself to the moment and leaned back, not caring much where he was being taken. Now and again the car was held up in the mazes of the traffic and Glyn, peering through the windows that ran with the rain, caught glimpses of the outside world, the normal chattering hurrying absorbed world. He realised that they were in a neighbourhood of mean streets; he saw shop-fronts lighted and people huddled in the doorway; he caught the faint blare of human voices roaring above the traffic and the rain; once they passed a cinema house, the lights flashing above a picture of a young woman in a scarlet gown, lying prostrate at the feet of a man in evening dress, who stood above her, knife in hand. He saw that picture quite clearly, but it did not impress him as being any more unreal than his own experience. Then with a jerk they drove on again. Newspaper-men stood in doorways, their posters saturated and clinging against their knees. Racing News—Earl in Divorce Action—Body found in . . . the car moved on, and he couldn't see where it had been found.

He said on impulse, "That isn't another development of our case, is it?"

Dupuy started. "What is not . . .?"

"We're not on our way to find another body, are we?"

Dupuy stared. "But, *mon ami* . . ."

And then Glyn remembered. Of course, they were going to see Brémond, and suddenly a realisation of whither they were bound and what they were going to do held him dumb. A dozen questions trembled on his lips, but he uttered none of them. The lawyer in him resented unnecessary examination; the events of the evening would explain themselves soon enough.

They left the long line of shops behind them and were now travelling uphill. The trams, that had accompanied them for some miles, had ended with the shops, and only an occasional omnibus came plodding in their wake. Then the car stopped altogether and Dupuy opened the door. Following him, Glyn saw, as he had anticipated, an expanse of black iron bars, and a great gate standing ajar, with a little stone lodge on the right. So this was the graveyard where they'd laid him, that wretched mysterious little French tradesman who had unexpectedly become the crux of the whole affair. He walked in silence through the sheeted rain through the gate where several men were waiting; the undertaker, some gravediggers, representatives of the police, a man whose face Glyn thought he had seen before, but now could not name—Field was there, too, greeting him laconically, and heading the little procession that wound round to the right.

"He is buried in this part of the cemetery," Dupuy whispered to his companion. "He was a Catholic nominally at least, though he may not have practised."

The night had turned so dark that it was necessary to use lanterns; over their heads the sky was invisible; the rain whipped and stung their cheeks. The stolid police walked like mechanical men oblivious to any weather conditions; the lights flung pools of gold on their gleaming waterproof capes; Field wore a heavy trench-coat; Dupuy wore dark blue; Glyn walked in silence, the sense of this strange vigil imbuing him with a second personality that seemed alert to the remotest sound in this unfamiliar world. All round them the memorials of the dead, touching or ostentatious, reared their heads; great stone angels, hands in frilled cuffs pointing skywards and suggesting to Glyn the kind of signs you were accustomed to see in the gardens of country tearooms; flat tombstones, anchors, broken pillars and above all crosses, crosses of every size and formation, grey granite and white marble, crosses carved to resemble the whitened bark of a tree, crosses hung with stone wreaths, crosses supine on beds of pebbles, crosses like those ancient monuments you found in the northern islands and lonely parts of the world; and among all these immobile symbols the sense of a strange life stirring amid the drip of the rain and the crunching of men's feet. Glyn lifted his head and looked about him; nothing was in view but that long acre of graves; there was neither colour nor form beyond the first few inches of a man's vision; but beyond, in the shadow and the murk, what forms might not be gathering.

> And out the dead came stumbling
> From every rift and crack,

came the harebrained voice of memory.

It seemed to him that they walked a great distance through the teeming churchyard, but they had not actually been moving more than about five minutes when Field called a halt, and they gathered by the side of a new grave. The turfs had not long been replaced, and there were gashes of wet brown earth in the patched grass. Neither headstone nor wreath was here, nothing to mark the spot where this friendless wretch was houselled for his last sleep. Field gave a word of command and the grave-diggers moved forward and started to turn up the newly-placed sods. Glyn thrust his hands into the pockets of his coat and pulled his dripping hat more securely over his eyes. This was the first time he had assisted at such an operation, and the eerieness of the scene impressed his vivid imagination. Even Dupuy seemed less assured than usual; Field was imperturbable. The grave was a common one and more than one coffin was displayed when at last the spades of the grave-diggers grated on wood. One of the men went dizzily into the grave, and a constable leaned over, flashing a lantern on the discoloured simple brass plate that was inscribed only with a name and a date. He nodded. "That's him," he said, moving back, and the undertaker took his place, carrying the broad apparatus of webbing and straps with which the coffin was to be dislodged. It came wheezily and, to Glyn's distorted imagination, reluctantly to the surface. He looked round, expecting to see some form of bier on which it might be wheeled to a waiting van. He had heard no sound behind him, but there it was, and now the constables were raising the coffin, and it was being taken away, and the gaping hole hurriedly filled in, but not too carefully, because it was only a matter of a few hours before the box would be returned to its place in the earth. Glyn, curiously discomfited, turned and tramped back, still in silence, wondering vaguely why he had come here, and what it was all about. This secret and (illogically enough) to him impious resurrection of the dead seemed to destroy all sense of the dignity of man. Hamlet might cry, enraptured, what a piece of work is man! How noble in reason! How infinite in faculty! In short the highest of the creatures, but at the end he became a pitiful worthless bit of rubbish to be screwed into a box and thrust under the earth, out of sight, a creature devoid of all virtue and worth. Unable to account for the vagaries of this inexplicable mood, he went back to the waiting car, his feet splashing forlornly in the puddles as he went.

The coffin drove ahead of them all the way to the station, where it was again cautiously unloaded and placed on the floor of an empty room. The little assembly crowded in and two men knelt and began to unfasten the screws. The cheap deal wood already showed signs of weather, and cracked ominously under the vigorous treatment of the carpenters. At last the lid was flung back, to display the inner shell. Then that, too, was opened, and the dead man was revealed. Everyone instinctively moved a little nearer as the carpenters stood back, displaying not a scrap of interest in the result of their gruesome task. One body was much the same as another to them, declared their attitude. One thing, this one hadn't been underground long. Some of them—cripes, fair birthday treat they were. There was no feeling in their expressions as they looked at that deathly face, the thin cheeks sunken, the lines of the clean-shaved jaw looking as though they had been drawn with a pencil, the teeth unnaturally prominent. It was a ghastly sight, but not so ghastly, one would have imagined, to justify Glyn's sudden pallor, the widening of his horrified eyes, his low dreadful cry, " But— my God, that's Tessier. You—you've exhumed the wrong man."

In his ear Dupuy's low whisper said, " M. Brémond,

Mr. Glyn," and Glyn turned and stared at him, incredulously.

And now an extraordinary incident was taking place. On that thin sunken face, fragile and pitiful in its bluish corpse-hue, Field was placing a dark beard and a moustache; over the head where the delicate bones were clear to every observer he pulled a dark wig; he even set a pair of gold-rimmed glasses on the inhuman countenance. Then he stood back, and made a sign to a man behind him. The man turned and went out of the room; in a few seconds he came back accompanied by a slight figure wrapped in a dark overcoat. It was Goriot. As the young man's eyes fell on that ludicrous, that dreadful figure who had been half-lifted from his coffin so that he seemed like some frightful spectre endeavouring to flee, before it was too late, from the box that prisoned, the earth that suffocated him, he shrank back, but where Glyn to his shame had cried out, he only whimpered.

"It's—M. Brémond," he whispered. "My God, how did he get here?"

"You recognise him quite clearly, don't you?" said Field.

The youth nodded.

Field leaned forward and in a flash had stripped away the trappings of false hair and the gold glasses. "And now?" he said. "Do you know him now?"

Goriot's face was almost the hue of the corpse's. "That's M. Tessier." His voice was so low it scarcely carried through that still room.

"You never saw any likeness before?"

"Never, I didn't think . . ."

Dupuy spoke. "You thought me a strange fellow, M. Goriot, coming to see you in that so elaborate disguise, the whiskers, the beard, the shiny hat." He held his hand several inches above his dark head in instinctive mimicry. "But I had to learn whether you were easily deceived. If you did not recognise me, to whom you have been speaking not many hours earlier, then perhaps you would not recognise M. Tessier whom you might meet any day on your own staircase, when he greeted you behind the counter. I had no wish to make a fool of you, monsieur, as you perhaps believed," he touched the young man kindly on the shoulder. "But mistakes are not forgiven to the police. They must take no risks—with truth." He smiled as if to indicate that risks to their person was quite a different pair of shoes.

Goriot nodded speechlessly. He seemed to bear no rancour, only he stared in a shocked and pitiful amazement at the crumbled figure who still waited to be restored to the obscurity of his nameless grave.

Glyn was still trying to piece together the mystery, and not succeeding too well. He muttered, "So Tessier was Brémond, all the time. No wonder he disappeared. Are you sure he wasn't any one else, too?"

"So you have understood," said Dupuy gently and, as it happened, inaccurately. "He was also the murderer of Madame Lemaitre."

2

"But when did you suspect?" a bewildered Glyn was asking Dupuy.

Dupuy this morning was showing a commendable modesty. "From the beginning," he said. "Oh, he was clever in a way, monsieur, but it was his own way. You have dealt much with artists? They are a difficult lot—they have imagination and that is bad for us; but they are stubborn and that is good. They know that a thing they desire to do is right, and more, that their particular way of doing it is the best. They are, perhaps, narrow. Let me tell you." He leaned forward, interclasping his fingers, his eyes very bright, his body tingling with pleasure at the way the story was developing. " You have perhaps sometimes tried your strength, as you say, with a jigsaw puzzle. It is a strange occupation to take a picture, to mount it on wood, to cut it to pieces in the most fantastic and absurd shapes, and then to re-assemble it again—yet many people take pleasure in such a pastime. Now, if you are working at a jigsaw," he was like a lecturer, moving his hands impressively to make his points, " you will first of all roam your eyes over the pieces, and if there's a patch of brilliant colour you will pick out those pieces first and figure them together. But if there is no particular colour to catch the eye, if all the pattern seems very much alike, then you will be wise to start with the border, the frame into which the whole puzzle must be built. So with my puzzle. The first piece I found was the history of M. Brémond. Mr. Wilson of the Charing Cross Road, whom presently we must see again, tells us that he thinks he recalls M. Brémond as a customer two years old; now we at the Sûreté have no such record of him. It is only a year since we hear his name. And at once he is an object of suspicion. Now, monsieur, it would be reasonable for us to learn something of his past history, but no enquiry tells us anything at all. He has fallen into that house in the Rue Félice, and whence he came no one can learn. Not one particle of information have we about him. He has bought the shop from an old man who used it as a second-hand clothes store. He gets it cheap, and at once he opens a chemist's business. I have told you already why we should be suspicious of that. Well, I start from that point. Here is this M. Brémond sprung from nowhere. No society has granted him a degree, he has no friends, no family. When he vanishes no one misses him except his assistant, to whom he has said that he is going away for a few days. Oho, I tell myself, he is going of his own will, but where he is going he will not say. Now he has vanished. The last that is known of him is that a man answering to his description takes care to be seen at various times on the afternoon of the 9th May. Then we find the beard packed into a case with some cheap underclothes. Now from that you may argue two things. You may say, someone wishes to destroy him, and has imitated him, in disguise. Or you may say, he wishes to disappear. He wishes it to be known how he spent that afternoon, and then he destroys himself. You understand me, monsieur?"

"I understand you. You mean he deliberately discards one personality because for the future he is going to assume the other. He must guess that sooner or later the search would start."

Dupuy looked thoughtful. "And yet, monsieur, I think that was only what you call an emergency measure. I think he did not mean the search to start for him. He meant to make the grand gesture at the last, perhaps to disclose the whole story himself. Make no mistake about it, monsieur, his work was by no means ended when he came to the Robespierre that pouring night."

"I still don't understand how you identified him, Brémond, I mean, with Tessier. It seems to me it must have been mostly guesswork."

Dupuy was not offended. "Guesswork," he repeated, eagerly stroking his prominent jaw. "No, monsieur, I would not say that. Listen, I become interested in the disappearance of this M. Brémond. For some time I have kept my eye on him, I have had my suspicions. So it is natural that his movements should interest me. Then, behold—he is gone—like a puff of wind," he snapped his fingers. "So I go after him. First of all, I find out where he lived, but when I go there. I find, not a man but a shadow. You observed me in those rooms of his, monsieur. I was puzzled. There was something I could not understand, but I was sure, yes, sure that no man had ever lived there. You remember the bed; it was made up with clean sheets, and there was a clean pair of pyjamas laid out ready for use. Now a man does not take those pains when he is going away. And if the sheets were clean where were the soiled sheets that he had taken off the bed only that morning? Monsieur, they were nowhere. I argued, it is not likely but it is possible that a man will take with him the pyjamas he has been wearing, but he does not take his sheets. You may say, O they were at the laundry, but who handed them to the blanchisseuse? And during the week following his disappearance why were they not returned? No, Monsieur, there was a mystery there. Then the shaving stand. A man with a beard and whiskers needs no such elaborate apparatus. That made me believe that the beard was a false one. There was not one atom of food in the larder; he burnt practically no gas. But no enquiries of mine could produce one person who recollected seeing him dine or déjeuner at any local restaurant. Then I enquired further, and no laundry had ever called at that address. I said to myself, this is a blind, this man does not live here. Where, then, does he live? And if he lives elsewhere, why have no enquiries been made for him if he is missing? All border pieces, you see, monsieur, not a very attractive pattern yet, but nevertheless the frame for our picture. Then I begin to ask questions. This man whom nobody knows, disappears on the 9th May, and on the same day M. Tessier leaves Paris and arrives in London very late at night. I make enquiries. M. Brémond is traced to the Gare du Nord at a time

202

when M. Tessier must also be on the platform. I ask myself, are there any other links between these two messieurs? And the answer is yes. M. Tessier lodges with Madame Lemaitre. M. Brémond supplies Madame Lemaitre with medicines. Madame does not herself call at the shop, but M. Tessier brings them back to her. M. Tessier is out all day, and often at night as well. M. Tessier is seen one night leaving the shop by the side-door. He is searched, but no drugs are found upon him. What then is the reason for his visit? No one—mark you, no one has ever seen the two gentlemen together, or even had evidence of their simultaneous appearance. I begin to think this is very strange. Presently I am thinking, perhaps there is only one missing man to be found. Naturally, monsieur," a gleam of humour lit his intent face, "I am glad to think that. One likes to narrow the field, as you say. Then—for I am still interested in Madame Lemaitre, whose death it is my duty to solve—I remember that M. Tessier lodged with Madame Lemaitre, that M. Tessier was once seen leaving her room at a time when she herself was not in the house, that M. Tessier has access to M. Brémond's stores, that on M. Tessier's body is found a quantity of cocaine, that Madame Lemaitre has been poisoned by cocaine. And I put two and two together and there is your four as large as life. But I go further. Now you see the pattern appearing rapidly; now one can fit in pieces more easily. I tell myself that Madame Lemaitre had amassed a great deal of money that she most carefully hides. There is some mystery about this money; she does not wish anyone to know that she has it. There are many reasons why people conceal their fortunes. There are importunate relatives, there are charges they owe, they are afraid of thieves. But Madame Lemaitre has no one, she has no friends, no family, no creditors. And I do not think she is afraid of thieves. Moreover, when a woman is rich does she continue to live in so wretched a street, making a hard living? No. I assure myself that Madame has her reasons. Now there are not more than two or three ways in which a woman in her position can make money. You, I think, monsieur, suggested one. Blackmail. But where are her letters, her proofs, the sword she would dangle over the head of her victim? There is none. And how would she obtain such letters? She is a poor woman who has never been in good society or good domestic service; she has had no opportunity. I do not think she is enterprising; but she has a certain peasant stolidity of mind. She can carry out orders; she is pitiless; she is avaricious. She is the perfect tool. And then I have my puzzle almost complete. I know why Mademoiselle broke off her engagement, I know why Louis Tessier leaped from the Arc de Triomphe, I know why Réné Tessier is killed, I know why M. Brémond has disappeared, I know why Madame Lemaitre must die."

"I wish I knew a quarter of that," said Glyn, drily. "Why did Louis Tessier kill himself?"

"Oh, he killed himself because Mademoiselle would not marry him, and she would not marry him because he was a drug addict, a ruin."

Glyn started. "How on earth did you discover that?"

"I did think you'd have got that far, Mr. Glyn," put in Field's reproachful voice. "You were there, you know."

"I was where?"

"Why, with me when that young Mr. Lecontre gave us the clue."

Glyn looked surprised and ashamed. "I still don't follow you."

"I asked him how long he'd been taking the powder, which was clearly cocaine, and he said about two years and a half ago he'd met a man called Tessier who put him on to it. You didn't think he meant Réné Tessier, did you?" he asked in sudden enlightenment.

"Of course I did. All the current reports about the old man were that he was going about with a drug-ridden lot and doping himself."

"But not so long ago as that. No, no, clearly he meant the son, and once we had that information we were on the track. I'd always wondered why a man of Réné Tessier's character should give way so easily. But of course he didn't give way at all. He knew about the drugs, he knew Louis was ruined and death was really the only possible way out, and in fancy he made up his mind he'd discover how Louis had started taking drugs. Tracing back Louis's history wasn't so easy. He'd never been anything special, though at one time he'd shown great promise. Then something went wrong, though I couldn't at first find out what it was. But that must have been when he started taking drugs. For a time his father helped him with money, then he shut up his purse. He'd had a hard fight, he said, and his son must do the same. People thought him heartless, particularly as he was supposed to be so fond of the boy, but he knew that every penny he gave him was going into the pockets of the dealers in drugs. After Louis died he resolved, with Mlle. Dulac's help, to find out the source of the supply. I doubt if he'd been on the job long before he realised it was a much bigger thing than he'd supposed. You could stumble on an individual agent, as eventually he stumbled on Madame Lemaitre. That's where her money came from; you remember she said she'd met Louis. That was another brick in my wall, but he wanted, as we want, to get right back to the originators of the plot. It was extremely widespread; there were agents all over Paris, and I fancy there are agents also in London. I think Tessier must have discovered that the headquarters are on this side of the Channel. He'd never have accepted Fleming's offer if it hadn't made a fine excuse to be over here with money in his pocket. There was Mlle. Dulac; he enlisted her from the beginning of the campaign. From all we've been able to learn, Louis Tessier was enormously important to her. I've discovered a friend who was living with her at the time of the engagement and she said that when Mademoiselle broke it off she was like a dead creature. So there had to be some very powerful reason to account for her absolute refusal to reopen the engagement at any cost. Oh, there's no mistake at the time he died Louis was, humanly speaking, beyond redemption. No man who hasn't had a good deal of experience of drug addicts will credit the effect of the drug upon them. And he'd been taking it in large quantities over a long period. After Louis's death we next hear of her in a third-rate cabaret. I do not think it was ever necessary for her to work there for the sake of a living; we've had the café watched, and there again we've found one of the agents. But, like Tessier, we're not going to be satisfied till we've scotched this snake in its hole. We've been tracing stray members of this gang for years—three years—and this is our great chance."

"And what did Tessier mean to do when he got here?"

"Do you remember he said he had another appointment the next day—he told Mr. Lane that? And so he couldn't see Mr. Fleming till the afternoon. I think that appointment might have led to great results if it had been kept."

" And we don't even know the name of the man or woman he was expecting to meet."

" I could make a good guess," returned Field, drily. " I'd say he lived in the Charing Cross Road."

" Wilson ! "

" You ought to be pretty careful with your dates when you're dealing with the police. He told us he remembered Brémond two years ago. Well, that was a year earlier than anyone else could remember him. And no passport office had any record of him, either. And if Wilson was an honest man, then Brémond had been using that name, whatever his own might be, for two years at least. But he couldn't have come over here without the passport. No, there was something wrong there. Mr. Wilson's our next step."

" Do you think he's the force behind the whole scandal? "

" I wouldn't care to bet on it. No, I think it's a much bigger man, a man of influence, who can pull strings. If criminals can't get far without money, gangs of this sort can't get on without someone of importance, someone socially beyond reproach. We've some rungs to go yet, but the man we want is at the top of the ladder. I'm convinced of that."

Dupuy, his patience breaking under this long imposition of silence, here chimed in, " But you are forgetting M. Glyn's question. He asked what M. Tessier was resolved to do. I think beyond doubt he did not bring that cocaine in the aspirin tube for nothing. I think he was resolved to stamp out the man he regarded as the murderer of his son, as already he had stamped out—or would in a few days —this Madame Lemaitre. Do you remember that he said to her, ' I may return to Paris, but I do not think we shall meet again '? He had been living in that house for a year; he had become friendly with its owner; he knew her habits, and one of these was to take a pill without fail when she went to bed. These drug devils do not taste their own wares; she would have no suspicions. Do you, by the way, remember that the inquest on Tessier said nothing of his taking drugs? He had them, but I think he hated them. Sometimes, as Brémond, he was forced to give them to young men and women who were sent to him. Otherwise there might be suspicion and all his fine plans would be spoiled. But often he would lay his plans, he would give them bismuth, he would cheat them, he would rob them of their drugs after they had left his shop.

"And all this time he kept up the pretence and no one suspected? It sounds like a fairy-tale. Réné Tessier leaving the Rue de Rossignol and Thomas Brémond entering the Rue Félice."

"Oh that," exclaimed the detectives together. "That was the easiest part of his work," Dupuy continued triumphantly. "That was his trade. Do you not recall how Madame Lemaitre said he was such a droll fellow, he could always make her laugh? How he would mimic the other lodgers, the men and women he met in the streets?"

"And Fleming, who's no fool, was convinced he could make that film. Yes, I see. I accepted the general report that he was under the weather for good and all. Great heavens, what an object-lesson for the law. Accept nothing you can't prove. Of course he depended on the general public being as gullible as myself and accepting him at his surface value."

Dupuy heaved a long sigh. "It is usually a safe game to play, monsieur."

Glyn was following up his own train of thought. "Of course, if I had begun to put two and two together, I might have realised that it was cocaine that Tessier carried and cocaine that was used to poison Madame Lemaitre."

"And Tessier himself was poisoned with hyoscin. Naturally, his murderer never dreamed that he might be carrying a poison himself, when he placed hyoscin on the body. Well, one cannot guard oneself at all points. Chance always plays the longest suit."

"And do you know now who murdered Tessier?"

Dupuy looked at him with round eyes. "But, monsieur, surely that is clear? There can be no doubt there." And he exchanged glances with Field.

Glyn was beginning to smile faintly, and blame his own denseness anew when their meaning flashed into his mind, and he rose to his feet, staring at them incredulously. For a minute he was beyond speech. And when his words came he said them in a loud voice, quite unlike his usual cool precision.

"No, gentlemen," he said, as though he were addressing a board meeting, "no, that isn't true. You've made a mistake at last. That couldn't ever be true."

But as he spoke there came into his mind the picture of Eve Dulac sitting in the rosy firelight, bathed in its glow, and the inexplicable premonition of terror with which that instant had filled him.

CHAPTER XIV

GLYN's light burned till four the next morning as, oblivious to all other considerations, he turned feverishly this way and that in an endeavour to make of Dupuy's brilliant and mocking pattern some picture more pleasing to his own desires. To say that he was alarmed at the danger that beset Eve Dulac is an understatement; he was dizzy with fear on her behalf. That she should so much as hear the police suspicion seemed to him an outrage. Again and again he reminded himself of his first sight of her, outlined in her slender youth against that panelled wall. And then quite unbidden flashed a vision of her standing in the empty ballroom, one urgent hand on Lane's sleeve, whispering, " We have just time, Julian. But be careful. He is armed." He told himself fiercely that she only wished to warn the young man of possible danger to himself; Rene Tessier, thwarted in some cherished design, might prove an ugly customer. These men with nothing to lose, he thought, observe no rules and no limitations. But his own mind seethed in such a chaos as he had never before known. Sometimes, when conflicting evidence faced him in his professional life, he would wrestle with the devil of doubt, both of his client's innocence, and of his own propriety in proceeding with the case; but never had he been confused by personal issues on this scale.

"Lane himself suggested that he might be suspected," he told his troubled heart. " Is that the act of a guilty man? "

And his heart told him cynically that it was. As for women, looking the picture of innocence, and deceiving even the elect, that happened every day of the week.

Nevertheless, in this instance, he refused to believe that either detective had sufficient ground for the accusations he would shortly make in public. He debated the possibility of warning Eve and her lover of the danger in which they stood, that they might realise how their lightest word or act might be mis-construed, but a most powerful disinclination to let them guess their peril vetoed the idea. Besides, to put them on guard might make them awkward and unnatural; they might suspect pits where none had been dug.

"I can't do anything," groaned Glyn, and simultaneously determined to discover the flaw in the authoritative argument. He knew how easy it is to turn quite trivial details to a man's disadvan-tage, and build up a case that rests largely on mis-construction of innocent words and deeds. Midnight chimed and he didn't hear it. One o'clock and he had scarcely moved. At two he was standing by the window staring over the dark and quiet streets. At three he perceived the flaw in Field's argument and at four he was happily asleep.

He had not finished his breakfast next morning when he received a telephone message from Field. The net was closing round the culprits, though much still remained to be done. Field suggested that Glyn might like to be in at the next move; it was even possible he might be of use. Field said nothing on the telephone as to the nature of the day's enter-prise, but Glyn, resolved not to miss the most meagre opportunity of seeing the official hand, said recklessly that they could count on him, and hurriedly rang up his clerk and told him to cancel the morning's appointments. The fellow clearly thought Glyn was mad: he said several times, "It's Paris, I suppose, it's Paris," as though the very name of that city were a spell, and an evil one at that.

When Glyn met his companion Field said, " We're after Mr. Wilson this morning, and it's just possible there may be a rough house. We've no notion how much these scoundrels know, or how they get their warnings. They may have been trailing Dupuy and me these last twenty-four hours, so we'd like a layman on the job in case of emergencies."

The plan was for the three men to approach Wilson's shop separately but at short intervals, so that they should all be on the premises at the same time. Dupuy was to play the leading part, and Field would be on guard. Glyn thought grimly, " My impression is they want me on the spot because, if I'm in one place, I can't be anywhere else." With Mlle. Dulac for instance. He shook the thought aside and watched Field cross the street.

Mr. Wilson had one of the larger second-hand book stores in the Charing Cross Road. The entrance was on a corner, and the arms of the outside shelves stretched some distance in either direction. One assistant, a young boy, stood by the doorway keeping a stern eye on those who pore over the sixpenny and shilling racks. It's easy to get away with a book, if you know the ropes, and swear it was bought and paid for at the shop up the street.

Inside the shop was a second assistant, rather older, who packed up parcels and gave change and occasionally answered enquiries; and in addition there was Mr. Wilson himself, an elderly man with a shining bald forehead and long straw-coloured moustaches, an amiable, benevolent man in a pepper-and-salt suit with an efficient manner and a low persuasive voice. Field stayed outside and observed the young boy while the young boy, more intermittently, observed him. Glyn went in and was immediately obsessed by a shelf of books on necromacy, a subject that he found entirely fascinating; while Dupuy walked once round the long dark shop and then, approaching the proprietor, asked for a rare foreign text-book.

Mr. Wilson was a true bookman; he didn't have to look up a list or consult with an assistant. He knew at once the book to which Dupuy referred and also that he hadn't got a copy in stock. Dupuy looked disappointed. "And what's more, I don't know where to tell you to try," Wilson said candidly. "Been to Foyles, I suppose?"

"And the 'Times,'" amplified Dupuy. "Well, well, for this I am most sorry." The clipped precision of his English, not quite at home in this country that appeared to him the antithesis of everything he desired, gave him a peculiar interest to his companion. "It was M. Brémond who told me to come here," Dupuy continued.

"Oh yes." Mr. Wilson might be receiving emissaries from the mythical Frenchman every hour of the day for all the emotion—either of surprise, pleasure or apprehension—that he displayed. "Keeps well, does he?"

"He told me," Dupuy continued steadily, "that sometimes you have in another room books that are particularly required," and he thrust his hand into his pocket.

Mr. Wilson's demeanour remained admirable. "That's so," he admitted. "Price, if you want to know anything, I'm going up to the back room with this gentleman, to try and find him what he wants. Just call if there's anything."

Price, a curt young gentleman with a blue chin and an alert eye, nodded. "Right, Mr. Wilson." He took a book from Glyn, who began to ask questions. "Get as many of them engrossed as you can," Field had said. "Then if there is a rough house their attention will be elsewhere." He himself was talking to the boy at the door. The shop was a busy hum of activity; two students came in and hunted through the shelves; half a dozen women turned over books in the street; an old gentleman was absorbed in a book of reproductions of pre-Raphaelite masterpieces. " The colours," he kept saying to himself, " it's a wretched travesty. It's abominable," but he continued turning the pages, as though he could not tear himself away.

Upstairs Dupuy said, behind the closed door, " I've got the stuff. Make the most of it. It'll be the last you'll get for some time," and he slipped a small packet on the table. Wilson picked it up and looked at it in dismay. " How far d'you think this'll go among all my people? " he demanded angrily. " And you know what they're like if they can't get what they want. If you ask me, this game's getting too dangerous to be worth the candle."

" It is always a dangerous game," agreed Dupuy solemnly. " But then—it is a very fat candle."

Wilson was argumentative. " I often think it's not worth my while. I've got a good business here with the books, and some of these people cut up such a row if they can't get all they want, or if the supply's late as it is this time; I'm always in fear they'll go to the police and complain."

" Could they prove anything? " enquired Dupuy sharply.

" I don't say they could. I'm a careful man. But it wouldn't be pleasant. I've had them round here once already about that fellow, Tessier."

" That was a disaster," Dupuy agreed. " But happily it had no ill results for you."

" Except I went short of the stuff that week. What he wanted to do himself in for, unless the police had tumbled to him . . ."

" He didn't do himself in, as you say," expostulated Dupuy, softly. " He was—removed."

Wilson swung round sharply. "What's that you're telling me? He didn't take his own life?"

Dupuy shook his head. "He had become a little —inconvenient, as any of us may do at any instant. It was not so safe to let him continue to act. So he is gone. And indeed, you are right when you say the game is dangerous. They are after us at every turn, the police of both our countries."

"You just come over?" Mr. Wilson enquired.

"From Paris. I shall stay here a few days; they may be watching for me. As you say, in this kind of work one is never safe. And indeed," he added gravely, "of late there have been too many of these accidents. There was M. Tessier; now there is M. Brémond. That is grave."

Wilson looked up with a shocked expression, and even in that instant of anxiety Dupuy had a thought to spare for this rascal, so sober, so eminently respectable, standing in this dark room with walls of books in dim covers reaching from floor to ceiling. Through the square window he could see the roofs and backyards of London; a smoke coloured cat moved stealthily along the wall, crouching on its belly, seeking for meat, and Dupuy thought, perhaps I too am like that; slinking in alleys for a word that may be my candle. Then he remembered that vast army of men and women who are ruined and depraved by the very traffic he was attempting to stamp out and all compassion and self-contempt faded from his heart. "Brémond?" Wilson was repeating incredulously. "But—what has happened to him? Has he also been—removed?"

"He's disappeared absolutely. No one seems to know where he is. Of course, he may have been under suspicion by the police and have run from them; he may be safe somewhere, but I am informed by an authority that I trust that he is dead."

Wilson let his voice rise to an incautious pitch. "It's not good enough, and I've said so for a long time. Here are we taking all the risk and getting a small commission, and when there's trouble it's us who are dropped on. These big men don't take chances—no fear."

"You know your leader in this country?" asked Dupuy, and Wilson shook a derisive head.

"Not much. Didn't I tell you they don't take any chances? If the police were to make themselves unpleasant to us we might be tempted to turn King's Evidence, try and save our own skins by giving the name of the man at the top of the ladder. Well, that would never do, so we learn nothing."

"How do you know then when to expect the stuff?" asked Dupuy in some perplexity. "They seem to treat us all in a different way."

"I have a note—a careful non-committal note that couldn't do anyone any harm in a police court. I had one when Tessier was expected, and I couldn't understand why he didn't come down that morning."

"And you had one telling you to look for me to-day?"

"No, I didn't and that's a fact. It's the first time it hasn't happened. What does that mean?"

"That those at the head are getting scared. It is known that the police of two countries are making what you call a drive to stamp out our industry. They are getting afraid—the danger is getting too great."

"And they'll sacrifice the lot of us to save their own greasy skins," ejaculated Wilson in a tone of great rage. "Why can't they tell us how far things have gone?"

"I will tell you how things are in Paris," his companion promised. "Now—you have perhaps

heard of a man at the Sûreté called Dupuy. He is
a very important French detective."

Wilson shook his head. " Search me," he returned
simply. "What's he got to do with this, anyway?"

"It is he who is resolved to have the credit for
annihilating this work of ours. He is like a spark
of lightning; one instant he is here, and another
moment he is in a field a mile away. He is like
quicksilver, you cannot pin him down. I warn you,
he is a dangerous man. I have my belief that he
crossed to England with me, on the same ship. He
may be watching us at any time. He may come
here asking for books. He is a large man, with a
black beard and a deep voice; he is very conceited,"
and Dupuy stuck his hands behind his back and
began to laugh.

"I've had enough of this," said Wilson quickly.
"Anyone can have my job. The shop does quite
well, and I don't want to see the inside of a prison
for five years."

"Then, if you have any of the little notes of advice
sent you by a higher hand, you would be wise to
destroy them."

"I keep them as a rule till I've been paid," said
Wilson in surly tones. "There's still something
owing." He went to a shabby secretaire standing in
a corner of the room, and pulled out a letter. "There
you are," he said. "That's what I get. I don't
know how they run things your side, but that's what
they call themselves here."

Dupuy took the page; it was a sheet of ordinary
paper, such as is used by several thousands of firms
in London, and the typewriting was uncharacteristic
enough though, as Dupuy knew, it's generally
possible to identify the machine on which a specific
letter has been written. The sheet was headed The
Anglo-French Book Company, with an address in

Endells Lane, Mansion House, and had an inde-cipherable signature. The letter ran:

> Dear Sir,
> With reference to the volumes of Roote's Philosophy for which you enquire, we hope to be able to send these by special messenger on Friday next. Cash payment on the usual terms.
>   Yours faithfully,

No amount of ingenuity could distinguish the signature. "No telephone number," reflected Dupuy. "Besides," he held the sheet up to the light, observing the commonplace watermark of a crowned lion standing on the globe, "what firm of repute uses this cheap paper with a printed heading? At least they'd go to the expense of having a die cut."

"You have been to the offices of the Anglo-French Book Company?" he asked politely, laying the letter back on the flap of the secretaire.

"Not me. That's only what they call an accommodation address. One room there, I should think, no one ever goes near. P'r'aps not even that. There are plenty of bogus companies going about that pay a small amount to be allowed to use an address, and send up a messenger for post every day or so."

"It is not quite satisfactory," agreed Dupuy, cautiously.

"I'll say it isn't," agreed Mr. Wilson. "Trouble is if things go wrong you don't know who to get hold of. All you can do is write a letter to this address and wait and see what happens. Got to be careful, too, in case it gets into the wrong hands. And then there's always the chance one of these young fools that take the stuff off you will go and get religion or fall in love, and split on you, and, though it wouldn't be easy to prove anything, you don't want the police smelling around here. They're nosey enough as it is. You'd think second-hand books would be safe, but no. There's no vice we're not suspected of. Ask some young woman to come and run an eye over some of the books in the back, and you'll have a forest of ears sticking out a mile to make sure the respectability of the British book reading public isn't being abused. Why, I was once asked if it was necessary for that back room to be so dark. 'Easy to see you don't live among books' I told the fellow. 'Books naturally make a room dark!' And then I asked him why he didn't clamour for lights in the picture-houses. 'Never know what is going on, do you?' I asked him. Quite unpleasant, he was."

Dupuy was regarding the speaker with bright eyes. "Oh, my friend, but how rash. Let me whisper a word in your ear, the word of one who knows much of the police. Never quarrel with them—they are a spiteful body of men, and they do not forget. Speak sweetly to them, pour honey on their tongues. Then perhaps you may presently pour hemlock in their ears. They have been watching you since then?"

"I had a queer lot of customers for a bit. You get to know the real bookman soon enough. F'r instance, I knew there was something odd about you the moment you came in."

Dupuy looked rather offended. "I have a great many books in my own home," he said in a lofty tone, and Wilson laughed and put his hand on his shoulder.

"I daresay, but that's not the same as being crazy about them. Why, there are hundreds of people wander up and down this street, just looking. Haven't got the price of a decent book in their pockets, most of them, but that's their life, just reading and handling and sliding off again. They're not the kind that pinches books. You can always tell."

At that moment a foot came bounding up the stairs and the assistant's high-pitched, rather nervous voice said, " Excuse me, sir, but . . . " and the door swung open a couple of inches.

Wilson turned in a instant rage. " What's that? Didn't I tell you I was busy? Can't you even manage half a dozen customers?"

Price said in a sullen voice: " You said call if there was anything I couldn't manage, and there's a gentleman downstairs asking for Hurdle's Eastern Mystics. A very rare book, he says, but he'll give any price for it. We haven't got it, of course, but you might be able to get it . . ."

Mr. Wilson's demeanour changed. " All right, all right, Price. I'll come down. Just excuse me one minute," he nodded hurriedly over his shoulder to Dupuy. The little Frenchman smiled and intimated his willingness to remain in that room for the rest of the day if necessary.

" That strange English idiom," he reflected, as the two men went down the steep discoloured stairs. " To know one's onions. It seems to mean nothing, but at least it is true of Mr. Glyn. Even these lawyers," and he chuckled with pleasure, not having much opinion of lawyers in the ordinary way, " even they can be trusted to behave like human creatures now and again." He didn't know how long he had, but those creaking stairs would warn him of the approach of the owner of the shop, and with quick practised hands he began to rummage through the drawers and pigeon-holes of the desk. He didn't find much that was of value; Wilson had spoken truth when he said he was careful, and didn't want to come a mucker with the police. All his search discovered was a list of names and addresses, being presumably Wilson's customers. He took this and the letter and after waiting a few minutes came quietly down the stairs and into the shop. Glyn had surpassed all his expectations; not only was he keeping Wilson engaged in conversation, he had got the man enthralled. That second personality, that so rarely makes its public appearance, had chased out of the bookseller's mind all thought of the danger of his secondary activity; even when Dupuy appeared close beside him, whispering " *A bientot* " and smiling beneficently, he scarcely broke off what he was saying. His large pale face, with its bald forehead and long resolute mouth, was transfigured; he argued, he questioned, he debated. Glyn, who appeared equally absorbed, was opening and shutting one hand where it rested against his thigh.

"We have twenty minutes at least," Dupuy reported triumphantly to Field. "Your little friend is proving very useful. He is perhaps what that poor Wilson means by a bookman." For an instant he was meditative, then, reflecting that being a bookman did not seem a great advantage in itself and no advantage whatsoever in other walks of life, he uncreased his frowning brow, and continued his speech.

"How much further are we?" said Field. "It's clever of this chap, whoever he is, not to let the underlings know his identity. Wilson's right. Anyone of them might rat at any time. I take it we're on our way to Endell's Lane."

"Assuredly," said Dupuy in a complacent voice. "I am hoping that there we may learn what is our next step."

Endell's Lane is a small turning near the Mansion House. The buildings are tall and dark, and seem taller and darker than they are because the street itself is so narrow. All manner of secret activities flourish there, like anonymous bees buzzing obscurely in a dim hive. Names in a dozen languages appear on the boards in the halls; societies, of whom few save the founders have ever heard, hire their one or two rooms for purposes best not retailed. The Anglo-French Book Company was on the fifth floor of a bleak looking house, whose wire blinds at the ground-floor window intended to advertise the existence of a solicitor.

"Odd sort of solicitor if he has offices here," murmured Field. "One of the birds who's been struck off the rolls, I daresay, and is practising on the sly. They say there's no crime so dirty but you can find some legal man to defend you."

There was a shoddy little iron lift, at which Dupuy looked with frank alarm. "I am, so to speak, a young man, am I not?" he demanded. "I think so. Too young to die and not so old that I cannot contrive a few steps," and he began to run nimbly up the stone staircase. Field, who also distrusted the lift, but whose imagination was of the fatalistic type that accepts disaster as part of some plan it is no duty of humanity to question, got in and locked the gate. The lift rose warily and with groans. On the third floor he passed Dupuy, who was still running gaily in a spiral.

"You are a brave man," he called as he saw Field's face through the bars. "But," he added, when they met on the fifth floor, "you should not take these risks. Not until this case is ended, that is. For you are valuable to me."

The office they came to seek stood at the end of the corridor, a single room with a solid wooden door, and a painted plate.

"I notice the secretary discreetly doesn't advertise his name," Field remarked, turning the handle. As both men had anticipated, the door was locked.

"What now?" asked Dupuy. "What are your country's regulations?"

"I think the first step is to go into the next-door office and ask if they can tell us anything about the habits of the staff of the Company," returned Field, carefully. "Then at least we shall know whether there is ever anyone here—in the daytime. I should imagine most of the work, including the delightfully effusive letters sent to the various book-sellers, is done at night."

Dupuy looked at him and said honestly, "Not till this moment had I realised that, of course, here, at all events, all the agents sell books. After all, selling books may be done so quietly, and it is not very expensive. It is not strange if your customers linger in the shop. All manner of titles are used, and it is easy to explain that these belong to books. Yes, yes. In Balham and Mayfair and West Kensington—booksellers everywhere." He nodded, and followed Field into the office of the Continental Aluminium Company, where a tall dark young man, with his feet on a desk, was smoking and flicking through the pages of a monthly report. He stood up leisurely as they came in.

"Good morning," he said cheerfully. "Take a pew, won't you? If you've come to see Mr. Carroll, he's been called into the country and won't be back till Thursday."

"As a matter of fact, I only wondered if you could tell me when the Secretary of the next-door office will be back," said Field. "I've had a letter from him," absently he waved the headed sheet of paper Dupuy had stolen from the Charing Cross Road, "and I thought I'd come and discuss it in person."

The elegant young gentleman looked surprised and interested. "So there really is a Company," he said. "I've often wondered."

"Oh, but . . ." Field looked a little discomposed, "is there no one there during the day?"

"I've never seen anyone, and I've never seen the door open either. Our telephone went wrong once, and I went to ask if we could borrow theirs, but there wasn't anyone in the place, and the door was locked."

"That's strange," said Field, and he read the letter again. "I must write them. But will they get letters?"

"Probably got some arrangement with the office," said the young man carelessly.

"I'll enquire," Field agreed, and they came out of the room and went down the stairs.

"I wonder whether the office was engaged in person or by letter and who pays the rent," Field remarked as they neared the ground floor. "Who's the agent here?"

The hall porter said he couldn't tell them any-thing; the agent was Berkeley and Twining of Victoria Street. They owned the whole block both sides of the road. As for correspondence, there weren't any letters to speak of, and those there were were put through the letter-flap in the ordinary way. No, he couldn't tell them anything further about the company; he didn't recall anyone ever coming before and asking for the Secretary, and he'd never been one of the nosey kind. Leave other folks' business to other folks was his motto, and he thought it was a pretty good one come to that.

Field thanked him so adequately that the porter knew at once it was the police.

"And I'm not surprised neither," he told himself. "Always did think there was some funny business going on there. Well, well, it all makes a bit of a change."

Meanwhile the two detectives went on to the offices of Messrs. Berkeley and Twining, where they interviewed a lofty-mannered agent in a glass box. This gentleman required a great many assurances before he would consent to tell them anything at all. Field, a little reluctantly, was forced to disclose his identity.

"I'm an official of Scotland Yard," he said, "and we're making enquiries about this Company. No, I can't go into details, but we don't take all this trouble for our health."

Thus crushed, the lofty one descended a step and admitted that the rental of the single room was one hundred and ten pounds a year. "And a crying shame at that," was Field's inward comment. "They must have a nose for these bogus businesses, screwing them up to that pitch. Forty pounds is nearer the value of the room." The agreement had been made three or four years earlier with a gentleman named Percival, who had never reappeared. The rent was paid by Treasury notes in a registered envelope every quarter. No letter was enclosed, but the notes were folded into a sheet of headed paper. He had heard no complaints of the behaviour of the Company.

"That doesn't get us much forrader," grumbled Field, as they came away, "except that we know for certain that whoever does rent that room is taking quite extraordinary precautions to keep his identity dark. But even if we had a case, we couldn't make an arrest. We haven't got enough to go on. Even that letter could be washed out in court if you had a sufficiently subtle and unscrupulous lawyer."

"What we require," Dupuy agreed, "is the contents of that room. Now, we might break the door down, but I do not think we should learn all that we wish to know even then. The names of the agents—yes, we might get those, but the names of those behind the agents, those, I think, we should not discover."

CHAPTER XV

FIELD had arranged with Glyn to meet them for lunch and when they arrived at the rendezvous they found the lawyer deep in a book. He greeted them with no particular enthusiasm, and to Dupuy's disgust did not instantly break into questions as to the results of the morning's investigations. On the contrary, he seemed disposed to do the talking.

"Extraordinarily interesting chap, that fellow Wilson," he said. "Books are actually his life; it's like going into an inner room—the rest of the world simply doesn't exist when he finds himself among books. I don't know when I've met anyone who was a better conversationalist on his own subject."

"Make the most of him, monsieur," advised Dupuy, with a fine scorn. "You will not have the opportunity long."

"What do you mean? You're not trying to link him up with this disreputable business?"

"He is one of the agents," Dupuy told him, rather maliciously. "I have his own acknowledgment."

Glyn was quite silent for a moment. Then he sighed. "Human nature's inexplicable, isn't it?" he said. "It's no good trying to size it up. One of the most attractive and most generous men I ever met made a tremendous fortune floating a bogus company that he knew—knew, mark you—meant ruin and death for thousands of small people all over the country. The fact is we all have a blind spot. I remember meeting a woman once who'd been concerned in a murder and had done twenty years' penal servitude. When she came out she married a middle-aged man whom she treated with the greatest kindness. A little later she began to suffer atrociously from neuritis in her arms, and she'd walk up and down the room crying, 'Oh God, what have I ever done to deserve this pain?'" He fell silent and listened as first Dupuy, and then Field, told him the history of the morning's activities. But he wasn't, as Dupuy observed discontentedly to Field afterwards, a really satisfactory audience. It was far too obvious that his interest was for Wilson, the bibliophile and not for Wilson the crook. However, when the story was finished, and he was ordering Grand Marnier with his coffee, he did make one useful suggestion. The three were discussing a plan of campaign for the immediate future; various suggestions had been made and rejected. They were now at the most critical stage of the adventure; a false step now and they might lose their man altogether. And then Glyn looked up and said, "I wonder if it's occurred to you to take Fleming into your confidence. He's absorbingly interested in the case, though, unless Lane has warned him to the contrary, he believes Tessier took his own life. He's an influential man, he's got this departmental job that would lay open to him statistics and files to which we haven't access. He may have some information about illicit smuggling of drugs. It's worth considering. Besides, if there is trouble later on, he's a good man to have behind you."

He had scarcely finished speaking before Dupuy reached out a hand and seized his impulsively. "My dear monsieur, that is a brilliant notion. Always, in spite of the copybooks, influence is useful. To be a policeman is not enough."

Glyn was a little surprised at his enthusiasm and sufficiently under his spell to be pleased by it. It was arranged that he and Field should visit Fleming, while Dupuy went off on a ploy of his own. When the two entered Fleming's office, the big man pushed aside a mass of work and started up, surprise and eagerness obvious in his expression.

"My dear Glyn! How do you do, Inspector? I must confess myself intrigued by this visit. I gather from my secretary that she knows more about the affair than I do, but I can't get her to speak. Has something else fresh turned up about Tessier?"

"Fresh things have been turning up ever since he was discovered," admitted Glyn, cautiously. "I suppose now, when publicity is inevitable, it's safe to tell you that the police have been pretty sure of foul play from the outset. They've kept it dark because they didn't want their nest fouled. Now we're in an *impasse*, the dark hour before the dawn, you might almost say, and it occurred to us that you might be able to lend us a hand. Inspector Field will tell you what the position is. It's amazing enough for one of your own films."

Field said, "I don't want to take up too much of your time, sir, but the fact is that after Mr. Lane left M. Tessier that night someone got in and we're pretty sure poisoned him. You know he'd had a lot to drink and would be an easy mark. Of course, the idea was to make it look like suicide."

"But I don't understand. What was the motive? Tessier couldn't have harmed anyone. He was beyond anything constructive. It was a great risk bringing him over here, and I knew I was chancing a small fortune making him the chief character in my film. But I'm a rich man and I don't mind taking risks. But as to his being dangerous . . ."

"He was extremely dangerous, sir," put in Field, quietly. "It suited him to accept your offer and come over here. He could put his enemies off the track that way; but he came intent on murder."

Fleming was aghast. "But who—the victim, I mean?"

"That's the point we thought you might help us to clear up. But I'll tell you this. Tessier came over with enough cocaine to poison the lot of us half-a-dozen times. I haven't a doubt that he meant to unearth this enemy—and put him out of the way. Don't make any mistake about it; he was quite ruthless. He poisoned a woman just before he left Paris in the most cold-blooded manner and he was prepared to do the same again." And he detailed the whole position.

Fleming still looked as if he couldn't quite believe what he heard. "He put up an amazing bluff," he said at last.

"That isn't surprising if you come to think of it," suggested Glyn. "Acting was his job. And he didn't stop acting when his son came to grief. His landlady in Paris, the woman he poisoned, said he was a constant source of entertainment. That ought to have warned her he wasn't the derelict wreck she supposed him to be."

"Did she suppose him to be that?" asked Fleming, and Field broke in, "She spoke as if she did, but then she may have been bluffing, too. It's a big affair, sir, and we're reckoning to get a netful. But you'll understand we don't want to act too soon and lose the men at the top of the tree. Anyone can get the catspaws; we're out for big game."

"I appreciate your point," Fleming agreed. "It would be ruin to be precipitate. Look here, I'll tell you. Trentham's your man. If anyone knows anything of these internal ramifications he does. I'll get in touch with him to-night. What about time? Is that a great object?"

"Not so long as these fellows don't know we're after them. So far we've managed to keep it pretty dark."

"I fancy Mr. Lane has an idea," Glyn put in. "He's

been in such constant touch with Mlle. Dulac, and she in a sense is behind the scenes all through."

"Then, suppose I tackle Trentham to-night, and you come and see me in the morning? Come to my private house if you like. You can get a warrant to search this mysterious room, I take it? It sounds as though the crux of the matter might lie there."

"I'll manage that, sir," Field promised. "And to-morrow will be all right. Of course, it's important no one should learn anything that isn't absolutely necessary."

"If you're thinking of Trentham, I'll guarantee him." Fleming smiled for the first time during the interview. And then the two men left.

Field went to the Yard; he said he must make final arrangements.

"You do confidently expect to get your men?" asked Glyn, who found this assurance in the normally cautious inspector a little surprising.

"Once we get that door open we'll learn a lot," said Field, grimly. "Only it wouldn't be any good to break it down and raise no end of a stink, and find we hadn't got our bird after all. He's a wily fellow and knows how to use his wings."

Glyn, having nothing more to do, went back to his chambers, where he proposed to make up for lost time. The Miller case came on in forty-eight hours —luckily it had been postponed from the original date marked for the hearing or it might have gone hard with the unfortunate plaintiff—and his mind was so full of this Tessier affair that he had to read through the documents from the beginning to get a proper grasp of the case. He was bowed over the papers, oblivious, as was his custom, to such trivialities as meals, when his telephone rang. At such an hour he might have let it peal unanswered but for his feeling that at any moment some new development in this affair nearest his heart might arise, so twitching off the receiver he said gruffly, "Yes," and gave his own number.

"That you, Glyn? Thank God I've got hold of you. Look here, do you know where Eve is?"

Glyn recognised the distracted voice of Julian Lane, and his own reaction was as gratifying as that young man could have wished for.

"Mlle. Dulac? What do you mean? Has anything gone wrong?"

"She's disappeared. Stay where you are and I'll come along in a taxi. I'll be with you in ten minutes."

Glyn, all thought of Miller banished, walked, panic-stricken, up and down the room, until the noise of a bell at the outer door sent him racing down the stairs. Lane was as white as paper; for a moment he could scarcely speak. His story, when Glyn got it, was as follows.

At about six o'clock, shortly after Fleming's interview with Field, a telephone call had been received for Mlle. Dulac, purporting to come from Lane, and asking her to meet him at a certain rendezvous. "As a matter of fact I did telephone her, but not till nearly seven. I knew Fleming was frightfully rushed, and she would be pretty sure to be there. When I got through they told me she'd left; that surprised me because it had been arranged that I should ring her up. We were going to dine together and go on to see this new dancer at the Loyalty. I got into touch with Fleming, who said that Mlle. Dulac had told him that I had phoned and had asked if she could get off a bit early. Fleming had at once said yes. I went round to the place, but of course all the staff had gone and no one could tell me a thing."

Glyn was as agitated as he. "Do you know where Mlle. Dulac was supposed to be meeting you?"

" We were to dine at the Berkeley, but I was going to call for her at her flat. I've made enquiries and she never turned up there."

"I've no notion where she could be." Glyn was terribly agitated. "I haven't seen her since the day I came round to her, the night that you were there. Why should anyone want to do her any harm?"

" She might know an embarrassing lot in connection with this Tessier ramp the police are running now. Curse them! I'm sorry enough about Tessier, but all the police forces of the world can't restore him, and to involve a girl like that . . ."

A sense of justice made Glyn interpolate, " Ah, she was involved on her own account before the police touched the case. But do you think someone thinks her dangerous? How could she be?"

" I don't know how much your infernal police have found out," exclaimed Lane, " but she knew quite a lot about Louis Tessier's death that the people morally responsible for it mightn't care to have broadcast. She might be dangerous, you see."

" But—has she got any names?"

" If she has, she hasn't confided them to me, but she might be able to give information that would lead to discovery. Anyway, who else would have any motive for getting her out of the way? I came to you because," he hesitated, then went on defiantly, " we may as well have gloves off and cards on the table at this stage—because, even if you didn't share their view, there's no doubt your precious police did suspect her of being to some extent involved in Tessier's death. Just as they suspected—and perhaps still suspect—me."

It was impossible for Glyn to give the warm reassurance he would have liked; there was too much truth in the assertion. He could only say, " I've never believed such a thing for an instant," to which Lane made the grim and rather humiliating rejoinder, "Unfortunately you aren't the police."

Then he leaped up. "We can't go on sitting here, talking, not knowing where she is or what she's doing."

"Have you tried the police stations or the hospitals?" asked Glyn rather foolishly.

"If she's been decoyed away they wouldn't be able to help us. No, the people I suspect are the folk behind all this ramp and how in heaven's name we're going to get hold of them defeats me."

Glyn began to reflect aloud.

"It was a damp night; according to the message she was urgently required. Most likely she'd take a taxi. There's a rank close by the door, and we might be able to discover the driver who picked her up."

Eager to be doing anything, he seized his hat and the two men hurried down the stairs. It occurred to neither to ring for the lift; they were at the stage where inaction is intolerable. At the rank Glyn took command, but he had to stop to ask Lane if he had any notion how the girl would be dressed. But Lane was as ignorant as himself. The chase seemed doomed from the outset; no one remembered picking up a young lady from the—Office anywhere near six o'clock; no one remembered seeing her emerge. Fleming had said that she left within a few minutes of the hour; and after that she seemed simply to have disappeared.

When he thought of her possible fate, of the pitilessness of these public enemies into whose hands she had fallen, of their total disregard for life, of their cunning and anonymity, he was frantic with dismay. The two men made enquiries in all conceivable directions; they even went to the mortuary at Westminster, where it was reported that the body of a girl had just been brought in badly mutilated, but there was no resemblance, and they came out again staring at one another with blank faces, almost incoherent in their terror.

"We've got to get her," cried Julian Lane. "If your police know so much, why in God's name don't they afford her proper protection? They must know she'd be one of the first people to be put out of the way."

Presently they separated, each to pursue enquiries on his own account. Glyn continued the search till dawn, but without success. And when he tried to get into touch with Field he found that he also was out and nobody could tell him where.

2.

In an empty office on the top floor of a building in Endell Street, Messrs. Field and Dupuy summoned their patience, smoked and talked in low tones. The hour was ten o'clock, and they had been waiting here since nine.

"Now that we're so near the end of the trail I'm taking no risks," Field remarked grimly. "It would be more than I could bear if at the eleventh hour—no, later than that, just before the clock strikes midnight, some rumour of our activities escaped and we got into that room and found every scrap of evidence had been destroyed."

So great was his native caution that he had brought with him a posse of police officers, who waited in the corridor and leaned over the well of the stairs. They were less fortunate than their superiors, in that they must not smoke. "If anyone should turn up we don't want to advertise our whereabouts," Field assured them.

And now it was getting later and later; ten had struck and the hands were creeping round towards eleven, and nothing whatsoever had happened. In the street below they could see an occasional lurking bird of ill-fortune slink past, but this was too narrow a thoroughfare for taxis or any night traffic.

"It would be a good place to knock a man on the head," said the bloodthirsty Dupuy. "How often does a police constable patrol this street, my dear Field?"

"It's a blind alley," said Field patiently. "There couldn't in the nature of things be much traffic. Anyway our men have all got their orders."

Dupuy was silent for a little. Then he said in a queer tone, "That girl!"

Field nodded. "A rotten business. But, thank heaven, she's safely under lock and key. Did she make much difficulty?"

"I said only a little, as little as need be. She made no fuss when she realised that there was nothing she could do. Only she asked that she might be allowed to speak to her lover; but that, of course, I could not allow."

Field nodded; there seemed nothing to say. This affair was one long string of tragedies and defeats, and before they were finished who could guess what pitiful developments there might not be?

"You said nothing to Glyn?" he asked suddenly, and Dupuy looked up in surprise.

"*Mon vieux,* have we not enough on our hands for this one night? We have these rascals to take, we shall be fortunate if we escape with our own lives. Do we desire to make complications? And that one, I would like to have him with me in a tight corner for he is loyal and to be trusted, but he is governed by his heart, and to-night we must rule by our heads alone. Had I told him the truth what might he not have done? Almost certainly he would not have believed it. And he might have overset all our plans and there is danger enough, God knows."

"And besides," said the more practical, the less, the far less romantic Field, " we are the police. Our lives are comparatively unimportant. We're paid to be shot at, put under ground, if necessary, in order that the public may go safe. But Mr. Glyn's one of the rate-payers that support us. This is going to be a dangerous game as you said; we can't involve him any further. Ah!" The door opened noiselessly, and a policeman became partially visible in the narrow beam of light cast by the single electric torch that illumined the room. It was important for the issues of this evening that no gleam should be perceptible from the street.

" The outer door's just been opened and shut," said the new-comer.

Field hurriedly extinguished his pipe; Dupuy crushed the thin black cigar he habitually smoked.

"Find out how many men have come in," Field commanded. "If there are two, wait till they're safely inside that room—they're pretty certain to lock the door from the inside, and there are no glass panels to betray them—or us for that matter—and then get four men under the window of that room in case there's any question of an escape that way. That leaves four more, as well as our two selves. We compliment these chaps," he added drily to Dupuy, " but they're fairly sure to be armed. Men in their position don't take risks."

The policeman disappeared. There was a long minute of silence. Straining their ears, the two men could hear the faint sound of feet on the stone stairs. So sure were the newcomers that they had the building to themselves that they made no attempt to lower their voices, though no actual words were audible.

The feet stopped a floor below; through the crack of the door you could hear the scrape of the key in the lock, the muttered exasperation of one of the men as the door stuck; then it creaked open and a moment later the key turned again.

" Now," said Field, " we want to give them a chance to open their secret drawers—people in their position won't take any risks about leaving things in open desks, and I don't believe in doing any work you can persuade your criminals to do for you—and then we come in. We don't want to give them time to destroy anything."

The four policemen were already in place under the window; four more lurked noiselessly in the passage outside the locked door. Field, with Dupuy at his side, came down the stairs, making no effort to disguise his footsteps. All this time there had been faint sounds, muffled by the intersecting door, but now they ceased abruptly. Field rapped smartly on the door.

" Police here," he said, and instantly slid to one side, the constables following his example. Through the wood of the door a bullet came tearing and flattened itself in the opposite wall. Field let out a realistic cry. Dupuy cried in a high-pitched note, " You are wounded, then? Ach!" And a second bullet followed the first.

" What wood!" muttered Field contemptuously, whose father had been a master-carpenter. " Oughtn't to be hard to smash that down."

A constable, crouching at the top of the stairs, now began to make a fervent onslaught on the lock, leaning against the wall so that no bullet could touch him.

" How much ammunition will they have?" asked Dupuy, anxiously.

Both men knew that time was short; while one man kept up this barrage of fire, the other might be destroying documents that, from the police point of view, were of paramount importance. A second constable suddenly lunged forward and they heard the door crack under his weight. He dropped back hurriedly, but not quite soon enough. This time a bullet found its mark. A colleague hastily pulled him back on to the stairs.

"Got his shoulder," he muttered, but there was no time for first aid now. An ominous crackling sound could be heard from within the locked room. The entrapped men were lighting a fire. Taking their chance, all the five on the landing made a concerted rush, the door creaked and trembled, and then a panel gave way. Instantly they dropped to the level of the floor, and more bullets sang over their prostrate bodies. In the room all light had been switched off; it was impossible to see where the enemies were moving, or what were their activities. The fire had gone out in the sudden draught; and now Dupuy, lifting himself cautiously, saw a dark shape leap for the window. The second was invisible in the shadows of the room.

"One more chance," he gasped. "We dare not ..." Once more the human battering-ram charged the door; a policeman went down like a log as the guns spat again, but the door was down also. From within, two figures, having drawn themselves back for this final effort, hurtled on to their attackers who were spent and bowed by the effort they had been making; the revolvers flashed again; Dupuy heard a groan as, reaching out with professional zest, he brought down one of the men on top of the squirming heap of humanity. Field, who had been dragged to one knee, and had blood pouring from a flesh wound in his upper arm, made a dive at the second, and a sergeant of police caught the fellow a neat upper-cut that laid him out on the back of his head.

"Good man!" muttered Field, "and if you've killed him it doesn't matter. Save the hangman a job." He got his whistle between his teeth and blew a shrill blast. Up the steps came the heavy hurrying steps of three of the policemen who had been left on outside duty; the fourth prudently remained where he was, his whistle at hand, in case this was another of the bastard's dirty tricks, and he (Mortimer) wasn't going to risk his promotion whatever the rest of the party might feel.

The man on the floor came round slowly to find himself hemmed in by the police; the other, a younger and lither specimen, fought savagely with smothered grunts of rage. But they had no chance. They were hopelessly outnumbered, even without the wounded man who had fainted quietly on the stairs, and the other who lay on his face with one arm twisted under him.

"Murdering a policeman on top of everything else," said Field, impatiently making a wad of his handkerchief and endeavouring to stop the bleeding. "Damn this wound! I shall look like a Christy Minstrel with all this dust on my face and all these scarlet patches on my clothes."

A constable turned on the light and revealed the two prisoners. It was a pity, in the interest of melodrama, that Glyn could not have been there to exclaim, as he certainly would, " My God! Fleming! Fleming of all men!" so that he wouldn't have any breath left to express his dismay at his recognition of Julian Lane as the younger of the pair.

Neither Field nor Dupuy seemed surprised. Only the latter, seeing the wicked look on the film producer's face, said to his English colleague, " I think, my dear Field, the handcuffs might be employed there. I have still a great expectation of life, and I have learned to recognise danger."

Julian Lane flung back his head as a constable approached him, but with his wrists held and his revolver missing he could do nothing. The room itself was in complete disorder; papers were scattered on the floor, drawers stood open, a basket was half full of documents torn or crumpled ready for the flames.

"That will be a nice morning's work for someone with neat fingers," observed Dupuy, with satisfaction.

Field said nothing at all; he was wondering whether he was going to follow the example of the fellow on the stairs, and how soon the ambulance would come and collect them all.

CHAPTER XVI

"MONSIEUR," said Dupuy, earnestly, for the fourth or fifth time, "I tell you, it was not safe. I dared not speak. If you had known the truth about mademoiselle you might have been tempted beyond your strength when M. Lane came seeking for her. For he was a very desperate man. It was his life and he knew it. Oh, make no mistake. When you and Field had warned M. Fleming that the game was up, as you say, then at once mademoiselle's life was in danger. She knew so much, you see, so much about Louis Tessier and his father; she knew that it was drugs that had ruined her lover; she is passionate and loyal; she does not know fear. Then, too, she would not believe any ill of her lover. Wherever he took her she would follow, thinking no harm."

Glyn, white-faced and aghast, laid one hand on the table. "Are you trying to tell me that Lane would have murdered her?"

"But certainly, monsieur. Why should he hesitate? He has—how many murders on his conscience? It is so simple and who will suspect that this ardent young gentleman has poisoned his sweetheart? No,

monsieur, the only way to save mademoiselle's life
was to put her where neither Lane nor any friend of
his could approach her. All night, while you sought
her, while we waited, while the battle raged, while
our prisoners were thrust into their cells, she has
waited also."

"Does she know the truth?" Glyn demanded.

"She knows it now. We could not tell her then.
Only I said, Mademoiselle, your life is in danger;
to-night we shall take the murderer of Réné Tessier,
the virtual murderer of his son. You must wait
somewhere secure; we do not wish to have a murder
on our minds."

"And she came with you quietly?"

"She asked if she might telephone to M. Lane. I
said, 'No; there are spies at every hole to-night.
Nothing is safe, the walls have ears. You must
remain here, without speech, till the last act is over.
This is your battle.' She was very quiet; she said, 'I
think he will be anxious.' As indeed, monsieur, you
can testify."

Glyn felt deathly sick. "I still can't really believe
it. Lane—why, he suggested it himself, and I
thought at the time, that's often a criminal's bluff.
But that it should be true. And how well he played
his part."

"How should he not, monsieur? Was not the
screen his world? Oh, he had opportunity enough,
believe me."

"I still don't know how you suspected Fleming.
Were you on to Lane from the outset?"

Dupuy nodded. "Who else was there?" he asked,
simply. "You see, there is one little piece of evidence
of which until this time nothing has been made. That
little flake of mud on the top of the gas-tap. Now,
M. Rentoul might have murdered Tessier, though I
was sure poison would not have been his method.

But remember—M. Rentoul had worn espadrilles; he had come over the roof, and that fire was extinguished by a man wearing boots or outdoor shoes, and he kicked the tap with his foot to save himself the trouble of stooping down. It is these little things, monsieur, that help to hang men. Now this man, whoever he was, did not, I was sure, enter the hotel through the open door. M. Pecheron was like a spider in the entrance, and no fly, no matter how smooth on his feet, could have got past him. Then how did our murderer enter? and to that there is but one answer—the fire-escape. And who knew that the escape wound past M. Tessier's room, but the man who had been inside that room, who had stood at the window and looked down, who had noticed that no man, except a policeman every few minutes, moved in that alley? All this, monsieur, pointed to Lane as our murderer. Then there was the letter. How should a stranger know that M. Tessier was left-handed? But Lane had just seen him sign the visitor's book. So then it seemed most probable that M. Lane was our man. For it was stretching the arm of coincidences too far," he opened his own arms as he spoke with a gesture of something snapping incontinently, " to believe that yet a third man found his way into that dreadful room in the early morning of May 10th."

" And that's all?" asked Glyn, still not altogether convinced.

" No, monsieur, that is not all. What does M. Lane do as soon as he leaves the hotel? I will tell you. He enters a telephone booth. Ah, you will say, that is wise; he is going to tell Mlle. Dulac that all is well. But no, he telephones to M. Fleming with the message—all is well. Does not that seem to you, monsieur, a very strange thing to do? M. Fleming has not asked him to meet M. Tessier, he has shown no interest, publicly, that is, in his arrival. True, he has received a telegram, but he has made no arrangements for the gentleman to be met. It is Mlle. Dulac who pleads furtively with her lover to go down to Victoria, and she warns him to be careful. Now that is not an official reception and assuredly it is nothing to do with M. Fleming. Yet it is M. Fleming to whom M. Lane telephones, saying, All is well. What can that mean but that some plan that has been made has been carried out?"

"Then he was poisoned before Lane left the hotel for the first time?"

"Oh, but certainly, monsieur. That short period of restlessness, almost of delirium, of which Pecheron spoke, that is a symptom of hyoscin poisoning. Of course, he did not know that M. Tessier carried poison also, and a man who carries cocaine does not normally destroy himself with another drug. So we began to enquire. Yes, monsieur?" for Glyn had made a sharp movement, as though recalling some detail hitherto disregarded by the mind.

"Do you know, when I was talking to him in Mlle. Dulac's flat he spoke of the picture Tessier made, slumped down in his chair, *with the empty plate beside him, he said.* If he didn't go back to the room, how did he see the plate empty? Everyone agrees the old man hadn't touched the sandwiches."

"It is in these foolish ways that men deliver themselves into our hands," returned Dupuy, grandiloquently. "Then, of course, our enquiries began. But they were clever, these scoundrels. No one knew their names, and we could only suspect. And it might be a horse's nest, after all. So we played our little trick on M. Fleming: if he were involved, then he would press for delay, for sufficient delay to destroy the evidence against him, and we should have our chance. If no one came to the office that night, then we were on a wrong trail, and must start again. But, of course," he wound up, with a superbly characteristic gesture, " we were not on the wrong trail. Some things, monsieur, proclaim themselves."

" To you, perhaps," agreed Glyn, heavily. " I feel like a blind man by comparison. I still haven't quite grasped it. Fleming to be involved in this. A man of his standing!"

" It is because he has so much to lose that M. Tessier must die, die before he can learn the truth, die, particularly, before he can whisper a word to Mlle. Dulac. Such a scandal about such a man would—how do you say it?—stink to heaven. A smaller man—well, even then it was difficult. The English judges, I think, are not disposed to be kind to a drug trafficker, and even we in France do not— shall we say?—love them. No, no, Tessier must be put out of the way, and quickly. For mind, once he knows that M. Fleming is concerned, then also he must learn about M. Lane. Him, at least, he could not suspect."

" You're right," Glyn agreed, " and I know it. But I don't realise it yet. That such a man should ever start on that course."

Dupuy shrugged. " You yourself have said it, monsieur. Human nature is inexplicable. And remember, he was most ambitious, and ambitious men require money. Here was a way to make a great deal of money. Or perhaps it was M. Lane who showed him the road. That we may learn later."

" Perhaps," said Glyn in a hopeless sort of voice. " Presumably Fleming picked on Mlle. Dulac for his secretary because he knew of her association with Tessier. I doubt whether he was deceived by Tessier's deception; I believe he knew he was out for revenge, and saw through his elaborate pose of decadence. He never meant to make that film; it was nothing but camouflage to match Tessier's, ding-dong all the way, and heaven help the loser. What he didn't know was that Tessier was double-crossing him and would win in the end—if you can call it winning. Naturally, in the circumstances, he'd prefer to have the girl under his eye. She might be in communication with Tessier and he wouldn't want to give them a chance of getting together, if by any means he could prevent it."

"Precisely. And then he could—rub her off, do you say?—when the hour struck—if it should ever strike."

"But she knew nothing of Fleming's side-line, surely?"

"I think—nothing. No, I am sure she knew nothing. I question if even Tessier himself knew the names of his enemies when he came to England. That they were in England I think he believed, and I think also he encouraged mademoiselle to come to England. Then he had someone whom he could trust, to whom he could turn. Perhaps M. Tessier hoped to learn the truth from M. Wilson. How can one tell? But I am sure, yes, sure, that when he learned those names he would have no more mercy than he had had on Madame Lemaitre, who was one of the great gang that helped to ruin his son."

"Not much consideration for mademoiselle's feelings," remarked Glyn, with bitter restraint. "No one seems to have thought much of those. Not even the police."

Dupuy, who was not bitter, said in a gentle voice, "At least we saved her life, monsieur."

"Yes, and for what purpose? What's she going to do now? Twice to have men failing her in such appalling ways. What sort of life has she left?"

"I thought, monsieur, you might be able to be of service to her. It is, I know, what you have wished from the beginning. And you are her friend. You cannot expect her to turn very readily to us; we are a uniform, an organisation, not flesh and blood. But you—oh, for you it is different."

Glyn could feel the painful colour surging into his drawn cheeks. "If she doesn't identify me with the tricksters," he said, roughly. "Anyway, I can't break in on her now. It wouldn't be decent. You can't ask a girl who's gone through what she has to trust another man."

"And yet," Dupuy urged, "what other life is there for her? She is so beautiful and so young. Oh, believe me, she was not born to wither like so many of these others."

"You flatter me if you think I have anything to offer that would have any value for her," returned Glyn, oblivious to the amazing nature of his conversation, so deeply were his feelings involved.

Dupuy came a little closer; his mask of mockery fell from his expressive face.

"Monsieur, attend to me. Suppose you are rich and happy and you have a big house and all goes well with you; and then one day your house is burnt to the ground and your friends desert you and you have nothing left; and suppose then that someone offers you, perhaps, a bed-sitting-room, some place where you can be safe, where no one will touch you again, where you can start to make your new life—do you think you would turn your back and say, 'I will lie out on the cold ground and catch pneumonia and die in the infirmary'?"

Glyn stared with incredulous eyes; he could play battledore and shuttlecock as agilely as the next man in the Courts, but he couldn't deal with this kind of attack. He tried for an instant to picture himself telling Eve Dulac that she was to regard him as a bed-sitting-room, and was staggered at the prospect.

" At least, be her friend," Dupuy was urging, " for this morning she has none. Already London is beginning to talk of this great drug scandal; her name will be freely mentioned; the story of Louis Tessier will be dragged up. They will nudge one another and say, ' She is unfortunate, that one; the men who love her come to a strange end.' They will laugh and point . . ."

" Oh, get to hell out of here," exclaimed Glyn, but without giving his companion time to obey the mannerless injunction he had flashed down the stairs and an instant later the irrepressible little Frenchman saw him emerge on to the pavement and imperiously shout to a cruising taxicab.

" Of course," he reflected, drawing back into the room, " it will not be easy for him, but then he is a lawyer, and a lawyer's life is to fight. I think he would fight well in a case he—loved. And one day, perhaps not too far off, I have a faith that that may be a very snug little bed-sitting-room. But will they say, ' Aha, that wise M. Dupuy. What a man! What a romantic! What—what . . ." his imagination failed him and he began to laugh.

He had much to do that day and during the afternoon he went to see his friend, Field, who was raging in bed with an aching shoulder and a murderous temper.

" Tut, tut," Dupuy rebuked him. " It is only a little holiday and you have deserved that. No, no, do not say, ' Get to hell out of here.' I have been told that by an Englishman once already to-day."

" How much holiday are you taking?" demanded Field, who could hear the news boys under the window shouting raucously, " More about the Drug Case," and thought of all the things he'd like to do with them for thus rubbing in his own inadequacy.

He loathed the thought that other men were following up his story.

"Alas!" Dupuy shook a mock-mournful head. "My country, she is a driver of slaves. No time am I allowed. For, see here," he waved a copy of the "Matin" at his companion. "Do you see that one we call the Tiger is back in Paris?" He threw back his head and laughed. "Generally he is more prudent. But now he must be thinking, 'That fox, Dupuy, he is in England, he is after other game, so my playground will be safe for me.' He comes back brazenly, thinking no one shall touch him. He does not know that to-night I return, that before dawn perhaps I shall be as his shadow. Oh yes, I must go back, for without me what will Paris do?" He laughed again. His exuberant spirits reduced Field to a quivering silence. If a thunderbolt had struck the little demon at that instant he would have seen a providential hand behind the deed. "But now," Dupuy continued, leaping up and opening a little case he had been carrying, "before I go we will drink one little toast together. I will give you," he was pouring out the golden liquid into glasses as he spoke, "I will give you a lady. Not a wife, monsieur, for I have no wife but Paris—but a mistress." He beamed, lifting his glass. "I will give you the most beautiful, the most wonderful, the most intriguing mistress in the whole world—Crime."

THE END

>>> If you've enjoyed this book and would like to discover more great vintage crime and thriller titles, as well as the most exciting crime and thriller authors writing today, visit: >>>

The Murder Room
Where Criminal Minds Meet

themurderroom.com